Kissing Carly

KISS A COWBOY SERIES BOOK THREE

Deanna Lynn Sletten

Kissing Carly
Kiss a Cowboy Series Book Three

Copyright 2015 © Deanna Lynn Sletten

ISBN – 10:1941212247
ISBN – 13:978-1-941212-24-0

Editor: Samantha Stroh Bailey of Perfect Pen Communications
Cover Designer: Deborah Bradseth of Tugboat Design

Kissing Carly

KISS A COWBOY SERIES BOOK THREE

Chapter One

Carly Stevens slowly drove up the long driveway leading to the ranch house. With every crunch of gravel under her tires, her heart beat faster. As she came to a stop near the familiar home, she brushed back her long, blond hair and bit her pretty, full bottom lip.

Well. Here I go.

Carly put the car in park and turned off the ignition as her blue eyes scanned the windows of the house. It was just after one o'clock on a sunny June afternoon, but she didn't see any movement inside the house. She looked over at the barn a short distance away and the pasture dotted with grazing horses and cattle. There were four trucks parked in the driveway and a midsized SUV, so she knew people were here. She was surprised no one was walking around or working.

Carly stepped out of her car and stretched. The day was warm and the sun felt good on her back. She'd driven to the Montana ranch from Seattle in two days, even though she could have easily made it in one. She hadn't been in a rush to arrive. No one was expecting her, and the longer she put off talking to her sister, Andi, the better. But now, here she was. She could no longer postpone the inevitable.

Carly slowly spun around, taking in the beauty of the Brennan ranch. To her right was the classic red barn and fenced-in pastures. To the left of that was the trail that headed up into the hills where the summer pasture lay and from where there was an amazing view of the ranch. As she continued turning left, she saw the house, then the highway, and across from that, the Clark Fork River sparkled just under the hill of pine trees that rose to the sky. Carly sighed. She was definitely a city girl, but she couldn't deny how beautiful it was here.

The creak of a door opening caught her attention and Carly looked up at the house in time to lock eyes with her handsome brother-in-law, Luke Brennan, as he stepped down the back stairs. Behind him was Randy Olson, Luke's longtime friend who also worked on the ranch.

Luke's dark blue eyes stared at her in surprise. "Carly?"

Carly took a deep breath and pasted a sweet smile on her face. "Luke!" She sauntered over to wrap her arms around his broad shoulders. "Aren't you looking as handsome as ever?" From the corner of her eye, she saw Randy behind them, rolling his eyes. She ignored the crabby ranch hand and kept the smile on her face as she moved away from Luke.

"Where is everyone?" Carly asked. "It's like a ghost town around here."

"We were all inside eating lunch," Luke said, still looking dazed by the fact that Carly had shown up out of nowhere. "Did Andi know you were coming?"

Carly shook her head. "No, but won't she be surprised?" she asked sweetly. Carly turned to Randy. "Hello, Randy. How have you been?"

Randy nodded. "Hello, Carly." He tapped Luke on the arm. "I'm heading off to the pasture. See you in a bit." Then he strode off toward the barn.

Carly frowned as she watched Randy walk away. He wasn't a bad looking man. Some might even call him ruggedly handsome. His dark brown hair was a bit shaggy, and he always looked like he'd forgotten to shave. But in the past, she'd seen his brown eyes sparkle when he joked with family and friends and she knew he could be nice when he wanted to. He never paid a bit of attention to her, though, and that irked her. Men fawned over Carly wherever she went. Everyone, except Randy.

The back door opened again and Carly's frown turned into a warm smile. "Colt, my hunky cowboy!" Carly ran over to give Colt Brennan a hug. Colt stood there, stunned, but wrapped his arms around Carly and gave her a squeeze.

"Carly? I didn't know you were coming here." He glanced over at his brother, but Luke just shrugged.

Carly pulled away and beamed up at him. "I'm surprising everyone," she said, running her hand down Colt's muscular arm. "You look gorgeous, as always," Carly told him. "Married life is treating you well." Carly sighed as she gazed up at Colt. A year ago, Colt had left the ranch to live with Carly in Seattle, but their relationship hadn't worked out. Carly hadn't been ready to settle down with one man. However, Carly's roommate, Beth, fell for the sweet, hunky cowboy and she and Colt were married just two months before here at the ranch. As Carly looked up into Colt's baby blue eyes, she couldn't help but regret not wanting to marry him when he'd asked. Deep down, though, she knew it would never have worked.

"Thanks," Colt said, grinning. "You look just as beautiful as ever, Carly."

"You're such a sweetheart," Carly told him with a smile.

"What's all the commotion out here?" Virginia 'Ginny' Brennan asked from the top of the steps. Her eyes grew wide when she saw Carly. "Carly! My goodness, but what a wonderful surprise." Ginny hurried down the steps to hug Carly, with Bree, their black and white Australian Shepherd cattle dog, bounding at her heels.

Carly hugged Ginny tight. She adored the older woman who

always welcomed her at the ranch with open arms and never judged her no matter what awful stunts she pulled. Since her own parents had died in a car accident when she was only fourteen and Andi was eighteen, Carly had been missing a mother figure. Ginny filled that role with ease, and Carly appreciated her for it.

Ginny stood back and looked Carly up and down with a smile. "You are still just the cutest thing ever. Why, I'm surprised Andi didn't tell us you were coming."

Carly tried looking contrite. "I didn't tell her. I hope you don't mind my showing up like this."

"Oh, darling," Ginny said, pulling her close again. "You're family. You can come here whenever your heart desires."

Carly looked into Ginny's kind hazel eyes. With her dark blond hair pulled back into a ponytail, and only a few wisps of gray running through it, she barely looked old enough to be Luke and Colt's mother. She was a tad taller than Carly and stayed slender from working hard around the ranch. It was her kind heart, however, that won over everyone who came to the ranch. "Thanks, Ginny. You're too good to me."

Ginny swiped her hand through the air to brush away her words. "It's easy being kind to you, sweetie." She turned and called out toward the house. "Andi, come on out. There's a surprise waiting for you in the driveway."

A moment later, a young woman with long, dark red hair and brilliant green eyes came to the door, holding a small baby on her hip. The little girl in her arms was a tiny replica of her mother. Andi stood there, surprise clearly marked on her face. "Carly? What are you doing here?"

"Andi!" Carly cried with delight. She ran over and met her sister at the bottom of the steps, pulling her and the baby into a hug. "I'm so happy to see you. And Jessi. She's grown so much. She's so adorable."

The baby backed away from Carly, her eyes as big as saucers. Tears began to well in her little green eyes.

Carly pulled away. "Oh, no. I'm making her cry," she said, truly distressed. "My own little niece doesn't even know me."

"She's fine," Andi said as she bounced little Jessi on her hip. "She's only six months old, so of course she doesn't remember you. But she'll get to know you, if you stay a few days."

Carly looked at her big sister, her eyes questioning. "Are you mad that I just showed up?"

Andi shook her head. "Of course not, but I am surprised. Whatever made you drive all this way without letting us know?"

Carly set her pretty, pink lips into a pout. "I missed you. All of you. And my baby niece too. Isn't that enough to make me want to come here for a visit?"

Andi looked at her in a way that made Carly think she didn't completely believe her. Andi knew her too well.

"Well, boys," Ginny said, turning to Luke and Colt. "Why don't you two carry Carly's things up to the guest room? Carly, come on in and have some lunch. You must be starving." Ginny headed back into the house.

Carly turned to Luke and Colt and hit the unlock button on her car key. Luke opened up the back of her Honda CR-V and looked inside. A crease touched his brow when he saw the luggage in the back. "You want all of this in the house?"

"Yes, please," Carly said sweetly. She walked over to the car, retrieved her purse and a large handbag, and then slung them over her shoulder. "Thanks, guys," she said, walking back over to Andi.

Andi watched as Luke and Colt unloaded four large suitcases. "Why so many bags?" she asked her sister.

Carly shrugged. "A girl can never have enough clothes along with her."

Andi shook her head and headed back inside the house with

Carly on her heels.

* * *

Randy strode out into the pasture beside the barn and retrieved his gelding, Black Jack. The horse came to him immediately, and Randy stroked his silky neck a moment before leading him into the barn to saddle him. Black Jack was a tall Tennessee Walker, seventeen hands high, and had a sleek black coat with an even darker mane and tail. He'd broke Black Jack himself, ten years ago, and trained him, and they'd been constant companions ever since.

As Randy saddled his horse, his thoughts turned to Carly and he rolled his eyes again. *What is that girl up to now?* Randy had a soft spot for Luke's wife, Andi, and he also liked Colt's wife, Beth, very much. Both women were genuine, honest, and hardworking, and neither one had a phony bone in their bodies. But Carly was different. That girl put on a show wherever she went. Just because she had a curvy body, long, silky blond hair, and those big blue eyes, she thought she had every man wrapped around her perfectly manicured little finger. Every man, that is, except Randy.

He chuckled when he thought of the many times she'd tried to win him over these past two years with her pouty lips or hip-swaying walk. He just ignored her as if she weren't even there. He knew it drove her crazy, and that made it even more fun for him. Randy wasn't generally a mean spirited person, but he wasn't going to be had by a five-foot, five-inch tall spoiled brat. For the life of him, he couldn't understand how Carly and Andi could be sisters. Andi was so sweet, smart, and reliable, and Carly, well, she wasn't any of those things. He supposed losing her parents at such a young age hadn't been easy for her, but she'd had Andi to take care of her, so she had no excuse for her behavior. A lot of people lose a parent when they're young, and they turn out fine. He did. So what was up with her?

Of course, Randy had been lucky enough to have the Brennans take him under their wing when he was eight years old. He'd lived with his mom in town, but he'd spent most weekends on the ranch learning everything he knew today under the tutelage of Luke's father, Jack. Jack had been a hard-working man who cared deeply for his family, and between him and Ginny, there had been enough love to spread around, even to a little boy whose own father hadn't cared enough about him to stick around. Every day of his life, Randy was thankful for the Brennans and all they'd done for him, because God only knew what would have happened to him without them.

Randy finished saddling Black Jack and then slipped on the bridle. The afternoon was heating up and the barn was sweltering. He lifted his black cowboy hat off his head, ran his hand through his hair, then replaced the hat. He knew he needed a haircut, but he hadn't gotten around to it. He'd try to get one Saturday so he'd look respectable on Sunday, not that it mattered. His mother probably wouldn't notice anyway.

Randy led Black Jack out of the barn and then slid up into the saddle and took off toward the trail that led to the back of the property. A few of the cows and calves had been left in the lower pasture instead of being brought up to the higher summer pasture, and he was going to check on them. The calves had been born later than the others had and two of them weren't growing as fast as they should. If it was necessary to supplement their diet, then they would. He'd go see how they were faring first, and tomorrow he'd drive his truck up and bring the barrel of grain up there to feed them if he felt it was necessary.

Before he hit the trail, Randy turned back a moment and saw Luke and Colt walking into the barn. He waved and they waved back. Randy knew that Colt was heading back over to Ray's place to help with the haying. The Brennans and their neighbor, Ray, shared the haying fifty/fifty. Ray had the equipment and the Brennans had the fields, so it worked out well for both of them. Luke was going to work on the riding lawn mower because it was acting up again. There was always work to be done on a spread as big as this.

Randy turned Black Jack back toward the trail, clicked his tongue, and off they galloped.

Chapter Two

Ginny insisted Carly have lunch before settling in. Carly loved being fussed over by Ginny. She made her a turkey sandwich on freshly baked bread, put out a jar of homemade pickles, poured her a glass of iced tea, and set out a plate of peanut butter cookies. Andi sat across from her with Jessi on her lap. The old oak kitchen table sat in the front corner and had a bench that ran along the wall on one side and chairs on the other. The cozy, country kitchen was large and held enough space for Ginny to cook as well as for the family to dine. There were counters along both walls, an old-fashioned farm sink, and plenty of cabinets for storage. Even with the new stainless steel appliances, the warm and welcoming kitchen felt like it was from another era. An old telephone hung from the wall by the doorway that led into the sitting room, their old-fashioned name for the living room, and a staircase ran along the back wall, leading up to the bedrooms. At the foot of the stairs, a worn pillow lay where Bree slept at night, and she was lying on it right now, watching everyone with interest.

"Where's Beth?" Carly asked between bites of her sandwich. "Everyone was here except her."

"She's working at the hospital in Superior today," Andi told her. "She works there part-time. She'll be home for supper tonight."

"Oh, yeah, that's right. I guess I forgot." Carly smiled over at Jessi who stared at her with round eyes. "I can't believe how big Jessi has grown in just a few months. She looks so much like you, Andi. I bet your baby pictures would mirror hers."

Andi smiled warmly. "Yeah, she does look like me when I was little. I'm happy you get a chance to see her. Time goes by so fast when they're this age."

Ginny sat down beside Carly. "Isn't she a cutie? Every day I'm in awe of her. This house used to be full of testosterone, but the women are starting to take over. I'm enjoying every minute of it."

They talked for a few more minutes while Carly finished her lunch, then Andi announced she was heading home to put Jessi down for a nap.

"Why don't you come along, Carly?" Andi said. "We can catch up while she sleeps."

Carly knew that Andi really wanted to get to the bottom of why she was here. She nodded, and followed her outside after thanking Ginny for lunch. They rode the short distance to Luke and Andi's cabin in Andi's car. Luke had built the cabin years before when he was married to his first wife, but she'd left him shortly after it was finished. She hadn't been able to bear living so far out in the country after growing up in California. When Andi's car broke down near the ranch two years ago, she'd knocked on his door to use his phone. What started out as an annoyance to Luke, ended up with them falling in love and Andi staying on. They were married in December that same year and one year later, Jessi was born.

Andi pulled up to the log home and parked, then gently took the sleepy baby out of her car seat and carried her into the house. Carly followed Andi across the covered, wooden porch and through the door, into the living room.

"Will you hold Jessi while I warm her bottle?" Andi asked,

handing the baby to Carly.

Carly held her, hoping she wouldn't make her cry, but the little girl only looked up at her with sleepy eyes. She was so adorable, just like a little doll. Carly smiled down at her as she gently rocked her.

"I'm so happy you decided to name her after both our mother and Ginny," Carly said softly while Andi heated a bottle of formula. "Jessica Virginia Brennan. It's the perfect name for a little cowgirl, don't you think?"

Andi chuckled. "We like it. And Ginny was over the moon when her name was included." She walked back into the living room with the bottle and sat in the wooden rocker that stood next to the leather sofa. Carly laid Jessi in Andi's arms and the little girl eagerly accepted her bottle.

Carly walked over to the river rock fireplace across from the sofa. She looked all around the cabin, loving how cozy it felt. There were large windows on the front of the house as well as on the far side in the dining room, letting in plenty of natural light. The kitchen was open with an island separating it from the living room. Beyond that, down the hallway, were the two bedrooms and the new addition Luke had built this spring for Andi to use as an art studio for her painting.

Carly looked up at the mantel and saw a row of photos sitting on it. There was one of their parents taken a few weeks before they died. Another of Ginny and her late husband, Jack. There was also a wedding photo of Luke and Andi taken in front of the fireplace at the main house where all the Brennans had been married since the ranch began in the 1860s. There was also a family photo from the wedding, including herself and Colt, standing together, looking happy.

Carly smiled as she gazed at that photo. She and Colt had become very close after the wedding, and that was when Colt had moved out to Seattle to live with her. She adored Colt. He was sweet, kindhearted, and extremely handsome. Unfortunately, it hadn't worked out between them. Colt wanted so much more than Carly could give him. But now he was married to Beth, and she was sure they were happy. She didn't regret not staying with him, but she did envy Beth a little for being lucky enough to have a man like him. He was the kind of man every woman dreamed of.

"No regrets, I hope," Andi said quietly so as not to wake Jessi.

Carly shook her head and turned toward her sister. "No. He's happy with Beth, so I'm happy for him."

"Good," Andi said with finality. She stood and carried Jessi off to her room, then returned a minute later. After rinsing out the bottle, she came back into the living room and sat in the corner of the sofa. "So, do you want to talk?"

Carly sighed and sat opposite her on the sofa, curling her legs up under her. "Okay. About what?"

Andi crossed her arms. "About why you came here out of the blue. I'm happy to see you, but something must be up. Tell me what's going on."

Carly pouted. "Can't I just come and visit my family and see my little niece? Does there have to be a motive?"

"Carly, it's me you're talking to. All the pouting in the world won't get you out of telling me the truth. Now, what's going on?"

Carly lowered her eyes. Her sister was right; she'd never been able to fool her. "Okay. I had a little trouble back home and I wanted to come here and spend time with family." She looked up at Andi. "You're the only family I have, and I think of the Brennans as my family now, too. I needed to be around people who care about me."

Andi's expression turned serious. She leaned forward. "What type of trouble? Are you okay?"

"I'm fine. It's just, well, I'm having a little financial trouble."

Andi sat back, looking relieved that nothing serious was wrong. "What do you mean?"

Carly took a breath. "I haven't been able to stay current with some of my bills. It's been hard paying for everything by myself since Beth left and I no longer have the extra rent income. And last summer, Colt was helping to pay the bills, too, and now that's over. It put me back a little."

Andi frowned. "I don't get it. You earn a good income. The townhouse is paid for, so all you have are the basics like electricity, water and sewer, and gas. How are you not able to pay your bills?"

Carly let out an exaggerated sigh. "All those things are expensive. Plus, I have to eat and I need clothes for work, and I have to maintain things in the townhouse. Like last month, the dryer broke down and I had to have it repaired. All that costs money."

"Yes, but you should earn enough for the basics plus a few extras," Andi said. "Maybe you need to tighten your budget. You don't have to eat out every night, you know. Or go drinking with your friends. That gets expensive."

Carly frowned. "I suppose Colt and Beth told you that I go out too much."

Andi shook her head. "Actually, they say very little about you. You aren't exactly the center of their universe. And they didn't have to tell me anything. I know you. And I know you like to go out a lot. You also like to shop a lot."

"Hey, I try to buy everything at the outlet stores where the prices are cheaper."

"Yeah, but designer clothes and shoes are still expensive, even in outlet stores. Carly, you have a degree in business management. You know how to handle money. How can you be behind in your bills?"

Carly crossed her arms. "This is why I didn't want to tell you about it. You're just getting angry with me. That won't help solve my problems."

Andi stared at Carly a moment before replying. "Okay, Carly. Just tell me what's going on and how I can help."

Carly bit her lip. "I came here because the power was shut off at the townhouse. The gas too. They won't turn it back on until I pay the bills in full."

Andi's eyebrows shot up. "Turned off? How much do you owe?"

"Like, three thousand dollars between the two."

"Carly! How could you get so far behind? That's more than just a couple of months' worth."

Carly looked down at the floor. "I got a little behind this past winter, but then it got worse as the months went on. Plus, I haven't been working for the past six weeks, so I couldn't pay the bills at all, and they shut me off."

Andi's mouth dropped open. "You lost your job? How could that happen? You've been working at the gallery since you were in college. You're the manager there, for Pete's sake. Why would they let you go?"

Carly stood and walked across the room, flinging her arms in the air. "I don't know. I mean, I took a few sick days here and there and they told me I was through. They gave my job to Everly. Can you believe that? Everly doesn't even have a management degree." Carly still had trouble understanding how they could have replaced her with Everly. Carly and Everly had been friends and she was part of the group that Carly went out with all the time. But Everly didn't have the schooling or experience to be a manager. Carly didn't begrudge her getting the job—Everly hadn't had anything to do with her getting fired—but she knew that Everly wouldn't be able to handle the responsibility. Of course, Carly knew that if she'd taken her job more seriously, she wouldn't have lost it in the first place.

"This is ridiculous," Andi said, standing up. "I'm calling the gallery right now. Our parents used to own that place. Mr. Barnett said you would always have a job there. If he fired you, I'm removing all of my paintings from there this instant."

Carly's eyes grew wide. "Wait, Andi. Don't call him."

"Why?"

Carly dropped back onto the sofa. "They weren't exactly mean to me about it. They said I could come back and have my old job as soon as I…" Carly hesitated.

"As soon as you what?"

"If I stop missing work so often. Sure, sometimes I had a little too much to drink and was too hung over to go in, but everyone does that occasionally. I'm only twenty-six, for cripes' sake. I'm allowed to have a little fun every now and then."

Andi sat back down. "Oh, Carly," she said, sounding gravely disappointed.

"Don't be mad at me, Andi. If you get mad at me, too, I have nowhere to go."

Andi shook her head. "I'm not mad at you, but I am disappointed. Partying all the time, not paying your bills, that isn't what I taught you. Don't you remember the mess we were in when Mom and Dad died? All the debt we had to pay off? We would own that gallery if we hadn't had to sell it because Mom and Dad were so irresponsible with money. I thought you knew better."

"It's not like I tried losing my job or being in debt. It just happened," Carly whined.

Andi sighed. "Okay, tell me how much you owe, besides the utility bills. Is there more?"

Carly didn't meet Andi's eyes. "I have a few credit card bills."

"How much, Carly?"

"Twenty, maybe twenty-five thousand," Carly said softly.

Andi's eyes grew wide. "Twenty-five thousand dollars? What the hell did you buy?"

"It adds up fast," Carly said, knowing how pathetic she sounded. "I was paying on them regularly until the gallery fired me. But now I can't make the payments, and I can't pay the utility bills."

Andi just stared at her, speechless.

"I'm sorry, Andi. I don't know how it happened. It just did, and I can't do anything about it now. I just feel like I'm so far down that I can't dig my way out of it. I need your help."

"Do you have any money?" Andi asked. "How did you pay to drive here?"

"I used the last credit card I have available," Carly said meekly.

Andi sighed. "Carly, I don't know what to say. You have no job, you can't pay your bills, and you have a pile of debt. What can I say?"

Carly looked up at her hopefully. "Well, I was wondering. Maybe we could get a line of credit against the townhouse and I could use that to pay my bills. The interest is cheaper, and I could start paying it off, little by little."

Andi shook her head. "No. Absolutely not. The townhouse is paid for. There is no way I'm going to let you jeopardize losing the townhouse so you can pay off your debt. No."

"But it's half mine," Carly whined.

"No, Carly. You obviously aren't able to handle money properly, and you're not going to put our one investment at risk just to pay off your bills. Don't you realize that if we lose the townhouse, you'll have nowhere to live? You'd never be able to afford rent somewhere else."

Carly knew her sister was right. She felt like such an idiot for getting into so much trouble with money in the first place. She knew better, yet, she'd done it anyway. And having to tell Andi made it even worse. "I'm sorry, Andi. I am. Tell me what to do to fix it and I will."

"First you have to stop acting like a child and grow up," Andi said, exasperated. "No more going out drinking and partying all the time. And no more shopping. And you have to get your job back, fast. How do you expect to pay any bills if you aren't working?"

Carly sighed. "I don't want to go back there, yet. I've made a mess of things, and I know I have to fix it, but not there. Can't I just stay here a while? I'll help around the ranch house and I can help you with Jessi."

"You have to do more than that, Carly. You need to start making money. We can't let the townhouse sit there empty. What if someone breaks in?"

"The neighbor is keeping an eye on it for me and I've had my mail forwarded here, to the ranch, until I figure out what I'm going to do."

"You're staying here?" Andi asked, surprised. "For how long?"

Carly looked at Andi, her eyes sad. "I know that if I go back to Seattle, I'll just go back to all my bad habits. I need to be with family right now. Please, Andi. I want to stay here for a few weeks. Maybe even for the summer."

Andi stood and looked at Carly sternly. "Fine. But if you stay here, you not only have to help around the ranch, but you have to get a job. You need to start paying on your debt."

Carly nodded, but for the life of her, she couldn't understand how she'd ever get a job in one of the small towns around here.

Andi left the room and returned with her laptop. She took it to the dining room table and waved Carly over. Carly followed her and they both sat down.

"What are you going to do?" Carly asked, looking at the computer.

"We're going to go through all your bills and figure out how much you owe. Then we'll see if you can consolidate some of your credit card bills onto a lower interest card. I also need to make arrangements with the power and gas companies to make payments to them."

Carly nodded. She went back to the sofa and took her wallet from her purse, then brought all her credit cards over to Andi so they could look up each account. "Thanks, Andi. I promise I'll do whatever you want me to do so we can fix this."

Andi looked her in the eye. "Yes, you will. Because if you don't, I won't help you again. Do you understand?"

"Yes." Carly hated having anyone tell her what to do, but she had no choice. She couldn't do this without Andi's help.

"I'm also going to talk to Luke tonight about helping you pay off the electricity, gas, and water and sewer bills."

Carly's eyes brightened. "You mean you'll pay those for me?"

"If we do pay them off for you, you'll still owe us the money. I have to talk to Luke first, though."

"Why do you have to ask Luke? You earn your own money from your paintings."

Andi shook her head. "Luke and I are a couple. We share our money and we discuss how we spend it. I'd never spend this much money without talking to him first and neither would he."

"Geez, I'm glad I don't have to ask permission to spend my own money," Carly said.

Andi raised one eyebrow. "Really, Carly? Well, guess what? From now on, you don't spend a dime without discussing it with me first. If you're going to get out of this mess, you'll have to do things my way. Understood?"

Reluctantly, Carly nodded. She really had no other choice.

Chapter Three

Randy pulled his truck up near the barn door and got out. He'd spent the last two hours in one of the upper pastures checking on the calves that weren't gaining weight. At supper last night, he'd discussed the problem with Luke and they'd both agreed they should add grain to their diet to see if that would jumpstart their weight gain. The calves weren't nursing from their mothers any longer and their main nutrition came from grazing. Since they weren't growing as quickly as the others were, it was time to help fatten them up.

Randy chuckled to himself as he pulled the heavy bucket of grain from the back of his truck and carried it into the barn. Supper last night had been interesting to say the least. He'd watched as Carly greeted Beth with a stiff hug and her awkward attempts at conversation with her. Randy supposed it wasn't easy acting normal when your former roommate was now married to your ex-boyfriend. And Carly was usually anything but normal. The old Carly would have flirted her way through supper, making eyes at every man at the table. But last night, this new Carly seemed very quiet and reserved, and it made him wonder why. Did the hardworking, confident Beth intimidate her? Or was she just on her best behavior? As Randy placed the bucket in the corner of the barn, he figured Carly's newfound quietness wouldn't last long. Not that it mattered to him; he just found it entertaining.

Randy headed up to the house for lunch. He was late, but Ginny always left a plate of sandwiches on the table so everyone could eat at their convenience. He noticed Glen Parker's car in the driveway before he walked inside. Glen and Ginny were sitting together at the table, eating lunch and drinking coffee.

"Hey, Randy," Ginny said, smiling up at him. "Figured you'd make your way in here eventually. Would you like coffee, or maybe a soda with your lunch?"

"Thanks, Mrs. B, but you just sit and enjoy your food. I'll grab something out of the fridge. Hey, Glen. How are you?"

"Hi, Randy. I'm doing fine. Mowed the lawn at my place this morning before coming here. The older I get, the bigger that lawn seems to be," Glen said, chuckling.

Randy grabbed a soda and sat at the table. He selected a sandwich from the pile and took a bite. He liked Glen. Ginny had started dating Glen around the time Andi and Luke became a couple, and Glen seemed the perfect fit for Ginny. Glen had retired in his early fifties from a career as a real estate developer, and he'd made a good chunk of money right before the bottom fell out of the market a few years before. He had a nice place on the river just down the road and he also had a home in San Diego where he wintered. He was a hard worker and was always willing to help out around the ranch, which earned him respect from Randy, Luke, and Colt. But his best attribute was he made Ginny happy, and Randy thought that Ginny deserved some happiness after being alone for so many years.

Ginny brought Randy a slice of strawberry pie and set it on the table in front of him. He smiled. He loved how Ginny mothered him, even though he was thirty-four years old. But Ginny mothered everyone who came in her home. That was her charm. He'd never met anyone who didn't like her. Well, except his mother.

Randy headed off to the barn after lunch. He was going to saddle up Black Jack and head out into the west pasture to check on the few cattle there. Most of the herd was up in the summer pasture, but they kept the few here that needed attention.

He stopped short when he came out of the storeroom at the back of the barn, carrying his saddle, blanket, and bridle. Carly was standing in the barn, looking around with a lost expression on her face. When their eyes locked, he could tell she was disappointed to see him.

Randy ignored her and set the saddle over a fence rail beside an empty stall. As he turned to leave the barn, Carly's soft voice stopped him.

"Is Colt around? Or Luke?"

Randy turned and looked steadily into Carly's blue eyes. "Nope."

"Do you know where they are?"

"They both went to Ray's to help with the haying."

"Oh." Carly frowned and bit her lip. "Andi said I could ride Abby anytime I wanted to since she rarely gets to go out much anymore."

Randy shrugged. "So, go ride Abby."

Carly smiled sweetly at Randy. "Would you mind getting her for me?"

Randy crossed his arms. "I'm not the stable boy, Carly."

A crease formed between Carly's perfectly shaped eyebrows. "Colt used to get a horse for me. And he'd saddle it too."

"Yeah, but Colt was madly in love with you. I'm not. Go get your own horse." Randy turned and walked toward the back door of the barn. He heard a rustle in the hay behind him and glanced back in time to see Carly stomping her foot. *What a spoiled brat.*

"I don't even know how to get a horse to come to me," she whined.

Randy rolled his eyes. He strode past Carly and over to the grain bin, filled a small bucket, and then handed it to Carly. "Take this out to the field, go up to Abby, and offer her the grain. She'll be easy to catch that way." He turned and headed out of the barn.

Randy walked to the pasture, where the male horses were kept, to get Black Jack. As he led his horse back to the barn, he watched Carly walk tentatively into the adjoining field and approach Abby. Randy chuckled. Abby was a spirited horse, and she knew that if someone was coming for her, they wanted to go riding. Sometimes, Abby didn't want to go riding. As soon as Carly drew near, Abby trotted off. This happened several times. Randy could tell that Carly was getting frustrated. He could have easily jumped the fence between the two pastures and gone to help her, but he was having too much fun watching the horse make a fool of the spoiled city girl.

Finally, Carly coaxed Abby to eat some the grain from the bucket and then she grabbed on tightly to the harness. Randy saw a satisfied smile spread across her face. Before he could look away, she caught his eyes with hers and her mouth dropped open. It was apparent that she hadn't known she was being watched. Her expression turned into an angry frown and she turned away, pulling Abby along with her.

Randy headed into the barn and tied Black Jack to a post with a lead rope. He grabbed another lead rope from the storeroom for Carly to use. She walked into the barn with Abby just as he brought out the rope.

"You could have helped me," Carly complained.

"Yep, I could have. I chose not to." Randy handed her the lead rope.

Carly looked at the lead rope in her hand. The she stared blankly up at Randy.

"Oh, please. You don't even know how to tie a horse to a post? Where the heck did you learn to ride?" Randy took the rope from her hand, snapped one end on Abby's harness, and then tied the other end in a slipknot around the stall post.

"I learned at a place that saddled the horses for us, that's where," Carly said.

"Well, guess what, missy? You'll have to do all this for yourself from now on. There are no single men around here anymore who will trip over themselves to impress you."

Carly put her hands on her hips and stared daggers at Randy. He tried hard to hold back his laughter. Damn if she wasn't a pretty thing, though, standing there in her tight blue jeans tucked into brand new boots and her skimpy T-shirt that scooped low enough to show off her ample cleavage. Her light blond hair was up in a ponytail but was so long it still brushed against her shoulders. And those damned blue eyes. They sparkled like sapphires. Not that it mattered to Randy. He was immune to her charms, although he was a man and could appreciate a beautiful woman when he saw one.

"Why are you such a mean old cowboy?" Carly demanded.

Randy's eyebrows raised. "I'm not mean, and I'm also not old. I'm thirty-four. The same age as Luke."

"Well, that's old to me," she mumbled.

Randy stood there a moment, locking eyes with Carly until he couldn't stand it any longer. He laughed so loud it spooked the horses. Abby moved quickly and bumped into Carly, sending her flying toward Randy. He quickly reached out and grabbed ahold of her right before she could fall face first on the floor.

Randy stood there a moment with his arms wrapped tightly around Carly. Her eyes were wide with fright. He held her so close, he could feel her heart pounding in her chest. He held onto her until she found her balance again, and then slowly let her go, completely aware that they were only inches apart.

Carly stood up straight and stared at Randy. "What's wrong with you? Are you trying to kill me?"

Randy took a breath. His own heart was beating wildly. From the scare of her almost falling down, he told himself, not from having her in his arms. But for that one instant, when he'd held her so close, she sure did feel good. *Cripes! Get ahold of yourself.*

"Sorry about that," Randy said, looking contrite. "I'll go get you what you need to saddle up Abby. Then I'll teach you how to do it yourself." He turned and walked into the storeroom.

* * *

Carly watched Randy walk away toward the storeroom with her heart still pounding in her chest. She'd thought for sure she was going to hit the floor after Abby bumped into her. But quick as a wink, Randy had grabbed ahold of her and kept her safe. It all happened so fast, she hadn't even realized she'd stopped falling until she'd looked up into his brown eyes. Even though she'd been scared out of her wits, she'd still noticed how amazing his eyes were. They weren't just brown, they were an amber brown with a ring of dark brown circling them. Why hadn't she ever noticed them before?

She watched him carry out the heavy saddle with the horse blanket and bridle sitting on top of it. He was wearing a short-sleeved, cotton T-shirt with his worn out blue jeans, and she saw the muscles in his arms flex as he easily lifted the saddle up and set it on the fence rail. Those same arms had held her tightly just moments ago.

"What?" Randy asked, staring at Carly.

"Huh?" Carly looked up at him, dazed. There were those amazing eyes again, gazing at her. And why hadn't she ever noticed his strong jawline or high cheekbones before? Under the brown shaggy hair and unshaven face, he was actually a very handsome man.

Randy frowned at her. "Are you okay?"

Carly blinked and saw his face wrinkled up in a frown, staring at her. She couldn't believe she actually thought he was handsome. "Yeah, of course, I'm okay. No thanks to you," she said snidely. "You almost killed me. How am I supposed to feel?"

Randy shook his head. "Okay, princess. I'll show you how to saddle a horse. I hope you don't break a nail."

Carly narrowed her eyes at Randy, but she paid attention as he showed her how to saddle Abby. She knew he wasn't going to show her again.

Carly was very proud of herself after she'd saddled Abby and put the bridle on without any help from the crabby cowboy. Well, she'd needed help lifting the heavy saddle up onto Abby, but other than that, and the fact that Randy had to help her cinch the saddle tight, she'd pretty much saddled her.

She led Abby outside the barn and climbed up on her. The day was warm and it felt good to be outside, but deep down, Carly wished she had someone to go riding with, but no one had been available. Andi had put Jessi down for a nap and was painting. Ginny was working on ranch business in her office, and Glen had gone back to his own house to do some work. Beth was working at the hospital, and Luke and Colt were gone too. The only one left was Randy, and she sure wasn't going to ask him to ride with her.

Carly glanced around her. She sort of knew the trails here from riding with Colt last summer. She decided she'd ride up the center trail and then go out past Luke's property and come back around from there. Just as she started to walk Abby away from the barn, she heard Randy call to her.

"You know, you really shouldn't be out riding alone."

Carly sighed. She turned Abby around to face him. He was sitting on Black Jack, looking down at her. His horse was taller than hers was, and his long, lean body sat tall in the saddle. The cowboy hat made him seem even taller. She felt small, even though she was sitting on a horse.

"I really have no choice. There's no one to ride with," Carly said. "I'm sure I'll be fine. I know the trails."

Randy squinted at her. "Which way are you going?"

"Up the middle trail. Why?"

"Well, I'm heading that way too. Might as well follow you for a while," he said, sounding like he was doing her a big favor.

Carly turned Abby around and headed up the trail.

They walked the horses in silence, Carly in the lead and Randy right behind her, until they made it to the top of the hill. Carly stopped Abby, and then turned the horse around. The view from here was beautiful, and she wanted to enjoy it before turning onto the other trail.

"Why did you stop?" Randy asked, bringing Black Jack around to stand beside Abby.

"Because I love this view," Carly told him. From here, the ranch sat in a rich, green valley with pine trees sprinkled about. Beyond the house and barn was the highway, and beyond that the Clark Fork River snaked its way past the property. Above the river rose the hills, covered in evergreens. Carly sighed. She may be a city girl, but she could appreciate a beautiful view when she saw one.

"It is a nice view," Randy said, admiring it.

"Have you seen Andi's painting of it at sunset?" Carly asked.

Randy turned to her. "Of course. It's amazing. She's a very

talented artist."

Carly nodded. Even though she and her sister had their disagreements, she loved her dearly and had always been proud of her talent. That's what Carly did for a living—sell beautiful works of art in what used to be her parent's art gallery, including paintings by Andi. Well, that used to be what she did for a living. Now, she had no idea what she'd do.

"Well, I'm headed west," Randy said. "Got to check on the cattle in the pasture there. You coming that way?"

Carly stared at him, confused. "Which way is west?"

Randy chuckled. "Right. I'm going right. Does that help, city girl?"

"Why didn't you just say that?" Carly asked angrily.

Randy rolled his eyes.

Carly sat up straight in her saddle. She turned Abby and headed on down the trail with as much dignity as she could manage.

Chapter Four

There was a full table at supper that night. Carly had helped Ginny and Andi prepare the food, in-between holding Jessi so Andi's hands were free. Carly loved that Jessi was already warming up to her. She was so cute, like a little doll, and Carly couldn't wait until she grew a little older and she could take her shopping for tiny clothes. Well, that is if she ever had money again.

Carly, Colt, and Beth sat on the long bench against the wall and Andi, Luke, Glen, Ginny, and Randy sat in the chairs opposite them. Jessi's high chair was at the end of the table next to Andi, and, unfortunately for Carly, Randy sat right across from her. Even though she tried hard not to, Carly found herself bumping knees with Randy under the table. Each time she'd pull away as if she'd been burned, and each time Randy slipped her a wicked grin. He appeared to enjoy how uncomfortable she was, and it made her angry.

"So, I hear you and Randy went riding together this afternoon," Ginny said, smiling at Carly. "That was nice."

Both Carly and Randy looked up in shock and blurted out, "No!"

Everyone glanced up and stared at the two at the end of the table.

"Oh," Ginny said, seemingly confused by their answer.

Red faced, Randy returned to shoveling mashed potatoes into his mouth while Carly searched for a way to explain herself. "I went riding," she said. "Randy was just on his way to a pasture to check on cattle."

Luke grinned and looked directly at Carly, his deep blue eyes sparkling with mischief. "So, you were both on horses, riding in the same direction, but you weren't riding together."

Andi elbowed Luke, but some of the others around the table chuckled.

Randy glared at Luke.

Ginny acted as if none of the teasing was happening around her. "I'm just happy you weren't out riding alone, Carly. It really is safer to ride with someone else along."

Carly sighed and picked at her food. She noticed all the good-natured ribbing hadn't hurt Randy's appetite. He was shoveling his food in faster than he could swallow it. *Caveman.*

Later, Randy made a hurried retreat after thanking Ginny for supper. Luke took Jessi home and Colt went outside to finish chores. The women stayed behind to clean up the kitchen.

Beth spoke to Carly as she loaded the dishwasher and Carly put away leftover food. "I'd be happy to go riding with you on my days off. I work Monday, Wednesday, and Friday every week. Just let me know if you want to go riding any of the other days."

"Okay, I'll do that," Carly said with a smile. She doubted if she'd ever ask Beth to go riding, though. What would they talk about? What a great kisser Colt was? Yeah, she doubted that.

"Oh, and Andi asked me about jobs at the hospital. They have an opening in the kitchen, but right now that's all there is. The pay is okay, but I'm not sure it's the kind of work you'd like to do. If something opens in the office, I'll let you know."

Carly nodded and gave Andi a sideways glance. She hated that Andi had told Beth she needed a job while she stayed here.

That meant everyone would wonder why, and the last thing she wanted to do was tell everyone her business. "Thanks, Beth," Carly responded with as much enthusiasm as she could muster.

They finished cleaning the kitchen and Beth left to go home. Before leaving, she invited Carly to come over sometime to see the house. Carly said she would. She wanted to see it since she hadn't in December when she was here last. She really didn't mind that Beth and Colt were together; it just felt a bit awkward sometimes.

Andi hugged her goodnight and left soon after Beth. Glen and Ginny had gone into the sitting room to watch television. Carly knew that Glen stayed over every now and then, so she didn't want to bother them. She felt a little lost. It was too early to go to bed and too late to do anything.

She grabbed her jacket and headed outside into the cool evening. It was still light out and would be for at least another hour. She pulled her phone out of her pocket, looked at the tower bars, and sighed. She knew there was no reception here at the ranch, but she thought she'd try anyway.

Carly wandered over to the fence by the barn and climbed up on it, standing on the bottom rail. She watched as the horses ambled about and grazed. Night creatures chirped and croaked. Although Carly had no idea what animals made those noises, it added to the country charm of the scenery.

If Carly were home, she'd be out eating with friends and possibly listening to a band and dancing. She and her friends always had fun when they went out. Of course, having a few glasses of wine helped. She wondered what everyone was doing right now. Adam, an artist friend of hers, had gone to Paris for a year with his boyfriend to, as he put it, soak up inspiration from all the classic art. Her other friend, Chelle, had been dating Quinn for over a year now. She'd met Quinn through Colt when he'd lived in Seattle last year. Quinn's father owned a large grocery market in downtown Seattle and Colt had worked there for a few months. Quinn was a great guy, but now that he and Chelle were a serious couple Carly didn't see Chelle as much as she used to. And then there was Everly. She hadn't talked to Carly since taking her job. Not that Carly blamed Everly for being given the job, but it seemed that Everly just stopped being her friend after that.

Carly sighed. Everyone she knew was now a couple, or had deserted her. Even her family had paired off. Andi had Luke, Beth had Colt, heck, even Ginny had Glen. And all she had was a huge pile of debt, no man, and no job.

"I hate my life," Carly said aloud to the horses in the field.

"What's the matter, princess? Someone step on your glass slipper?"

Carly turned sharply and lost her balance. A strong set of hands grabbed her around the waist to keep her from falling. She hopped off the fence, turned around, and found herself looking up into a familiar pair of amber eyes.

"What's wrong with you? Are you trying to kill me?" Carly asked, her face inches from his.

Randy chuckled. "No, just the opposite. I was making sure you didn't fall on your cute little behind."

Randy's hands still circled her waist. She was so close to him, she could smell his aftershave. It was light and spicy but also mixed with the smell of horse sweat. She pulled back as soon as her mind cleared enough to realize they were too close.

"Let go of me," she insisted.

Randy dropped his hands but didn't move.

"Why are you still here? I thought you'd gone home to wherever it is you live."

"I was on my way to my truck when I heard you complaining to the horses about your life," Randy said, smirking. "Why do you hate your life? You get everything you want by pouting and batting your eyelashes. How can that be so bad?"

Carly glared at Randy. "What would you know? Besides, I'm not discussing my life with a *ranch hand*."

Randy tightened his jaw and narrowed his eyes. "That's fine with me. I could care less what goes on in your life. You're just a spoiled little brat who needs to grow up." He turned and strode off toward his truck.

Carly's mouth tightened into a thin line. How dare he insult her and then walk away? She ran after him. "I don't care what you think of me!" she yelled at his back.

Randy ignored her and kept walking. He reached his truck and hopped up into the cab, slamming the door shut. The engine roared to life and he backed the truck up to turn it around. When he put it in drive and looked up, Carly stood right in the way, her hands on her hips.

"Get out of the way!" Randy yelled at her.

Carly stood firm. "Not until you apologize."

Randy slammed the truck into park and jumped out of the cab. He strode over to Carly, who widened her eyes the closer he came. He picked her up easily and swung her over his shoulder like a sack of grain.

"What are you doing?" Carly screamed. She pounded her fists on his back, but to no avail. Randy carried her over to the house and set her down next to the steps. When he looked at her, his eyes were spitting fire.

"Goodnight, missy," he said through clenched teeth. Then he walked back to his truck.

Carly's face grew hot with anger. "I hate you!" she screamed at him as he opened his truck door. "Do you hear me, you crabby old cowboy? I hate you!"

Randy glanced over at her, grinned, then hopped up into his truck and drove away.

Carly stood there, seething with anger. She stomped her foot hard on the ground. Then she turned on her heel and walked up the steps and inside the house.

* * *

Randy drove the few miles west to his home as the sun began to set behind the hills. Many nights, he stopped at The Depot for a beer or two before heading home, but not tonight. After his scrap with Carly, he didn't feel much like being around all the regulars at the bar.

He turned his truck into the long driveway that led down to his small mobile home. It sat on ten acres of land that lay on the edge of the Brennan property. Jack Brennan had deeded him the land as a gift when he'd turned twenty-one. Although he'd been hanging out at the Brennan ranch since he was a child, he'd actually started working part-time as a ranch hand when he was sixteen and had become a full-time hand at eighteen. He wasn't much for schooling, and ranching was really all he knew, so working for the Brennans, alongside his best friend, Luke, was perfect for him.

Randy parked in front of his home and sat in the truck a moment, gazing at nothing in particular. *Ranch hand.* When Carly had called him that, she'd said it with great disdain, as if he wasn't worth a nickel. It had made him feel less than what he was, and that was what had angered him. He knew he shouldn't have let her upset him, but she had. The Brennans had always treated him like family. Andi and Beth had too. No one had looked down their nose at him for being just a ranch hand in years. Well, no one except his mother, but that was different. His mother had always treated him as if he was less than nothing.

Sighing, Randy stepped out of his truck and headed inside

his home. It wasn't new, and it wasn't large, but inside, the mobile home was cozy and comfortable. It was fine for his needs.

The front door opened into a tiny entryway where there was a closet for coats, a hat rack on the wall, and a space on the vinyl floor for his dirty boots. He slipped off his boots, set them on the rug by the door, and then plopped his hat on the rack. To his right was a small bedroom that he used for storage and a bathroom. To his left was the living room where a cushy brown sectional sofa sat in the corner against two walls and a widescreen television sat on the opposite wall. A potbellied stove stood in the farthest corner surrounded by tile flooring so it was safely away from the carpet. Even though he had propane heat, he preferred wood. It was warmer and cost less to heat with during the long, cold winters.

Randy walked through the living room and into the kitchen. It was compact but had all the necessary appliances as well as a dining table with four chairs in the corner. Down the hallway, past the kitchen, were his washer and dryer in an alcove and then another bigger bathroom and his bedroom. Nothing was fancy, but it suited him fine. Plus, it was all he could afford for now. His money was earmarked for more important things these days.

Randy grabbed a beer from the refrigerator and sat down on the sofa. He picked up the remote and switched on the television. Flipping through the stations, he landed on a crime drama show and left it there. The pretty policewoman on the show reminded him of Carly, and he shook his head.

I hate you, she'd yelled at him as he'd driven away. Well, she probably did. She'd never been a big fan of his and today had proven she really didn't like him. It was no surprise to Randy.

Randy thought of how twice that day he'd held her close just as she'd started to fall. Even though he'd never given her more than a cursory thought, both times she'd been in his arms, he'd had to pause a moment. She'd smelled of a light lavender perfume and her hair had felt silky as it brushed across his arm. Her sapphire-blue eyes had looked up at him, wide and beautiful. But then she'd opened her mouth and ruined the moment both times. Why on earth couldn't she be as sweet and kind as her sister? Or as warm and caring as Beth? What was her problem?

"And why in the hell am I even thinking about her?" he said aloud to the empty room.

Randy chugged down the last of his beer, snapped off the television, and headed back to the bedroom. He shrugged off his clothes and took a hot shower before climbing into his bed. Alone. Exactly how he liked it. He adored women, but he was in no rush to have one run his life. Maybe someday, when he found the right one. If he found the right one. But certainly not a woman like Carly. *Thank God she isn't my problem.*

* * *

Carly lay in bed that night, exhausted, but unable to sleep. She was still boiling with anger over her fight with Randy. How dare he call her a spoiled brat? He barely even knew her. It was his fault she'd been angry in the first place. He was the one who'd startled her, making her lose her balance and nearly fall off the fence. And those snarky comments he was always making drove her crazy. *Princess.* He had no right calling her that. She didn't act like some high and mighty princess. Just because she was more educated and sophisticated than he was didn't mean she was a snotty little princess.

When she'd called him a "ranch hand", she'd seen the anger spark in his eyes. She'd realized she'd crossed a line, but she'd been so angry, she wasn't about to apologize. And then he'd called her a spoiled brat and that was it. But now, lying in her bed in the quiet house, she felt guilty for talking to Randy that way. She was a lot of things, but she wasn't a snob and she would normally never look down on a person. But she had with Randy, and she knew it was wrong. At some point, she realized, she'd have to apologize to him.

Carly sighed. Why couldn't Randy be nicer, like Luke and Colt? Twice today she'd been close enough to him to see how good looking he really was, beneath that shaggy hair, facial scruff, and that damned smug grin. There was no doubt he was strong. Both times when he'd caught her to stop her from falling, she'd felt how strong his hands and arms were. And then when he'd lifted her tonight and carried her over to the house, dropping her down unceremoniously, he'd done so like she was no heavier than a bag of feathers.

Indignation rose inside her again at the thought of him carrying her that way. Just who did he think he was? Well, from now on, she wasn't going to give him the time of day. She could care less about Randy.

So, why am I still thinking about him?

Frustrated, Carly pulled her covers up tightly around her, rolled over on her side, and closed her eyes, trying to block the crusty cowboy out of her thoughts.

Chapter Five

The next morning, Carly woke up later than everyone else and took her time showering and dressing. Breakfast was generally at six every morning so the men could get started with work, but that was too early for Carly. Besides, she didn't want to chance running into Randy yet. Just thinking about him made her blood boil, and not in a good way.

Carly pulled her hair up into a ponytail and applied a small amount of makeup to enhance her eyes and lips. She felt naked without at least a touch of color because her skin was so pale and her eyelashes were as blond as her hair. People thought she was vain, but the truth was, she looked very plain without a little makeup on. And one thing Carly didn't like was being plain and ordinary.

The kitchen was empty by the time Carly came downstairs. Even Bree was gone. A basket of blueberry muffins was on the table and Carly knew there was always fresh fruit in the fridge. She found a bowl of strawberries and poured a glass of milk, then grabbed a plate and sat down at the table.

Halfway through her breakfast, Ginny came in from the garden with a bucket full of strawberries and another of raspberries. Glen followed behind her, carrying little Jessi, and Bree pranced in and headed for her water bowl.

"Good morning, dear," Ginny said with a big smile on her

face. "It's about time you woke up and joined the rest of us." Glen grinned and said good morning too. He looked so cute, carrying little Jessi. She wore a tiny pair of pink striped bib overalls and a sweet little pink T-shirt and pink sneakers. Her red hair curled all around her face and her green eyes sparkled when she saw her auntie.

Glen set Jessi in her high chair beside the table and made sure she was strapped in securely. Carly scooted over to sit next to Jessi.

"Aren't you just the cutest thing I've ever seen," Carly cooed at her niece.

Jessi smiled and made a gurgling-laughing noise.

"Where's Andi?" Carly asked. Ginny and Glen were over by the sink, washing the freshly picked fruit.

"She went into town a little bit ago to pick up a few things," Ginny told her. "Do you want to give Jessi her bottle? It's time for her morning nap."

"Sure," Carly said. She picked Jessi up from the high chair and took the bottle from Ginny.

"There's a small crib in the office where you can lay her down when she falls asleep," Ginny said.

Carly nodded and walked into the sitting room. She sat in the armchair and held Jessi as she fed her the bottle. The baby quickly grabbed ahold of the bottle and started drinking it greedily.

Carly smiled down at her little niece. She'd never had much experience with babies, and had never really thought much about them, either, but she adored Jessi. She didn't know if it was the fact that Jessi was her sister's baby, or that she was so small and helpless, or maybe because she was so darned cute, but somehow this little girl had stolen Carly's heart. She wondered if this was how it felt to have a baby of your own. Carly was terrified of marriage, and had never thought of having children, but when she looked down into little Jessi's eyes, she could almost see herself with a baby of her own. Almost.

Jessi's eyes grew heavy and by the time her bottle was empty, she was sound asleep. Carly lifted her up on her shoulder and rubbed her back while she walked carefully across the sitting room to the office. Once inside, she gently laid the baby in the crib, slipped off her sneakers, and pulled the blanket over her.

Carly stood there a moment, watching Jessi sleep. The little girl tugged at her heart like no other living being had ever done. Yes, she'd definitely like to have a baby someday. She smiled down at the sleeping angel, then noticing the baby monitor, she turned it on and quietly left the room.

When Carly returned to the kitchen, Andi was sitting at the table sipping a cup of tea. The other baby monitor was on the table beside her. Ginny and Glen were gone. Carly supposed they'd headed back out to the garden for more berries. This was the time of year when Ginny made her special jams and preserves to sell in a booth she shared with her friends at the Western Montana Fair in Missoula.

"Is Jessi asleep?" Andi asked, looking up at Carly. Her red hair was up in a thick ponytail and curly tendrils fell softly around her face. Even without much makeup, Andi was beautiful. Carly had always thought so, but Andi never really gave much thought to her beauty. She liked looking nice, but that was where it ended.

"Yes. She fell asleep right away," Carly said as she rinsed out the bottle and set it in the sink.

"Good. I'm glad she's getting used to you," Andi said. "It's nice for Jessi to know her aunt."

Carly nodded and sat down opposite Andi.

"I think I may have found you a job for the summer, if

you're interested," Andi said.

Carly's mouth dropped open but she clamped it shut again quickly. "Already? Where?"

"At a little gift shop on this side of Superior called Margie's Mountain Gifts. She's a sweet, older lady who's owned the shop for years. She sells all types of gift items for tourists and also artwork by local artists. I have some of my latest prints there."

Carly frowned. "A gift shop? Like plastic dolls, stuffed animals, and bags of rocks?"

Andi stared at her. "It may have a few of those items, but like I said, she sells artwork too. She needs help and I thought you could bring new life to Margie's shop. It's not like you have that many options around here."

Carly sighed. "I suppose you're right."

Andi leaned forward. "You need to earn money to start paying off your debt, Carly. At least this is something you have experience with."

Carly nodded. "So, what do I need to do? Apply?"

Andi sat back, a satisfied smile on her face. "She said to stop by tomorrow morning and visit a while. I'm sure the job could be yours if you're polite."

"Hey, I'm always polite to people."

Andi raised her eyebrows.

Carly tightened her lips. "Fine. I'll go and be polite and get the job."

"Good. I'm sure once you get to know Margie, you'll be glad you're working there. It may even be fun."

Carly bit her lip. *Right. A load of fun.*

* * *

Saturday morning, Carly woke early, showered, and dressed

in a silky blue blouse and a pair of black pants and black heels. She was sure she could have gone to the gift shop in a T-shirt and jeans and still have gotten the job, but she thought she should at least try.

It was past breakfast time, but when she entered the kitchen, Colt was sitting at the table with Glen, and Ginny was pouring coffee. Colt looked up at her and grinned.

"Now, that's the Carly I remember from Seattle. You look nice."

Carly smiled. "Thanks, Colt." She sat down on the end of the bench and accepted a mug of coffee from Ginny. She was happy that Colt still felt comfortable around her after all they'd been through together. She knew she didn't deserve his friendship after dumping him the way she had the year before, but being the sweetheart that he was, he gave it to her anyway.

"What are you all gussied up for this morning?" Ginny asked, bringing over a basket of muffins, the butter, and a plate.

Carly selected a muffin and began buttering it. "I have a job interview this morning," she said. "Andi arranged it."

"A job interview? What about your job in Seattle?" Colt asked.

Obviously, Andi hadn't told everyone what was going on with her. For that, Carly was grateful. "They had to cut back. I'm going to work here this summer."

"Oh." Colt looked at Carly curiously. "So, you're staying the whole summer?"

Carly nodded. She glanced over at Ginny, who didn't look surprised by the news. "I hope you don't mind, Ginny. I don't want to overstay my welcome."

Ginny smiled. "Of course it's okay, dear. Andi already told me you'd be staying. You're welcome to stay as long as you wish."

Carly let out a sigh. She took a bite of her muffin and

washed it down with some coffee. She didn't mind Ginny's coffee, but she'd kill for a latte.

"I'd better get back to work or I might not have a job," Colt said, standing. "Good luck with your interview, Carly. Where are you going?"

"Margie's Mountain Gifts."

Colt nodded. "You'll like Margie. She's a sweetheart." He headed out the door.

"Seems everyone knows who Margie is," Carly said to Ginny and Glen.

"Oh, everyone around here knows Margie," Ginny said. "She's owned that shop for over thirty years. When the boys were little, they'd always beg me to take them there to buy a trinket. She's great with kids."

Carly sipped her coffee. That's what she was afraid of. She'd be working in a cheesy gift shop that sold toy bow and arrow sets and rubber snakes. Great.

After breakfast, Carly took off in her car and headed west on highway 90 toward Superior. Andi had told her to take the only exit into Superior and the gift shop was on the right. "You can't miss it," Andi had said. "It's the cute log building with the big windows and wind chimes hanging from the porch roof."

Carly found the building easily. She parked in a spot right in front of one of the two big windows and sat in her car a moment. She peered through the glass, but it was difficult to see what was on display because the window was so dusty. Sighing, Carly stepped out of her car and walked to the porch where, sure enough, wind chimes tinkled in the morning breeze.

Those could drive you batty after a while.

Carly opened the door and heard a bell jingle. She looked up and saw an actual bell above the door that jingled when the door hit it. She'd only seen those in old movies, never in real stores.

She stood inside the door and assessed the building. It was longer than it was wide and there were two large plate-glass windows on her right and one large window at the rear of the building. Freestanding units stood in rows in front of her with glass shelves packed with items. They looked in need of a good dusting. Artwork hung on the walls toward the back of the store. Toys, puzzles, stuffed animals, and the dreaded fake bows and arrows were just some of the many gift items for sale. There was a display of ceramic wildlife creatures and a huge barrel of colorful rocks that children could pack into a small drawstring pouch and purchase. In the back of the store were shelves of T-shirts and sweatshirts touting Montana. Dreamcatchers hung from the ceiling and swayed gently from the breeze of the old box air unit hung in the corner above the door. This was exactly how Carly had expected the shop to look, yet she was disappointed just the same.

"Can I help you, dear?"

Carly slowly turned around to see a woman standing behind a long counter that was waist-high and held an old-fashioned cash register on the left and shelves of trinkets on the right. One section of the counter was glass and had lights that showed off turquoise and silver jewelry.

Carly pasted a smile on her face and walked over to the woman. "Hi. I'm Carly, Andi's sister. You must be the owner, Margie."

The woman nodded and smiled. She was shorter than Carly and plump with short, straight, silver hair and bright blue eyes. She wore a simple pair of brown slacks and a flowered blouse with a tan cardigan over it along with a pair of sensible brown shoes. But her smile was warm and inviting and Carly felt comfortable immediately.

"Yes, I'm Margie," she told Carly. "My, but aren't you a

pretty girl. Andi told me all about you, and I was so pleased to hear you'd be interested in working in my little shop."

Carly glanced around but kept the smile on her face. Just a few weeks ago she would never have even considered working in a shop like this. Now, she really had no choice.

"Can you tell me a little about the job?" Carly asked, feigning interest.

Margie nodded. "I'll be up front with you. I have this shop up for sale, so if I'm lucky, it will sell by fall. It's been for sale for three years now, so I'm not holding my breath, but I can always be hopeful. I'm ready to retire and relax a bit. I have a daughter and grandchildren who live in California who I'd like to go visit in the winter. If I can't sell the shop, I'm closing for the winter anyway and will worry about what I'll do with it next summer."

"Okay," Carly said. She glanced around. She understood why no one wanted to buy the shop. It was cluttered, and a lot of the merchandise looked old.

"But until it sells, I need someone to come in three days a week and every other Saturday from nine to five. I'm thinking Monday, Wednesday, and Friday. I need someone to help customers and maybe help me clean this place up a little. Does that sound like anything you'd like to do?"

Carly held back a sigh. It sounded awful, but she smiled and nodded anyway. "Sure. That would be fine."

Margie's eyes lit up and she walked around the counter and over to Carly. "Wonderful. Let me show you around the store."

They walked up and down aisles. There were plenty of western toys, animal puzzles, and cute Native American dolls. On the far wall was a long row of books for children and adults, many on the history of Montana. Scattered around were framed prints and paintings by local artists as well as paintings on stretched deer hides. In the back corner there was a display of Native American craftwork including birch bark baskets, beaded deer hide moccasins, and woven blankets. Margie also explained that she sold jewelry made by local Native Americans displayed in the glass case by the counter.

As Carly wandered the shop, she saw many beautiful works of art that were hidden in shadowy corners of the store. Hand-carved wooden animals sat up on high shelves where they could barely be seen. All around, the shelves were covered in dust, making the products undesirable. As she passed the shelf of puzzles, she softly blew on them and dust went flying. *This place needs a lot of work.*

She turned to Margie who looked at her curiously. "You have an interesting array of items here. Have you thought about moving some of the artwork near the front of the store so customers can see it when they walk in?"

Margie walked over to Carly and patted her on the arm. "Sweetie, if you come and work for me, you can move the store around any way you see fit. I know I've been remiss in keeping the store up, and fresh ideas would be welcome. What do you say? Will you work for me?"

Carly looked into Margie's kind eyes. She saw instantly why everyone liked her. She reminded her of a sweet grandmotherly figure. "I'd love to work here with you," she said.

Margie clapped her hands together. "Wonderful. We'll get your paperwork done up and you can start on Monday. I know I'm going to love having you here with me."

Carly wasn't as sure, but at least she'd be making some money.

* * *

That evening, the family ate supper as usual around the big table in the kitchen. Randy was absent, but Carly knew it wasn't unusual for him to fend for himself on the weekends. Earlier in the afternoon while she'd helped Ginny prepare supper, she'd seen her give Randy a covered container of food. Randy had smiled and kissed her on the cheek before leaving. Carly had no idea what Ginny had given him, and she figured it wasn't any of her business. Maybe it was a few homemade cookies or some leftovers to heat up.

Carly was unusually quiet during supper and Andi didn't press her about her new job after hearing that she'd been hired. Andi had smiled happily over Carly already having a job, but Carly wasn't as excited. She knew Andi was just trying to help her dig out of her financial mess, but she wished she'd found something better. Although, in the middle of nowhere, what were her choices?

After helping clean up the kitchen and spending time with Andi and Jessi, everyone left to go to their own homes and Ginny and Glen sat in the sitting room, watching a movie. It was Saturday night, and Carly was stuck here at home. She'd tried talking the others into going to The Depot for a beer or two and to dance awhile, but everyone declined. Carly had thought about going by herself, but once she saw the warning look Andi gave her, she decided against it. It irked her that she couldn't go out. How dangerous could it be for her to go to the local honkytonk alone? She went to bars in Seattle all the time, usually not alone, but still, no one had ever accosted her there.

As evening settled over the ranch, Carly decided to go outside and stretch her legs. She grabbed a jacket and pulled her riding boots over her jeans before heading outside. The evening was chilly, but the sky was clear and the stars shone brightly in the blue-black sky.

Carly stopped halfway to the barn and looked up into the sparkling sky. She inhaled the mountain air, taking in the scent of freshly cut hay and the sweet smell of evergreens. She missed Seattle's bright lights and nightlife, but she also thought it was lovely here. Glancing up at the barn, she remembered the times she and Colt had climbed up into the hayloft and sat gazing out at the night sky. The thought lightened her mood, and she walked to the barn to do just that.

There was a light on in the back corner of the barn when she entered. A man wearing a plaid shirt and jeans stood over a saddle, rubbing something into it with an old rag. His shoulders were broad and his waist narrow. Carly couldn't see his hair because of his hat, but he looked like Colt. Smiling wide, she walked over and tapped him lightly on the shoulder.

"Hey, Colt. I thought you'd gone home."

The man turned around and stared at her. "Sorry. Wrong guy."

Carly sighed. "Oh, it's just you."

"Sorry to disappoint you," Randy said. He turned back to his work.

"I thought you'd left hours ago."

Randy shrugged. "I did. I went to The Depot and had a burger, but I didn't feel like hanging out there tonight. So I decided to clean my saddle and tack."

Carly leaned against an empty stall and watched as Randy rubbed cleaner into his saddle. "I tried getting someone to go out to The Depot with me tonight, but they're all boring. Everyone said they were tired and wanted to go home. It's depressing just sitting around here on a Saturday night. If I were at home, I'd be out dancing."

Randy turned and stared at Carly. "So, why are you here in the barn, looking for Colt? Did you think he'd dance with you out here or something?"

Carly rolled her eyes. "No. And I wasn't *looking* for Colt. I only thought you were him. I came out here to go up to the loft and look at the sky. It's beautiful tonight. Colt and I used to go up there and enjoy the stars."

Randy snorted. "Yeah. That's what you two were doing up there."

Carly glared at his back. "What would you know?" She walked past him and started climbing up the ladder attached to the back wall.

"Won't do you any good going up there," Randy said as he continued cleaning his saddle.

Carly glanced down at him. "Why?"

"The big door is closed."

"So, I'll open it."

Randy chuckled. "It's awfully heavy, for a girl."

Carly ignored him and continued up into the loft. "I can do it myself," she insisted.

"Just wait a moment," Randy hollered up the ladder. "I won't be blamed for you falling out of the loft trying to push open that door."

A moment later, Randy was up through the hatch. He carried a small cooler in one hand as he walked past Carly toward the large door.

Carly watched as he unlatched the door at both ends and then slowly pushed it aside. She walked over and stood next to him, admiring the view.

"You were right. It is beautiful out tonight," Randy said.

Carly gazed out at the night sky. The stars were twinkling high above and the half-moon shone bright over the fields. It was soothing to look at after today. Randy stood next to her, his hands on his hips. He had a small smile on his lips. She glanced behind her at the cooler that he'd set on a square straw bale.

"What's in there?"

Randy turned to her and grinned. "Figured since you didn't get to go to The Depot, you might want to have one of these."

He stepped over, opened the cooler, and pulled out two bottles of beer. "Want one?"

"Sure. Thanks," she said. Randy twisted off the top and handed it to her. They both took a drink of their beer and Carly sighed. "I really needed this after my crappy day."

"Why was your day so crappy?"

Carly looked at the straw bale. She moved the cooler to the floor and sat down but stood up again quickly. She glanced at Randy. "Colt used to lay his coat down on the straw so it wouldn't be so prickly."

"Yeah, but Colt wanted to impress you. I don't." Randy sat down on the bale. "Feels fine to me."

"That's because you're prickly," Carly shot back.

Randy shook his head and stood. "Fine." He unbuttoned his flannel shirt, slipped it off, and spread it over the straw. Underneath, he wore only a white T-shirt.

Carly tried not to stare at his chest muscles stretched tautly under his T-shirt or at his upper arms that were thick and hard. She sat down beside him and took another sip of her beer. Sitting on the shirt helped, but she still felt the straw poking her.

"So, why was your day so crappy?" Randy asked. He removed his hat and took another drink from his beer.

"You cut your hair," Carly said, staring at him. No wonder she hadn't recognized him from behind. His hair wasn't shaggy anymore. In fact, it looked kind of nice.

"Well, yeah, I got it cut. What's the matter? Can't a guy get a haircut?"

"You don't have to get all grouchy. I just noticed, that's all. It looks…nice."

"Oh." They sat there a moment, both staring out into the night. Finally, Randy spoke up. "So, are you going to tell me why your day was crappy or not?"

Carly sighed. "Oh, yeah. Andi found a job for me that I'm not very excited about, for one. And then no one wanted to go out dancing. All in all, it hasn't been that great of a day."

Randy cocked his head. "Why did you get a job? I thought you had some fancy schmancy job in Seattle."

Carly slid her eyes over to Randy. She didn't want to tell him her business. "I did, but I'm staying the summer here, so I needed a job."

"You're staying the whole summer?"

"Yes, I am. Is that a problem for you?"

Randy chuckled. "No, not for me. I didn't realize you were staying that long. So, where did you get a job at?"

"Margie's Mountain Gifts."

"What's wrong with that? Margie is a sweetheart."

"I know. Everyone says that. And I agree. She is a sweetheart. It's just that her gift shop has a lot to be desired and I'm used to things a bit more upscale."

"Oh, that's right. I keep forgetting. You're so much more sophisticated than the rest of us," Randy said.

Carly frowned, but then she realized how she'd actually sounded. She turned to Randy and laid her hand on his arm. "I didn't mean it that way, okay?"

Randy glanced down at her hand, then back up into her eyes. He nodded.

Carly bit her lip. "I also owe you an apology for last night. There's nothing wrong with being a ranch hand and I sounded like a snob. I'm sorry."

Randy stared at her in disbelief. "I appreciate that," he said quietly.

They sat there a while longer, sipping their beer and staring out into the sky. It was so beautiful and peaceful.

"You're not staying the summer to try to get Colt back, are you?" Randy asked bluntly.

Carly's mouth dropped open. She glared at Randy. "No, I'm not. How dare you ask such a thing? He's married to Beth now, and I'm fine with it." She stood and walked closer to the door, staring out into the night. She was so angry with Randy she could have hit him. She'd just apologized to him and then he hit her with a question like that. Now she wished she hadn't apologized.

Randy walked up beside her. "Sorry, Carly. I just had to make sure. After what you did to him last summer, I'd hate to see you hurt him again. Colt and Beth are happy together. They belong together."

Carly looked at him. "I know they belong together. I was the one who told Beth to come out here and be with Colt. But I can still care about him even though he's with someone else."

Randy nodded.

"Colt will always be special to me," Carly said softly. "He's so sweet and kind. He knows how to treat a lady. And he's a really great kisser." She sighed.

Carly glanced up at Randy and saw him staring at her strangely. Then, he reached out and pulled her to him, dropping his lips over hers. She was so shocked, she didn't move at first, but his kiss grew deeper and she responded. Randy's hands slid down to her waist and her spine tingled with delight at his touch. She raised her arms around his neck and pulled him closer. As quickly as the kiss started, it ended. Randy stepped back, glaring at her.

"That's how a real man kisses," he said. Then he stormed across the loft and down the ladder.

Carly stood there, dazed, wondering what had just happened.

Chapter Six

Sunday afternoon, Randy drove east along the highway toward the nursing home where his mother lived. On the seat beside him sat the food container Ginny had given him yesterday. He smiled when he thought of Ginny. She was such a sweet person. She always sent along a treat for him to bring to his mother. He wished his own mother had been more like Ginny, but that was like wishing that money grew on trees. It was never going to happen.

As the road pounded under the truck's tires, Randy thought back to last night and his encounter with Carly. What had he been thinking? Everything had started out just fine. They'd passed their snide banter back and forth as usual, which for some reason he enjoyed. Sitting up in the loft, having a beer, and enjoying the starlit sky had been nice. Even though Carly drove him crazy—and not in a good way—what had happened was not something he would have ever planned.

Why in the hell did I kiss her?

Randy thought about how he'd grabbed her and covered her mouth with his. He was not an aggressive man, but at that moment, he'd acted like one. Her skin under his fingers was soft and her lips had felt silky against his. God, she'd smelled glorious. Like flowers. A field of lavender. When he'd felt her arms go around his neck, her body pushed up against his, it had jolted him back to reality. Not only were they kissing, but she was actually enjoying it.

Shit! I enjoyed it!

All night, Randy had pondered why he'd kissed her. He blamed the beautiful sky. He blamed how close Carly had sat next to him. When she'd placed her hand on his arm to assure him she wasn't going after Colt again, it had completely unnerved him. He hadn't expected to enjoy the feel of her touch. Then, to his utter surprise, she'd apologized for insulting him yesterday. All of it had been so out of character for Carly and he'd felt disorientated. But then she stood there with dreamy eyes talking about how wonderful Colt was and how he was such a great kisser, and that had set him off. Randy had nothing against Colt—they were like brothers—but he suddenly had to prove to Carly that he was a great kisser. *Why?*

Randy had no idea.

Carly was a player. He knew that, yet last night he hadn't felt like he was being played. For the first time since he'd met her, she'd acted like a regular person. No flirting, no pouting, no batting her eyes. He saw who she really was, and he'd liked what he saw. At least, he thought he had.

Well, that was as good a reason as any.

He drove into the nursing home parking lot and put the truck in park. Grabbing the food container, he stepped out and headed to the front door. He had to forget about Carly for now. Visiting his mother would take all of his energy.

Randy walked inside and immediately smelled what the residents had eaten for lunch. The community dining room was to his right, but the smell of tuna fish casserole seeped into all corners of the building. He walked up to the front desk and signed in, giving the young woman who worked there a friendly nod. She was a blond, blue-eyed cutie who always smiled wide at Randy when he visited. Sweet but much too young for him.

So he smiled and kept his distance.

Walking down the hallway toward his mother's room, he said hello to several of the residents who ambled past him assisted by walkers or awaiting a guest in wheelchairs in the doorway of their rooms. Sunday was the big visiting day around here, and everyone eagerly waited for family to arrive. Randy knew most of the residents after coming here for five years. Of course, many had passed away over the years, but new ones arrived and all were eager for a friendly face.

A nurse in blue scrubs came out of a room and smiled at Randy. She was in her mid-forties, sturdily built, and dark complexioned.

"Hey, there, Randy. How are you today?"

"Can't complain," he said. He always enjoyed talking to Renee when he visited. She not only gave him the rundown on his mother's current condition, but she had a wicked sense of humor, as well. "How's your day going?"

"Oh, it's another day in paradise," she said, her eyes sparkling mischievously. "I just helped your mother back to her room. She's in pretty good spirits today. She only snapped at me once. And she even sat in on Sunday services this morning before lunch without a complaint." She winked. "We both know how that usually goes."

Randy chuckled. Church attendance hadn't been high on his mother's list of priorities when he was growing up. For her, Sunday morning had been for sleeping off a hangover.

"I'm glad to hear she's in a good mood. I hope I don't darken it for her."

Renee shook her head. "Dear, you should be the sunshine of her week. But you know not to take it personally. It's the dementia speaking when she gets so ornery. It's not because of you."

"I know," Randy said. But it was difficult even though he

understood that.

Renee nodded to the container in his hand. "Another delicious treat from Ginny?"

"Yep. She's too good to me."

Renee squeezed his arm. "It's nice someone is. You deserve it." She headed off down the hallway.

Randy walked to his mother's room and peered inside the open door. She was sitting in a chair beside her bed, watching a silent television in the corner of the room. He knocked on the doorframe to catch her attention, but she just kept her eyes on the television.

Randy glanced around the room. Unlike a typical nursing home, this one allowed for private rooms and bathrooms. It had a small kitchen with a sink, two cabinets, and a mini-refrigerator. Beyond that was a table with two chairs, the recliner his mother was sitting in, and then the bed, covered in a cheery blue and yellow quilt. The television sat on a stand in the corner. It cost a lot more money to live here than his mother's insurance allowed for a care facility, but Randy had wanted his mother in a nice place. For the past five years, he'd paid the difference in cost, even though it left him with little to spend on himself. But he felt better knowing his mother was in a nice place.

"Hello, Ma," Randy said cheerfully, walking through the door and setting the food container on the counter. He took off his hat and ran his hand through his hair to smooth it down.

Evelyn 'Evie' Olson turned and glared at him. Her white hair was sparse and her face was pale and wrinkled. She had been a small woman when she was healthy, but each time he saw her she seemed even smaller. At five feet, four inches tall, she couldn't have weighed more than 98 pounds. Her striped blouse and brown pants hung loosely on her and the big chair seemed to swallow her up. After having had a stroke five years ago, and the damage caused by excessive alcohol abuse for decades, she looked much older than her sixty-four years. But her eyes, with their hard, cold stare, still had a way of scaring the daylights out of Randy.

"What do *you* want?" Evie asked in a deep, raspy voice.

Randy took a breath and then smiled. "I came to visit like I always do on Sunday, Ma." He walked closer and kissed her lightly on the cheek, then sat on the bed across from her. "How are you feeling?"

Evie slowly raked her eyes over him before answering. "I'd feel a hell of a lot better if I wasn't living in this prison."

"Now Ma, don't say that. This is a very nice place to live. The food is good and the nurses take good care of you."

Evie snorted. "That's what you think." She eyed him curiously. "Say, you got a cigarette on you?"

Randy shook his head. "You know I don't smoke, Ma."

"Then why the hell did you bother to come here?"

Randy sighed, but didn't answer. He stood and retrieved the container, setting it down on the small table. "I brought you something. It's apple crisp, your favorite. Ginny made it fresh yesterday, just for you. Would you like a bite?"

Evie turned in her chair and stared at the dessert. "Who'd you say made it?"

"Ginny. You remember, Ma. Ginny Brennan." He went to the cupboard and pulled down two plates, then picked up two forks and a butter knife to cut it. "Would you like me to get us some coffee to go with this?"

When Randy turned to look at his mother, she was sneering at him. "Ginny Brennan. I can't stand those Brennans. They all think they're so high and mighty, looking down their noses at everyone else in town. You know, they tried taking my son away from me. Well, I gave them a piece of my mind. No one was going to take my Randy away from me no matter how good-for-nothing he was. At least he earned money that helped support me. I needed the money. They thought because I was just a lowly bar waitress, they could take him away from me. Damned Brennans!"

Randy frowned and looked into his mother's face. It was turning red with anger. None of what she'd said about the Brennans was true, but there was no sense in arguing with her. She'd always been jealous of the Brennans and the way they took care of him. Truth be told, though, she had been fine with taking the money he earned as a boy on the ranch every summer. She was still getting money from him, money he earned from the very people she hated.

"Hey, Ma, how about some of this apple crisp?" he said, trying to distract her. He cut a piece and laid it on the plate. "I'll help you to the table."

"I can walk by myself," Evie snarled. "I'm not a cripple, you know." She gingerly pulled herself out of the chair and with the help of a cane, slowly walked the few steps to the table. She not only had minor damage to her left side from her stroke, but her years of drinking had damaged nerves throughout her body, making movement a challenge for her.

Evie peered up at Randy after she sat down. "Where's that coffee you were going on about?"

"I'll get it." He strode down to the dining room and poured two cups of coffee, then returned to his mom's room. She'd taken a bite of her dessert and was waiting for her coffee. "Here you go, Ma."

They sat there silently, eating the apple crisp and sipping coffee. He'd made sure his mother's cup was only half full so she wouldn't spill on herself. Her hands shook when she lifted the cup, and she had to work hard to bring the fork to her mouth. Randy knew better than to help her cut up it up, though. She would have had a fit.

He thought about how different her life was now compared to when he was a child. His mom had never been helpless. If anything, she'd been tough as nails and no one dared cross her. She'd always worked as a bar waitress, and he supposed that was what had made her so tough. After his father left them, she'd grown even more bitter and angrier. Randy remembered when he was twelve years old, and at least a foot taller than her, she'd reached up and knocked him so hard on the side of the head that it had made his ears ring for days. All because he'd been late getting home from school. Not that she'd cared about him, but because he was bringing home a bag of groceries she'd wanted before she headed off to work. His mother thought all men were useless, including him. Even so, she'd brought home a few men over the years when he was a boy, two of which he'd run out of their trailer home for hitting her. She was a mean, spiteful woman, but she was his mother and he felt obligated to take care of her despite how she treated him.

Randy looked up and saw his mother staring at him curiously.

"Who did you say you were?" she asked.

"It's me, Ma. Randy. Your son," he said softly.

* * *

Carly rose early Monday morning, showered and dressed, then sat at the kitchen table with Andi, Jessi, and Ginny eating a light breakfast that Ginny had insisted on making for her. After giving Jessi a quick tickle and kiss, she took off in her car for her first day of work.

As Carly drove, her mind wandered to what had happened up in the loft on Saturday night. Randy had kissed her. Why? He didn't even like her. And the surprising part was, she'd really enjoyed his kiss.

She'd been pondering his kiss almost every free moment since he'd bolted from her as if she'd electrocuted him. *He'd kissed* her. Why on earth had he run off as if she'd been the offending person?

Carly had been shocked at first when he'd grabbed her and covered her lips with his. So shocked, that she hadn't even reacted at first. But as his mouth opened hers and their tongues met, she slowly melted in his arms. Feeling his strong body against hers, his mouth warm and inviting, had erupted desire within her for the first time in weeks. She'd forgotten who was kissing her and given in to it. And dear Lord, how she'd enjoyed it.

Who knew the prickly cowboy was such a good kisser?

After two days, she still didn't understand why he'd grabbed her like that, and thought that maybe she didn't want to know after all. He hadn't come to the ranch on Sunday, thank goodness, and she hadn't run into him this morning. But she knew he'd be at the supper table tonight, and it made her nervous just thinking about him there, sitting across from her.

Carly shook her head to push thoughts of Randy away as she pulled into the gift shop parking lot. She stepped out of her car, smoothing the wrinkles from her pants and silky blouse. Pulling her purse up over her shoulder, she steeled herself for her first day of work and entered the gift shop.

Margie was behind the counter placing money into the old cash register. She smiled cheerfully at Carly. "Ready to start work?"

As ready as I'll ever be, Carly thought. She pasted a smile on her face. "I'm all yours."

Carly spent the day learning how to use the old cash register as well as helping a few customers who stopped in. Margie explained that Mondays weren't too busy, but as the week progressed, more customers would stop by. To keep busy, Carly began dusting and organizing shelves, moving some of the items that were less popular to the back of the store and some closer to the front. She made a mental inventory of the artwork and looked around for a more optimal place to display it. Ideally, she'd like to have placed it near the large windows in front, but paintings and prints needed to stay out of direct sunlight so as not to fade. She studied the area and decided that on Wednesday, she'd clean the large windows and begin moving some of the hand-carved and hand-made items to that side of the building.

When Carly told Margie her plans, the older woman nodded enthusiastically.

"I like your ideas. You just go ahead and move anything wherever you please, dear. I'll help you as much as my old back and legs will let me."

By the time Carly left that afternoon, she already had a good plan on how she wanted to reset the store, and she was actually smiling. Maybe working at the gift shop this summer wasn't going to be so bad after all.

* * *

At supper that evening, Carly had tried to maneuver herself to the seat farthest away from Randy as possible, but everyone sat down before she did and she was forced to sit directly across from him again. He didn't look her in the eye all throughout the meal and he was shoveling in his food even faster than usual. After a while, she grew angry. So, *he* wanted to get away from *her*? He was the one who should have been embarrassed about grabbing her in the hayloft. It was as if he wanted to run as fast and far away from her as possible.

The word *hayloft* drifted across the table, and Carly looked up to see who'd said it. Luke was the one talking.

"Does anyone know why the big door up in the hayloft was open Sunday morning? I'm almost certain it was closed before I left Saturday night."

Carly and Randy both stopped eating and stared at each other for the first time. Neither said a word.

Luke zeroed in on Carly. "It wasn't you who opened it, was it?"

Carly looked at him, not knowing if she should deny it or not. She wasn't even sure why she should lie. After all, it wasn't that big of a deal to have been in the loft. She was just about to answer when Randy spoke up.

"Sorry, Luke. It was me. I went up there to move a few bales around and it was so hot, I opened the door. Guess I forgot to shut it."

Luke sat back in his chair and stared at Randy with a mischievous glint in his eyes. "Was it so hot that you had to take your shirt off?"

"What?"

"I found a shirt spread over a straw bale. Oh, and a cooler with a couple of beers in it. Guess those were yours, too."

Every eye turned to Randy, and Carly watched his face grow red.

"Yep. Guess so."

Luke chuckled. "Right. You were moving straw bales up there."

Randy glared at Luke.

Carly couldn't help but smirk. *Serves him right for kissing me and running off.*

Randy turned and glowered at her.

"Luke. Stop teasing Randy," Ginny piped up. "Carly? How was your first day at work?"

Carly looked up so quickly, she dropped her fork onto her

plate with a loud clank. Now, all eyes were on her, even little Jessi's. From the corner of her eye she saw Randy grinning. *Jackass.*

Composing herself, she smiled over at Ginny. "It was fine. Like everyone says, Margie is a sweetheart. She's happy to have the help and said I could move things around in there as I please."

"I'm glad you had a good day, dear," Ginny said. She stood and retrieved the coffee pot, then began pouring coffee all around.

"No more for me, Mrs. B," Randy said, standing up quickly. "I'm heading home. Supper was delicious as usual. Goodnight all." He turned to walk into the back porch.

"I hung your shirt on a hook back there," Luke said. "If you decide to spend time up in the hayloft again tonight, just be sure to close the door." He chuckled as Andi hit his arm and shook her head.

Randy turned, glared at Luke, and then let his fiery gaze fall on Carly. She shrugged at him. She had no idea why Luke was giving him such a hard time. Before she knew it, Randy was out the door.

Chapter Seven

Wednesday morning found Carly up on a ladder outside the gift shop with a spray bottle of window cleaner in one hand and a large rag in the other. Margie had insisted she wear a long men's button-up shirt over her clothes. "I won't have you ruining your nice things," she'd told her. Carly knew she looked silly but hadn't argued with Margie. She was too much of a motherly figure to talk back to. It would be like talking back to Ginny, which she'd never do, either.

Cleaning the dusty grime off the windows was hard work. First, Carly had used the hose to spray the outside of the windows. A year's worth of gritty gravel dust slowly slid down to the ground. Now, she was trying to make the glass sparkle and shine, streak-free. She wasn't sure she was going to manage the streak-free part, though. Cleaning wasn't exactly her forte, especially windows. A janitor had polished up the windows both inside and out at the gallery in Seattle once a week, and she'd never cleaned the windows at the townhouse. Andi had when she lived there, and then Beth did, too. But Margie didn't have the extra money to spend on hiring a window cleaner, so here she was, doing it herself.

As Carly sprayed cleaner and rubbed the rag over the glass, cars continued driving past on the frontage road, spitting up gravel and dust. From time to time, men would hoot or holler at her as they drove by. *Cavemen!* She'd purposely worn jeans today, albeit a nice, designer pair, but the men's shirt was covering all her best assets. Obviously, the men around here were desperate for female companionship if they thought she looked hot in this shirt.

They're probably all Neanderthals like Randy.

"Hey. Looking good."

A male voice startled her and she turned so quickly to see who it was that she lost her balance and began to fall off the ladder. Right as a scream escaped her lips, a hand grabbed her backside and steadied her. The spray bottle and rag dropped to the ground, leaving her hands free to clutch onto the ladder for dear life as the hand stayed firmly on her backside. Carly turned and glared at the offender, and found herself looking into a pair of familiar amber-brown eyes.

"Are you trying to kill me?" she screamed at Randy.

Randy grinned. "Nope. But you sure startle easily. Are you steady yet?"

Carly swiped at his arm. "Yes. Get your hand off my ass."

Chuckling, Randy pulled his arm away. "Sorry. I didn't mean to scare you. I was just admiring your work."

Carly climbed down the ladder and stared hard at Randy. "I swear. I'm surprised you didn't throw me out of the hayloft the other night. You keep trying to kill me."

Randy's eyes sparkled and the crinkles that framed them made him look even more adorable. "If I remember right, you were very much alive when I left the loft."

Carly felt her face heat up and it made her even angrier knowing this cowboy had the ability to make her blush. "What are you doing here, anyway? Aren't you supposed to be shoveling manure or something?"

Randy bent down to retrieve the spray bottle and rag, then placed them on the ladder's steps. "I honestly didn't mean to scare you," he said. "You just looked so cute in that get-up and scrubbing that window that I had to come see what you were up to."

Carly looked down at the long shirt and couldn't help but smile despite her pounding heart from almost falling. "Margie made me wear it. She didn't want me to ruin my 'dressy clothes' as she put it."

"Well, we wouldn't want the princess to get dirty now, would we?"

Carly put her hands on her hips. "Don't call me that."

Randy grinned mischievously.

"Don't you have somewhere else to be?"

"Yeah, I suppose I'd better get back to the ranch. Just stopped in at the hardware store down the way to get a few things. Couldn't resist coming here to tease you, though."

Carly frowned. "Why?"

Randy looked surprised by her question. Then he shrugged. "Guess it's like pulling a little girl's pigtails on the playground in grade school. It's fun."

Carly shook her head. "You sure do have a mean streak, don't you?"

Randy leaned in closer. "Actually, I'm a pretty nice guy."

Carly smelled the spicy scent of his cologne and it brought her back to that moment in the loft. *And a pretty good kisser too.*

Angry at her own thoughts, she crossed her arms. "Well, if you're so damned nice, you'd help a lady out by cleaning these windows for her."

Randy laughed heartily. "Sorry 'bout that, but I'm on company time right now. Besides, it looks like you're doing a heck of a good job on your own."

As Carly glared at him, she watched his hand rise up toward her face. Gently, he rubbed the side of his thumb across her cheek.

"What are you doing?"

"Just removing a dirt smudge," he said, his eyes twinkling. "Can't have you looking anything but perfect now, can we?" Randy turned and strode off to the other side of the parking lot where his truck sat.

Carly stood stock still watching him, still feeling his gentle touch across her cheek.

He tipped his hat as he hopped up into his truck, and then was gone.

* * *

I've got to stop doing that, Randy thought as he drove down the road to the ranch. *Every time I'm near that girl, I want to touch her. Heck, I don't even like her. Do I?*

It felt like a ton of bricks had hit him head on. *Do I?* Could he honestly say yes to that? Was he insane?

I just enjoy picking on her, that's all. It was fun watching those pretty blue eyes spit fire at him or the way she wrinkled up that beautiful face of hers when she frowned. *Pretty? Beautiful? Come on, man. Get it together.*

Randy pulled into the ranch driveway. He grabbed the bag of nails he'd purchased at the hardware store and headed out back to the tool shed. One of the shed's walls was rotting and he and Luke were replacing the boards today. As he strode to the shed, he thought about how Carly had almost fallen off the ladder and he'd steadied her. He smiled to himself. She had a nice, firm behind, that was for sure.

"Took you long enough," Luke said as soon as Randy reached the shed. "What are you grinning about?"

"Huh? Oh, nothing." He handed the bag of nails to Luke.

"Well, come on over here and hold this while I hammer," Luke told him.

Randy held one end of the wood plank flush against the shed while Luke hammered in nails on the other end. They'd been working side-by-side like this since they were children. Riding, roping, branding cattle, fixing fences, and shoveling manure. They'd done it all together, so much so, that they sometimes sounded like an old married couple nit-picking at each other or grunting answers because they could read each other's thoughts. Luke was more than his employer—he was his best friend. They could say pretty much anything to each other, even if the other person didn't want to hear it. It was Randy who'd told Luke outright that if any woman was worth begging for, it was Andi. And he'd been right. Luke had been so stubborn, he'd have probably let Andi drive away two years ago if Randy hadn't intervened. Now, Luke was the happiest Randy had ever seen him, and it made him happy for his friend.

"You'll never guess who I saw cleaning windows in town," Randy said as Luke fitted another board flush against the previous one.

"Who?"

"You're sister-in-law, Princess Carly."

Luke's eyebrows rose and he stared at Randy. "Our Carly? Really? Well, will wonders never cease?"

"Yep. I couldn't resist teasing her about it. She was all covered up in an oversized men's shirt to stay clean and standing on that ladder, scrubbing her heart out. It was kind of cute, actually." Randy smiled as he thought again of how she'd looked. She'd had her hair up in a ponytail and it was so long, it reached down to the middle of her shoulders, like a golden horsetail. When he glanced up, Luke was staring at him oddly.

"What?"

"What's going on between you two? I thought you didn't even like Carly," Luke said.

It was a warm summer, day but the heat Randy felt rising up

his neck and face had nothing to do with the temperature. "Nothing's going on with us," he said gruffly. "I was just giving her a hard time, that's all."

"And were you giving her a hard time when you two had beers up in the hayloft the other night?"

"Who says I was in the hayloft with her?"

Luke snorted. "Who else would you be up there with? The only other single woman on this ranch is my mother, and I sure as hell hope you two aren't sneaking around, seeing each other. Glen wouldn't like that much."

Randy tightened his jaw. "We were just having a beer. Nothing more."

"With my mom or with Carly?"

"With Carly, you idiot," Randy growled.

Luke chuckled. He went back to pounding nails into the board. Neither of them spoke again until the last board was in place.

Luke took the tools into the shed and came back outside. "Would you put a couple of coats of paint on that side of the shed?"

"Sure."

"Mind if I give you a word of advice?" Luke asked.

"I doubt if I can stop you."

"Carly is a pretty girl, no doubt about it, and easy to be attracted to. If there's something going on between you two, that's your business. But keep in mind what she did to Colt, okay? I honestly don't think she means to hurt people, but she does just the same."

"Is that all you have to say?"

Luke slapped Randy on the back. "You're not as tough as you want everyone to believe. We all get hurt."

Randy didn't answer him.

"Come on. Let's go grab lunch before Colt eats all the

sandwiches," Luke said. He walked away toward the house.

Randy stood there a moment, thinking about what Luke had said. He knew Luke was right about Carly. So, why did he feel such a strong pull to her? Sighing, he followed Luke toward the house.

* * *

"My, but aren't those windows just sparkling clean," Margie said. She stood behind Carly inside the shop and admired the view. "I haven't seen so well out of those for a year or more."

Carly beamed, pleased with her work. After cleaning the outside, she'd spent a good hour cleaning the inside. Now, tourists would be able to see what was inside the shop from the road. Maybe it would be enough to entice more customers.

Margie walked back to the counter. "Was that Randy Olson you were talking to outside?"

Carly's smile faded. She'd been trying to forget about Randy all afternoon. She picked up her cleaning supplies and followed Margie to the front. "Yes, it was Randy."

"He's such a nice young man," Margie said. "Guess you know him pretty well from him working on the ranch. Doesn't he eat all his meals with the family?"

Unfortunately. Carly nodded. "Yes. Most of the time."

"I remember when he was just a little guy and he'd come into the shop. He'd have a little change in his pocket and want to buy caps for his cap gun. All the little boys bought their caps here. He was different, though. The other kids would get allowance money from their parents or a little money from chores, but not him. He'd sweep off the sidewalks in front of businesses or do odd jobs for people to earn a little money. He was only five or six then. So, when he'd come in here, I'd always give him a candy bar or soda for free when he bought his caps. It would make him smile, and goodness, that boy needed something to smile about."

Carly had stopped unbuttoning the big shirt and listened intently to what Margie was saying about Randy. "Why? Did he have a bad childhood?"

Margie nodded. "Bad doesn't even begin to describe it, sweetie. His mama is one mean woman. I know she's ill now, but to be honest, most of her problems were self-inflicted. She was a heavy drinker, that one, and ornery. But I shouldn't be talking about her or Randy, so just forget about what I said, dear. He's a fine man, despite his childhood, and I give him a lot of credit for that. And the Brennans too. They've always been good to him. They're a fine family. You're lucky to have them as your relatives."

Margie went off to the back room.

Carly stood there, pondering what Margie had said. She'd never taken much interest in how Randy ended up so close to the Brennans—he'd just always been around. She'd known that he and Luke were childhood friends, but that was about it. *Maybe his mother being so ornery had something to do with him being grouchy.* She had to admit, it all sounded a sad. She turned and looked out the window, trying to picture little five-year-old Randy, probably in his worn-out jeans, boots, and cowboy hat, sweeping the sidewalk across the way. *Wow, that is sad.*

Carly took off the big shirt and carried it and the supplies to the back room, all the while thinking about Randy. Today, he'd stopped to tease her about cleaning the windows. Why? He could have just as easily driven on by and ignored her, the way he'd been ignoring her for almost two years every time she visited. Was he just rubbing in the fact that she was doing dirty work now? He was always calling her things like princess and missy, which really made her angry. Was he trying to make her mad? Or was it like he'd said earlier—like pulling the pigtails of a little girl on the playground? *Did he like her?*

Carly pushed that last thought away. It was absurd. Ridiculous. He just liked torturing her. He thought she was stuck up, and he enjoyed making fun of her. In fact, he was a jerk. A real jerk.

But as the day wore on and Carly kept busy moving artwork up to the front of the store, she couldn't get the picture out of her head of little Randy Olson, sweeping sidewalks for pocket money.

Chapter Eight

That night at supper, Carly once again found herself directly across from Randy at the table. Everyone seemed to have their own spot, and, unfortunately, this had become her permanent one.

Randy had nodded at her when he'd sat down but that was about it. She'd been setting the bowl of mashed potatoes on the table then, and just ignored him. Now, as she sat there picking at her food, she glanced up from time to time to see if he was watching her, but his head was down and he was concentrating on his food.

Chatter floated around the table as everyone told stories about their day. Beth mentioned something about a kid with a broken arm and Ginny shook her head over that, saying she knew the boy's mother. "She was in your grade in school, Luke. Remember?" Luke nodded and then the conversation flowed from one topic to another. Ginny had made fresh preserves today and Andi had helped. Glen had mowed the lawn around the house and Luke was thanking him. The conversation went on and on, and all Carly could think of was Randy sitting across the table from her, shoveling food into his mouth like a hungry animal.

Under the table, something tapped Carly's leg, making her look up. Randy grinned at her and winked. Carly rolled her eyes.

"I'm going riding after supper to check on something," Randy said softly amongst all the other chatter. "If you want to ride a bit, I wouldn't stop you from coming along."

Carly smiled slowly. *Such a gracious invitation.* "Sure. I'll come. It'll be nice to get outside after being stuck indoors all day."

They grinned at each other, until Carly realized the room had fallen silent. She looked around the table. Everyone was staring at her and Randy.

"Well, isn't that nice," Ginny said as naturally as if Carly and Randy went riding together every night. "It'll be such a beautiful night for a ride."

Randy frowned and returned his attention to his plate. Carly did the same, but she still felt everyone's eyes on her.

Later, after helping Ginny and Andi clean up after supper, Carly changed into an old pair of jeans and a T-shirt, slipped on her riding boots, and grabbed her jacket from the back porch.

"Have fun," Andi called to her as she opened the back door.

Carly leaned back and glanced at Andi, who was sitting at the table with Jessi nestled in her arms, giving her a bottle. She could tell from the look on Andi's face that she was teasing her.

"Smartass," Carly mouthed, making Andi giggle.

Once outside, Carly stood on the back steps and inhaled the mountain air. She smelled pine mixed in with freshly cut grass. The sun was angled in the sky and the air had grown cooler, but it felt good after the warm day. Tying the sleeves of her jacket around her waist, Carly walked to the barn, prepared to get Abby and saddle her. To her surprise, Abby was already tied to a fence post in the barn, saddled and ready to go.

"Figured I might as well get her ready for you," Randy said, standing between Abby and Black Jack. "We only have a couple of hours of sunlight left, so no sense in wasting them."

"Thanks," Carly said, stunned. After his lecture on how she

could do everything herself, she was thoroughly surprised.

She walked over to Abby and ran her hand down the horse's smooth neck. Randy was saddling Black Jack, and Carly watched him with interest. He had his usual white T-shirt on, and the muscles across his back were taut underneath it as he moved easily to cinch the saddle. His arms and the back of his neck were tan, except for where his hair had once been before he'd cut it. His hat was pushed back on his head, and stubble ran across his jaw and neck. She decided she didn't mind the unshaven look on him after all. It looked rugged, like he did. It suited him.

"Ready?"

Carly jumped and her eyes focused on Randy's face. He was grinning wickedly at her.

"Don't tell me I scared you again. I've been standing here the entire time."

"I was just thinking about my day," Carly said tersely. She slipped up into the saddle and then leaned down to unhook Abby's lead rope. Out of the corner of her eye, she saw Randy take a long-sleeved cotton shirt off a hook and slip it on, then buckle on a holster with a pistol inside.

"What's that for?" Carly asked, pointing to the pistol.

Randy pulled himself up into the saddle. "Protection. Wolves and mountain lions roam the hills. Don't worry. I won't shoot you."

"Yeah, right," Carly said. She turned Abby and they walked out of the warm barn and into the cool evening air.

"Let's go up the center trail," Randy said behind her.

Carly moved Abby in the direction of the trail. They walked the horses slowly, and Randy moved Black Jack up beside Carly. At the top of the hill, they didn't veer off to the right as usual.

"I want to go up farther," Randy said. "There are some

calves I want to check on."

Carly nodded and they rode on. The trail was wide here from years of moving cattle back and forth between the summer and winter pastures. Evergreens and pines dotted the landscape along with aspens, birches, and maples. Carly took in the beauty of it as she thought of what Margie had told her today. She knew very little about Randy, even though they'd known each other for two years.

"Did you always want to be a cowboy?" Carly asked.

Randy's eyebrows rose as he turned and looked at her. "Where'd that question come from?"

Carly shrugged. "I'm just making conversation. I really don't know that much about you. I wondered if being a cowboy was what you dreamed about when you were a child."

"Did you dream about running a gallery and selling your sister's paintings?"

"Not when I was little. I wanted to be a dancer, then a movie star, and about a million other things before I realized I should learn to do something sensible. I worked at the gallery in high school, and I was good at it. So, I majored in business management in college."

Randy grinned. "A movie star, huh? Well, you would have been pretty enough to be one."

Carly glanced up in surprise. "You think I'm pretty?"

Randy frowned. "Did I say that?" He chuckled. "I'm not blind. Of course, you're pretty. In fact, you're drop-dead gorgeous. But you know that already, don't you?"

A small smile spread across Carly's face. "Men tell me that all the time. But I hadn't thought you'd noticed." She cocked her head. "So, is that why you kissed me? Because I'm pretty?"

Randy shook his head. "Nope."

Carly's smile faded. "Randy Olson. You are the most frustrating man I've ever met. Men trip all over themselves to get my attention, and you won't even give me the time of day. What's wrong with you?"

Randy laughed. "That's the problem right there. You think all you have to do is put on a show, bat your eyelashes, smile prettily, and a hundred men will do your bidding. From the first time I met you, all I saw was you putting on a show for Colt. You'd pout and smile and shake back your hair and he was putty in your hands. You know exactly how to manipulate men by being what you think they want, but the minute a relationship gets serious, you run away. You work so hard convincing a man you're something you aren't, that it scares you when you can't live up to your lies. You know how to reel them in by playacting, but you don't keep them, because you aren't being yourself. Your real self. Sweetie, you did fulfil your childhood wish. You became an actress after all, except that your acting leads to broken hearts."

Carly's mouth dropped open. She reined in Abby and stopped. "Is that why you invited me to go riding? So you could insult me?"

Randy turned Black Jack around and stopped, facing Carly. "That didn't exactly come out the way I meant it to." He moved closer, their legs touching. Quietly he said, "You asked me if I kissed you because you were pretty. What I was trying to tell you is, I kissed you in the hayloft that night because for the first time ever, I saw the real you. You weren't trying to impress me or flirt or do anything but be yourself. At that moment, I thought you were beautiful."

Carly took a breath. She stared into his eyes to see if there were any trace of teasing. There wasn't.

Randy slowly raised his hand and cupped her face, drawing her to him. Ever so lightly, he touched his lips to hers. No sooner had their lips met, he pulled away slightly and whispered, "Do you know why else I kissed you in the hayloft?"

"Why?"

His eyes met hers. The corners crinkled as he smiled. "Because you were going on and on about what a great kisser Colt was and I had to show you I was better."

Carly pulled away and smacked him on the arm. Randy laughed. Underneath them, the horses danced from their sudden movement. Abby spun around in a circle to get away from Black Jack until Carly reined her in.

"You are a mean, crusty old cowboy!" Carly yelled, her eyes spitting fire.

Randy laughed again, which only infuriated Carly more.

"I'm going home." She turned Abby and headed back the way they'd come.

"Carly. Aw, come on." Randy rode up to her and blocked her way. "I was only giving you a hard time. Follow me a little farther up, and then we can head back, okay?"

Carly glared at him, but agreed, and they continued on their way.

The sun was falling low in the sky and the air was cooling fast. Carly pulled on her jacket as she rode alongside Randy. She wondered how much of what he'd said was true, and how much was teasing. She'd thought for sure when he'd told her why he'd kissed her in the hayloft that he'd been telling the truth. But if that were true, then he'd also meant what he'd said about her being phony around men to get what she wanted, then getting bored with them. That thought unnerved her. Did she really do that?

"We're here," Randy said.

Carly looked up and saw an open pasture of lush, green grass dotted with cattle. "I thought the summer pasture was farther up the trail."

Randy nodded. "It is. It's about a three hour ride from here.

We use this pasture for the at-risk cattle that we want to keep an eye on. See over there?" He pointed to a cow and her calf. The calf was a good size, no longer dependent upon its mother.

"Yeah."

"That's one of the calves that was pretty scrawny still, so I've been supplementing his diet with grain to fatten him up. He's doing better now. There's another one, too, but I don't see him right now. He must be out farther."

Carly looked across the pasture and off in the distance. There was land for as far as the eye could see. "Is this all Brennan land?"

"Yep. In all four directions you look."

"I never realized how much property they own. It's huge."

Randy nodded. "Yeah. Two thousand acres is pretty big."

Carly peered up at him as he scanned the horizon. She could tell by the look on his face that he loved the land and the cattle as if it were his own. She couldn't help but smile. "You never answered my question earlier. Did you always want to be a cowboy?"

Randy glanced over at her. "I don't know. I suppose so. Like all little boys who live around here, I didn't think of much else except ranching. I started coming here to the ranch at eight years old and Luke's dad, Jack, taught me everything as if I were one of his sons. Never thought I'd do anything else."

"So, there you were, with your little cowboy boots and hat, your toy holster and cap gun, riding the range on a pony and learning how to care for calves."

Randy glanced down at Carly. "How'd you know I owned a cap gun?"

"Margie said you used to come in and buy your caps in the shop, like all the little boys."

"Ah, yes. Margie. What else did she tell you?"

"That you swept sidewalks and did small chores for pocket

money when you were five years old."

"I was more like six or seven."

Carly grinned. "Well, that makes it much better."

Randy studied Carly a moment. "Hey. Don't feel sorry for that little boy. I made a lot of extra money that way, and I scored a free candy bar or soda at Margie's every so often too."

Carly shook her head. "I'm not feeling a bit sorry for you. I just wondered what it was like for you to be out by yourself at that young of an age, trying to earn a little money. Where were your parents?"

Randy's face hardened. "We'd better go back before it gets dark." He turned his horse around and headed for the trail.

Carly watched him, frowning. He obviously didn't want to talk about his parents. She turned Abby around and followed Randy down the trail.

* * *

The next week and a half flew by for Carly as she continued reorganizing the gift shop and helping Ginny around the house, as well as occasionally watching Jessi for Andi so she could paint. That first Saturday after Carly had cleaned the shop's windows and moved some framed prints up to the front, they'd sold two of them. One had been Andi's and another was by a local Native American artist. Margie had been thrilled and told Carly it was all because of her. "You just keep doing what you want with the shop, dear," she'd told Carly. "It's all working."

Carly had been happy, too. She felt like she was making a difference for the gift shop and helping Margie out. After only a few days of working there, Carly had already grown fond of Margie. She was a sweet lady—the real deal. It felt good working to help Margie increase her business instead of only working for a paycheck. Carly had to admit, she felt more fulfilled here than she ever had selling expensive artwork in Seattle.

Even as busy as Carly was, she couldn't get Randy off her mind. She'd pondered often what he'd said about her being phony with men. Was that why she couldn't hold onto a relationship longer than a few months? And if it was true, had she played with Colt's feelings, too? That thought upset her the most. At the time, she'd told herself that she was falling in love with Colt, but the truth was, she'd never actually been in love with any man. She enjoyed having a steady man around, but she was scared to death of commitment. She had no idea why.

When Colt had proposed to her, she'd panicked and backed away from him. Now, looking back, she realized how immature that was, and how much she'd hurt Colt. That was why Randy's words had hit her so hard. If she really was playacting with men, then she had a lot to figure out so she wouldn't do it again.

It also bothered her how Randy had blocked her out after she'd asked about his parents. That night they went riding, when they'd returned to the barn, he'd unsaddled his horse as quickly as possible and left. He'd ignored any attempt she'd made to talk to him. She'd even apologized for bringing the subject up, but he hadn't responded. He'd just taken off.

Carly had dreaded sitting across from him the next night at supper, but he hadn't shown up. After supper, she'd asked Ginny why Randy hadn't been there.

"He went up to the summer pasture to stay a few days," Ginny said. "There's some fencing that needs mending and he wanted to check on the cattle."

So he'd run away from her as fast as he could. Or, was he running from his own past? Carly had a feeling it was both. One thing was for certain: he'd left her with more questions about their exchange that night than answers. She decided it was for the best he was gone. She had a lot of soul-searching to do.

Chapter Nine

Randy worked out in the hot sun, stringing new barbed wire across areas of fencing and pounding in nails wherever he saw a board sagging. He'd taken his shirt off and sweat rolled down his bare back. He stopped working a moment and pulled off one leather glove to wipe the sweat from his forehead. Closing his eyes, he stood there and listened, then sighed happily. Silence. Only the sound of birds chirping and a cow bellowing occasionally in the distance.

No one here to jabber at me and ask nosy questions about my childhood.

As it had many times over the past few days, his mind returned to his last conversation with Carly. It surprised him that she could ask a simple question that managed to take his mood from happy to angry in an instant. He realized she hadn't meant anything by it, yet it had thrown him for a loop. He wasn't going to rehash his childhood with anyone, especially a girl whose head wasn't screwed on any tighter than his.

Randy went back to work, stringing wire, stretching it taut, and tying it off around a post. He'd been pretty rough about telling Carly how phony she acted around men. He truly hadn't meant to say it that bluntly, but it had come out and there was nothing he could do about it now. Besides, it was the truth.

Honestly, he really didn't know how she acted around *all*

men. He'd only seen how Carly acted with Colt last winter and the summer before when she'd first come to the ranch. He'd seen through her act right away. She'd made Colt fall head over heels in love with her, then when it came down to him wanting to commit to her, she'd tossed him away. Okay, he didn't know the details, but he figured that had been the gist of it. In the end, Colt had fallen for Beth, a much better choice for him. But from what he'd heard from Andi about Carly's track record, she didn't hang onto a man very long. For some odd reason, she wasn't able to be herself around men. He'd called it as he saw it. If Carly didn't like what he'd said, so be it.

Then why do I feel so bad about saying that to her?

Randy pulled on his glove and began stringing wire again. It was thoughts like that which had made him decide to come up here and get away from the little vixen. She was warping his brain. He wanted to tell her off one minute and kiss her the next. That was insane. Being away from her for a while to clear his head was best.

Yet here I am, still thinking about her.

As he worked, Randy thought about her question, "Where were your parents?" He hadn't wanted to actually tell her the truth—sleeping off a hangover. On summer days from the time he was five years old he'd leave the house early and walk the short distance to town to find ways to earn money from the string of shops. He hadn't been aware of it at the time, but everyone around there knew his parents were drunks and had little money, so they kindly let him do small jobs and gave him a few dollars here and there. He would pocket the money, sometimes buying a trinket at Margie's or something to eat at the little coffee shop, and then sneak back into the trailer before either of his parents woke up. If his parents had known what he was up to, they never mentioned it. In fact, they rarely acknowledged him. They'd get up in the late afternoon, eat something, argue with each other, then his mom went off to work at the bar and his dad went off to work, or somewhere—he had no idea where. Randy would be left alone in their little trailer until about three in the morning when his parents returned, usually drunk, sometimes hollering at each other, and fall dead asleep again. The sad thing was Randy thought all parents were like that until he started hanging out at the Brennan ranch and saw how kind Jack and Ginny were to each other. By then, his father had driven away in their beat-up pick-up truck.

No, that wasn't really a story you wanted to tell someone, especially a princess like Carly. She'd be appalled.

But why did he care what she thought?

The sun moved off to the west and Randy decided he'd worked enough for the day. His arm and back muscles were sore and he was hungry. He tossed his tools into the back of his truck and slipped on his T-shirt, then drove to the little cabin they used when they worked the summer pasture. It was only a one-room cabin with two bunks, a sofa, and a small kitchen, but it was sufficient for his needs. He could heat up a can of strew and drink a cold beer, thanks to the generator that kept the refrigerator running, and wash up in the sink with the hand pump. That was really all a man needed. He didn't need a sweet smelling woman to coddle him and keep him company.

Although, it would be nice.

He planned on staying here until the end of the week and then returning by the weekend. He'd skipped visiting his mother last Sunday to stay up here, but he figured he should go there this Sunday. Not that she remembered, or cared, but it made him feel better at least to check on her.

Women. They were more trouble than they were worth.

Even so, as he lay on his bunk that night, he couldn't get the image out of his mind of Carly in her tight jeans and low-cut T-shirt with her blond hair flying behind her as she rode Abby down the trail.

* * *

Carly was dying to have some fun. All she'd done since coming to the ranch was work. The past two weeks, she'd moved everything in the gift shop around for maximum exposure of their best stock. She'd pulled down the old shelves behind the counter that once held cheap trinkets and hung quality artwork there instead. She'd displayed the handmade Native American items—birch baskets, dream catchers, beaded moccasins, and dolls—on the shelves in one of the large windows, and the many hand-carved animals in the other window so tourists would see them. The old toys were relegated to the shelves at the back of the store, and she'd moved the bookshelves that held books about the area and by local authors up closer to the register. She'd kept the printed T-shirts and sweatshirts in the very back where they'd been, but she'd created a display of colorful clothes up on the wall above the alcove so people would see them. She'd even rearranged the glass cabinets at the counter, separating the cheap jewelry from the handmade items. It had all kept her very busy on the days she worked, but it was worth it. Sales had risen. Artwork that had sat dusty in back corners was sold, and the local artists brought in new items, surprised, and pleased, by the sales. Andi's prints sold like wildfire, and even Andi was in shock at how Carly had changed things around so rapidly. And Margie? She was thrilled. She admitted to Carly that for the first time in years, she was excited to come to her shop every day and see what sold.

"You were definitely a godsend to me," Margie told Carly that Saturday as customers flowed in and out of the store all day, almost every one of them purchasing something.

Carly had to admit she'd enjoyed doing it. This is what she was good at—marketing and selling products. She'd always thought her expertise was art, but this proved she could take any type of shop and make it a success. And it was fun talking to the many tourists who passed through the area. They came from all over the country, many even from other countries. She'd been small-minded at first, thinking that only hicks and country bumpkins would pass through, but she'd been wrong. People with plenty of money to spend came into the shop, and she did her best to make sure they spent some of it here.

"Sweetie, you should buy this little shop of mine," Margie said in passing. "With your talent and people skills, you could turn this shop into much more than it is."

Carly had smiled and shook her head, but once the idea had been planted in her mind, she couldn't get rid of it. It was an interesting thought. Of course, with her present financial state, she'd never be able to buy this place, but it did give her pause.

Carly left late that Saturday afternoon and drove the few miles back to the ranch. She really wanted to go out and have some fun tonight. If she were still in Seattle, she'd get all dressed up and go out dining and dancing with her friends. She missed doing that. But trying to get anyone at the ranch to go out for even a couple of hours was like pulling teeth.

She thought about Randy and that he usually went to The Depot every Saturday night. As far as she knew, he was still at the cabin in the summer pasture. He'd been gone over a week-and-a-half, and no one had said when he'd be back. She thought about him often, much to her annoyance, and what he'd said to her about the way she acted around men. At first, she'd given it a lot of heavy thought, almost believing he'd been right. But then she'd grown angry with him. *Who is he to judge me? He hardly even knows me.* Besides, he was as screwed up as she was. Hadn't he run away the minute she'd asked him about his childhood? Who did that? He could have said he didn't want to talk about it and left it at that. He was the last person on earth to be analyzing her behavior.

Carly changed her clothes quickly when she returned to the ranch and then immediately began helping Ginny and Andi with supper. She told Andi they'd sold another one of her framed prints, and that they should pick out a few more for her to bring to the shop on Monday.

"You've really made a difference at Margie's," Andi said, impressed. "My prints sat there for months and I never sold one. Now, they're selling like crazy. I bet the other artists are thrilled, too, and Margie must be ecstatic."

Carly shrugged. She was poking the baked potatoes in the oven with a fork to see if they were done. "It took a lot of cleaning and moving of things so people could see them." She smiled. "But it is fun to see the happy look on Margie's face. It's revived her enthusiasm in the shop again. I think she'd grown so tired of it all that she'd lost interest."

Andi squeezed her sister's arm affectionately. "I like that it makes you happy, helping Margie. You're so good at what you do. The gallery in Seattle lost an amazing asset when they let you go. I bet they're regretting it."

Carly wondered if they were. She still hadn't heard from anyone in Seattle since coming here.

"Do you miss Seattle, dear?" Ginny asked. She was stirring the gravy she'd made from the roast drippings.

Did she? She'd been so busy here, she hadn't even thought much about it. "I'm not sure, really. I miss going out with my friends, but most of them have scattered or are in serious relationships now. Actually, I've been enjoying being here with family and working with Margie." She grinned at little Jessi who was already propped up in her high chair. "And I love being around my little cutie-pie," she said, tickling Jessi.

Luke, Colt, Beth, and Glen came inside and they all sat down to supper. Since Randy had been gone, Carly had ridden with Beth a couple of times on their days off. She actually enjoyed getting to know her again. When Beth had lived with her in Seattle, they'd been like two strangers sharing a house. Carly was the party girl and Beth was the homebody. Now that they'd spent time talking, Carly found she really liked Beth. They'd even gone down to Colt and Beth's house so Carly could see it. Carly didn't envy Beth marrying Colt—she knew they belonged together and she was happy for them. She did envy them their beautiful cabin home, though. It was lovely and cozy, just perfect for them. Carly knew that she'd never have made Colt as happy as Beth had. She wondered if she'd ever feel like settling down with just one man, forever. It seemed like a daunting idea.

Feeling restless, Carly tried talking everyone into going out dancing. "It's Saturday night," she said. "Don't you want to go have some fun?"

Andi shook her head. "Sorry, Carly. I'm beat after a full day of watching Jessi and helping Ginny. My bed is calling my name by nine o'clock."

Carly turned to Colt. "What about you and Beth? I know you love to dance, Colt. Wouldn't you like to go out for a little while and dance with your wife?"

Colt and Beth looked at each other, and Carly could tell that neither of them wanted to go out.

"Sorry, Carly," Colt said. "Beth worked at the hospital today, and I think we just want to go home and relax. We still have a lot of finishing work on the cabin that we'd like to do tomorrow."

Carly sighed.

After finishing the supper dishes, Andi packed up her baby

bag and put on Jessi's small jacket. Carly carried Jessi to the car, and Andi put her in her car seat. Luke had headed out to do a few more chores before going home.

Andi looked sternly at Carly. "I know you really want to go out, but please don't go alone. I don't want to worry about you drinking and driving on these mountain roads. Besides that, it's not safe for you to go alone."

Carly wrinkled her nose. Andi knew her too well. She'd already been thinking about going by herself. "Who says I'm going anywhere?" she lied.

"I know you better than you think," Andi said, giving Carly a quick squeeze. "Please stay home. Maybe tomorrow Ginny will watch Jessi and you and I can go riding."

Carly nodded and waved good-bye. Riding. That was all she was allowed to do around here.

She headed back into the house. It was only eight o'clock and she was bored. Ginny and Glen were sitting at the table, drinking coffee and playing Gin Rummy.

"Do you want to play cards?" Ginny offered.

Carly shook her head. "Thanks, but I think I'll go up to my room. Goodnight."

"Goodnight, sweetie. See you in the morning," Ginny said.

Carly stopped at the foot of the stairs a moment where Bree was laying on her pillow. She squatted and pet Bree behind the ears and Bree opened one eye and looked at her.

"You're even bored," Carly said softly to the dog. Then she stood and headed up the stairs.

In her room, Carly pulled out her phone and lay on her bed. There wasn't any cell service out here at the ranch, but Ginny did have wireless internet, so Carly was able to email and message friends. She scanned her Facebook feed to see what everyone was up to. Adam had posted a selfie at a crowded nightclub in Paris. Girls in short skirts and men in tight pants were dancing behind him. Some of her other friends had posted updates on where they were eating out in Seattle that night, or what dance clubs they were going to. Carly sighed. She really did want to go out and have fun, even if it was dancing to country western music.

"I'm a grown woman. I can do whatever I want," she insisted to the empty room.

Determined now, Carly got up and searched through her clothes for something cute to wear. She chose a silky blue blouse and a short, tight jean skirt. She pulled on a pair of western-style ankle boots, and ran a sparkly silver belt around her waist. Excited now, she applied makeup and then pulled her hair out of its ponytail and curled it loosely. Silver hoop earrings completed her outfit. She planned on grabbing Andi's white cowboy hat from the back porch before she left. Glancing at the clock, she decided to wait until ten to sneak out. Ginny should be in bed by then. She figured there was no sense in causing an uproar with Andi by letting anyone at the ranch know she was going out. She'd simply go to The Depot for a couple of beers and a few dances and be back by midnight.

Carly smiled. She couldn't wait to finally have fun.

Chapter Ten

Randy sat at a table in the far corner of The Depot over by the pool tables. He'd just finished eating a burger and was watching the guys play a game of pool. He figured he'd shoot some pool and then head on home. It had been a long day, and he was tired.

The place was bustling tonight as it usually was on a Saturday. A band played an old country tune in the other room and people were crowding the dance floor. Most of the tables and booths in the main room were filled. In summer, the area was packed with tourists who were visiting local dude ranches and drifters who found temporary work on ranches. On a winter night, Randy could name almost everyone in the bar, but tonight he recognized only a few faces.

The waitress came up and leaned over Randy to pick up his empty plate. She was dressed in tight jeans and an even tighter scoop neck T-shirt that didn't leave much to the imagination. Randy tried not looking down her shirt, but it was hard, considering she was only inches away from him.

"How about another beer, cowboy?" she asked, her pretty, made-up face close to his.

Randy glanced at his mug, which was still half-full. "I'll wait awhile, thanks," he said, smiling up at her.

She winked and turned around, walking away slowly.

Randy watched her hips swaying seductively. She was new here, and couldn't be much older than drinking age. She was a cute little thing, but he wasn't one to rob the cradle.

"She has her eye on you," Jeremy Colter said, tapping Randy on the arm. He was one of Randy's friends who was playing pool. "I'd bet all you'd have to do is say yes and she'd follow you home."

Randy shook his head. "She's too young."

"Too young? She has to be at least twenty-one to work here. And she's gorgeous."

"Like I said, too young. If you're so interested, you ask her out. She's closer to your age than mine."

Jeremy laughed and went back to playing pool.

Randy glanced across the room where the long, curved bar stood. He noticed a cluster of men standing around the end of it and wondered what, or who, was so interesting that they were all so eager to surround it. Probably that little waitress, he decided.

The band began playing a lively tune that brought more dancers to the floor. Randy liked to dance, but not tonight. He'd worked all morning up at the summer pasture, than packed up the truck and headed back to the ranch. He'd been up there long enough and he was tired of his own company. He'd stopped by the ranch house to let Ginny and Luke know he was back before he'd driven home. Ginny had anticipated he'd be home today, so she'd handed him a quarter of a freshly baked strawberry pie for him to take to his mother tomorrow when he visited. She was always doing nice things like that for him, and he appreciated her kindness immensely.

A soft giggling sound drifted across the room, causing Randy to look up. He frowned. The laughter sounded familiar. He scanned the crowded dance floor. Again, the sound of a woman laughing caught his ear. Standing to get a better look, his eyes zeroed in on a woman with long blond hair topped with a white cowboy hat and a curvy body dressed in a short, tight jean skirt and a billowing blue blouse. She had long, shapely legs that kept up with the tall cowboy she was two-stepping with. When they turned, Randy caught sight of her face. Carly.

Randy scanned the tables to see if Luke and Andi or Colt and Beth were there. He didn't see them. Had Carly really been stupid enough to come here alone? Then he remembered the cluster of men by the bar. They must have been surrounding Carly.

It's none of my business. She can take care of herself. Despite his thoughts, he couldn't stop himself as he strode across the room and onto the dance floor, stopping in front of her.

"May I cut in?" he asked the man dancing with Carly. Not waiting for a reply, he took Carly into his arms and began dancing with her as the other man stood there, stunned.

Carly looked up at him with wide eyes. The band started playing a slow song and Randy pulled Carly close as he moved her slowly around the floor. "What are you doing here?" he asked.

"I could ask you the same question?" Carly shot back. "I thought you were brooding up at the summer pasture."

A crease formed between his brows. "Brooding? What the hell would I be brooding about? You?"

Carly shook back her hair haughtily. "Well, you ran off fast enough and went to hide out. I figured you were hiding from me."

Randy snorted. "Don't think so highly of yourself, missy. I had work to do there. Now, you answer me. Why are you here alone?"

Carly glared at him. "I'm a grown woman. I can do whatever I want. And if I want to have a few drinks and dance, then I will."

Randy studied her face. It was flushed and her eyes were bright. Despite her being angry with him, she still looked damned pretty. Too pretty to be out here with a bunch of strangers.

"Listen, Carly. It's not safe for you to be out alone. Does Andi know you're here? Does anyone?"

"I don't have to ask my sister's permission to go out. This isn't the eighteen hundreds anymore, cowboy. Women can go out dancing. I go out all the time in Seattle and nothing ever happens. Besides, this is a small town. It's not like you don't know everyone in here. So stop acting so protective."

Randy hardened his jaw. "Actually, I don't know everyone in here tonight. It's summertime, Carly. There are tourists and drifters coming through here all the time. And you shouldn't be drinking and driving. I can already tell you've had one too many. I'm taking you home."

The song ended and Carly tried pulling out of Randy's grasp. He held on tighter. "Let me go. I came here to have fun and I intend to do just that. Go mind your own business."

Randy loosened his grip on her and she walked away. She hadn't gone more than five feet when another man was already at her side. Randy watched as Carly smiled up at the man seductively. She was playing her games again. Just like he'd told her she did. *Damned woman!*

Randy strode back to his table on the other side of the room. He downed the rest of his beer. When the waitress came over, he ordered another. Carly was right. It was none of his damned business. If she wanted to dance with strange men and let them buy her drinks then that was her problem.

Randy joined in on a game of pool, partnering with Jeremy and playing against two other guys. Unfortunately, he couldn't keep his mind on the game. His eyes kept scanning the bar to keep tabs on Carly. After losing two games, he gave up and sat down. Jeremy teased him about having his mind on women instead of pool, but Randy ignored him. His mind wasn't on the women in the room, it was on only one woman, and it irked him to no end that Carly being here bothered him so much.

An hour went by and Randy was still nursing his second beer and watching the dance floor. The crowd was thinning out, but there were still a few locals hanging around as well as some faces he didn't recognize. Duane Utley, a local ranch hand, was dancing with Carly to a slow song. Randy didn't like Duane. They were the same age and had gone to school together. He'd always been a bully, and had been married twice, each one ending in divorce. Word around town was he treated women roughly and that's why his marriages hadn't lasted. Randy could put up with a lot of things, but not a man who hit women. And he really didn't like seeing Duane with his arms around Carly.

Midnight rolled around and Randy had finally had enough. He'd watched too many men pawing at Carly. He walked over to the bar where Carly sat, surrounded by her admirers, and pushed his way through. When the other guys eyed him, he smiled wide and said, "Will you give us a moment, gentlemen?" They glared at him but backed off.

"Okay, Carly, you've had your fun. Let me drive you home."

Carly glanced up at him. Her blue eyes were glassy and she sat unsteadily on the stool. "I'm not ready to go home. I'm having fun," she insisted.

Randy sighed. If he thought he could get away with it, he'd haul her over his shoulder and carry her out of here. But he knew there'd be a dozen guys coming to her rescue if he tried it. He caught Carly's chin with the side of his finger and tilted her head up to look into his eyes. Quietly, he said, "Come on, Carly. Let's go. I can't leave you here alone. We'll come back another night and have some fun, okay?"

Carly gazed at him, and he wondered if she even recognized who he was. She brushed away his hand and slid off the stool. "No. I want to dance some more. Leave me alone." Randy watched as she wobbled away from him toward the dance floor.

He took a step toward her, but Duane moved between them.

"You heard the lady," Duane said with a sneer. "She's staying."

Randy glared at Duane. He clenched his hands into fists. He'd like nothing better than to knock Duane to the floor. Taking a breath, Randy turned and walked out the door instead. If Carly didn't want to go, he couldn't make her.

The night air helped cool Randy's anger as he walked to his truck. Leaving Carly in there with Duane and those other men was difficult for him to do, but he didn't have any other choice. She was so damned stubborn. As drunk as she looked, there was no way he could let her drive home, either.

Randy hopped into his truck and started it up. He sat there, his anger rising again. Damn that Duane Utley for nosing in where he didn't belong. And Carly, too, for not listening. He crossed his arms and sat back against the seat. There was no way he could live with himself if he drove off and left her here. If for no other reason, he couldn't do that to Andi. If anything happened to Carly, Andi would be heartbroken. He felt responsible for Carly, despite her being such a pain in the ass. The bar would be closing in less than an hour. He decided he'd sit here and wait, and when she stumbled out to her car, he'd drive her home.

A while later, Randy was startled awake by the sound of a woman's voice. He shook his head to clear it, and then remembered he was still in his truck. He panicked. What if he'd missed Carly coming out? He quickly looked around. Most of the cars and trucks had cleared out, but the lights were still on in the bar. The clock on his dash said it was one-fifteen. Most of the people had already left. Carly's car, however, was still in the parking lot. Randy let out a sigh of relief. At least she hadn't driven away yet.

He heard a woman's voice again and he glanced around to where the sound was coming from. A few parking spots down, he saw a dark truck and he thought he saw a man and woman on the other side of it. The woman had a white cowboy hat on.

Carly.

He hopped out of his truck and strode over to where they were. The man had Carly pressed up against the side of the truck. She was protesting that she wanted to go home.

"Don't you worry, little gal. I'll take you home," the man said, snickering. He lowered his head to kiss Carly.

Randy's blood boiled. He knew that voice. It was Duane.

Randy stepped up behind Duane, grabbed the back of his shirt, and pulled him so hard he fell over backward and landed on the ground.

"What the hell?" Duane yelled.

Randy ignored him and wrapped his arm around Carly. "Come on, Carly. I'll take you back to the ranch."

"Hold it there, Olson," Duane bellowed as he stood up. "She's with me. Get the hell out of here."

Randy let go of Carly. He turned and faced Duane. "Forget it, Duane. She's not going anywhere with you. She's Andi Brennan's sister. You don't want to mess with her, or them."

"Do you think I give a rat's ass who she's related to? I'm not afraid of the damned Brennans, and I'm certainly not afraid of you." Duane took a step closer to Randy. "Get out of my way and get the hell out of here."

Randy's heart pounded and his fists clenched. "Back off,

Duane. She's going with me."

Duane took a step closer and swung at Randy. He hit him on the side of the head. Randy stumbled, but he righted himself quickly. His adrenalin was pumping so fast, he didn't even realize he'd hit Duane until he saw him lying on the ground, dazed, holding the side of his face. Blood trickled from the corner of his mouth.

"You asshole!" Duane bellowed.

Randy ignored him, grabbed Carly's arm, and led her to his truck. His head hurt like hell and his heart was beating fast. His hand didn't feel all that great, either. He hoped he hadn't broken any bones when he'd hit that big oaf.

Carly was like a rag doll when he tried getting her in the truck. He finally pushed her in and closed the door, then hopped in the driver's side.

"I want to go home," Carly slurred, slumping in the seat. She passed out in seconds.

Randy sighed. He'd just punched out a guy to keep her safe and she had no idea what had happened.

Randy drove the short distance to his home. His head was throbbing too much to drive all the way to the ranch and then try to get Carly inside and up to her room without waking anyone. She could sleep it off on his couch and he'd drive her home in the morning.

After pulling into his driveway and parking, Randy stepped out of his truck. He walked around to the passenger side and opened the door. Carly was lying on the seat, sound asleep.

Princess. Right.

Randy pulled her across the seat and lifted her up, dropping her over his shoulder like a sack of grain. He heard her moan, but she was still out. He walked up the steps of his deck, and then awkwardly unlocked his front door before entering his trailer. He walked directly to the sofa and unceremoniously dropped Carly onto it. He stood there a second, staring down at her, wondering how she could sleep through everything. She must have drunk a lot.

Walking to the kitchen, Randy pulled a beer out of the refrigerator and placed the cold bottle against the side of his head. The pain was excruciating. He decided he'd better ice it, so he opened the beer and took a swig. He pulled the Tylenol out from the cupboard and took a couple to ease his headache. He went to his bedroom and slipped off his boots, then found a washcloth and returned to the kitchen. Filling the washcloth with ice, he walked back into the living room, sat on the opposite side of the sofa, and gently placed the ice to his face.

I bet I'll have a hell of a lump in the morning. And a black eye too, thanks to her. He stared at Carly. She'd curled up on the sofa and was fast asleep.

Damn. How can she look so darned cute even when she's passed out?

Angrily, Randy stood up and headed back to his bedroom. He thought twice about it, swore, then went back out to the living room with a pillow and gently placed it under her head. He slipped off her boots, and then covered her with the afghan that lay on the back of the sofa. Finally, he turned out the lights and headed off to bed.

* * *

Carly awoke to someone poking her arm. She tried opening her eyes, but the sunlight streaming into the room made it difficult. Her head pounded and her stomach rolled. Where was she? Someone poked her again.

"Wake up, princess. It's time to take you home."

There was only one person who called her princess. Randy. But why was Randy in her bedroom? "Leave me alone. I want to sleep," she mumbled, turning back into her pillow.

"Oh, no you don't," Randy said, pulling the pillow out from under her. "It's taken me ten minutes already to wake you. Now, get up."

Carly's head dropped onto the sofa. She realize she wasn't in her bed. She slowly opened her eyes again, and as the room came into focus, she realized she was in an unfamiliar living room. A long pair of legs jean-clad stood beside her. She followed the legs up to a button-up plaid shirt and then up to Randy's frowning face. She closed her eyes again.

Why am I here with Randy?

"Where am I?"

"You're on my sofa. I'll give you two more minutes to get up and if you're still lying there, I'm carrying you out to the truck."

Carly slowly pushed herself up to a sitting position. The room spun and her stomach lurched. She covered her mouth with her hand. "I'm going to be sick."

"Crap." Randy grabbed her arm, pulled her to the bathroom, and no sooner had he lifted the toilet lid did Carly lose all of last night's fun. He gently pulled her hair back, away from her face, until she was finished and then he went to his bathroom and wet a washcloth for her. When he returned, she was sitting on the bathroom floor against the tub, looking pale.

"Here," he said, handing her the cool washcloth.

Carly took it and placed it on her face. "Thanks."

Randy flushed the toilet. "Are you done being sick?"

"I'm not sure. Just let me sit here a moment, okay?"

Randy stood there, staring down at her.

Carly winced at the pounding in her head. "Do you have any Tylenol? My head is killing me."

He left and returned with two pills and a glass of water.

"Thanks."

"Ready to leave?"

Carly sighed. She tried standing up, but felt a bit wobbly. She steadied herself on the sink, and then leaned in toward the mirror. Her mascara was running down her face and her hair looked like a rat's nest. "God, I look awful."

"Well, that's what a night of heavy drinking will do to you," Randy said.

Carly ignored him and ran her finger under her eyes to wipe away the mascara.

"You can pretty yourself up when you get home. Let's go. I have somewhere to be."

Slowly, Carly walked back into the living room and fell onto the sofa. Her boots were on the floor, so she slipped them on. She had no idea where Andi's hat was. "How did I end up at your place? Why didn't you take me back to the ranch?"

"Because I didn't feel like driving you there, considering you were passed out in the truck," Randy said.

Carly looked directly at Randy and focused on his face. She gasped. "What happened to you?" There was a red lump on the side of his head and his swollen left eye was black and blue.

"My face fell into someone's fist. He wasn't so keen on letting you go."

Carly's hands rose to her face and her eyes grew wide. "Oh, Randy. I'm so sorry."

"Don't worry about it. Now, let's go."

Carly stood, but her legs were rubbery. Randy reached out his arm and let her lean on him out to the truck. He helped her up into the cab and then got in and took off toward the ranch.

"What time is it?" Carly asked in a small voice.

"Almost noon."

"Andi's going to kill me."

"I called this morning to tell her you were on my sofa so she wouldn't worry."

Carly turned toward Randy. "Did you really get into a fight

because of me?"

Randy glared back at her. With the swollen eye, he looked even more menacing. "Duane Utley was going to take you home. I'm sure to his home, not yours. Believe me, you wouldn't have wanted to go with him."

Carly looked down at her hands. She didn't remember anything past telling Randy that she wanted to stay longer and dance. Men were buying her drinks all night and she hadn't paced herself. Now, she wished she hadn't gone out at all. "I don't even know who he is," she said quietly.

"Well, you two almost got to know each other very well," Randy said angrily. "What the hell is wrong with you? Don't you know how dangerous it is to go out drinking alone and get that drunk? If I hadn't been there, I'd hate to think of what might have happened to you."

Tears welled in Carly's eyes. She knew Randy was right, and it embarrassed her that she'd been so stupid to go out in the first place. In Seattle, she'd always had her friends to look after her when they went out. She should have realized that going out alone was a bad idea.

"I'm sorry," she said again.

Randy didn't reply. He pulled into the ranch's long driveway and the truck bounced over the gravel road. Carly's stomach lurched, but she forced herself to keep down whatever was left in it. The last thing she needed to do was throw up in Randy's clean truck.

"Here we are," Randy said, pulling to a stop.

Carly felt like she should say something, but knew that anything she said wouldn't be enough. Randy reached over to the back seat and grabbed something, then handed it to her. It was Andi's white hat.

Carly took it, opened the door, and stepped out. Looking up at Randy one last time, she said, "I really am sorry about your eye."

Randy stared hard at her. "Don't worry about it."

Carly sighed and shut the door. He spun the truck around and drove off.

Chapter Eleven

Carly walked into the kitchen with her head down. It was almost lunchtime, but luckily the men hadn't come in yet. Ginny stood at the counter making sandwiches, and Andi was feeding baby cereal to little Jessi at the table. Both women glanced up at Carly when she entered.

"Can I get you anything, sweetie?" Ginny asked as if Carly had just come in for a bite to eat.

Carly was thankful for the way Ginny ignored the obvious and acted normally. Still, she felt ashamed. "No, thank you, Ginny. I'm going upstairs to shower." She slowly walked to the stairs.

"Are you all right?" Andi asked softly.

Tears filled Carly's eyes. She swallowed hard, and nodded her head, not daring to look at her big sister. "Yes."

"Then we'll talk later," Andi said.

Carly walked up the stairs, careful to hold onto the rail. Her legs were still wobbly and she didn't trust herself not to fall. She went into her room, closed the door, and fell across the bed, weeping.

* * *

Carly awoke an hour later. She'd cried herself to sleep and if it hadn't been for the mower humming outside, she'd probably still be sleeping. She sat up and was happy her headache had receded. Standing up, she walked to the mirror over the dresser and winced when she saw her reflection. Not only was her makeup from last night smudged on her face, but her eyes were red and puffy and her hair was a mess. Her stomach felt better, though, and her legs weren't as shaky.

She grabbed clean clothes and went to take a shower and wash her hair. As she stood under the hot water, she thought about last night and how foolish she'd been. It had all started out innocent enough. She'd wanted to go out and have a little fun. But she'd overdone it and it had ended badly.

Thanks goodness for Randy. A chill prickled Carly's skin as she thought of where she could have ended up waking up this morning—in a stranger's bed. She had never in her life gone home with a strange man, and the thought of it made her cringe. Yes, she was a flirt. Yes, she'd had a lot of relationships. But one night stands? Never. But then, she'd always had her friends to look out for her when they'd gone out drinking. Last night, thank God, she'd had Randy.

Carly thought about Randy's black eye and guilt crept over her. He didn't have to protect her like that, yet he had. Even after she'd told him to leave her alone, he'd still made sure she was safe.

Carly dried her hair and dressed, then went to her room and applied fresh makeup. She thought about waking up this morning on his sofa. He'd put a pillow under her head and a blanket over her. And when she'd been sick in the bathroom, he'd held her hair back for her and given her a wet cloth to wipe her face. He didn't have to do any of that for her, but he had. He'd even taken off her boots for her to sleep. Despite her telling him to bug off, despite getting punched in the face because of her spoiled behavior, he'd still taken care of her.

Yes, he was angry with her, but that was only because he'd cared about what might have happened to her.

He cared. That thought made her pause.

She decided she had to do something nice for him to thank him and apologize for his getting hit. She knew nothing could make up for what had happened last night, but she had to try at least.

Carly went downstairs into the kitchen. Ginny was the only one sitting at the table. She was labeling jars of preserves she'd made yesterday and tying cute little calico ribbons around them.

"Well, there you are," Ginny said, smiling at Carly. "I saved a sandwich for you. It's in the fridge. And there's some strawberry pie left, if you can stomach it."

Carly smiled. "Thanks, Ginny." She did feel hungry, so she took out the sandwich and poured a glass of iced tea, then sat down across from Ginny.

"Where's Andi?" Carly asked.

"She took Jessi to the cabin for a nap. I think she was going to work on her new painting. She'll be back in a little bit."

Carly took a bite of the roast beef sandwich. Ginny knew just how she liked it, with mustard and lettuce. She was so thankful for Ginny's kindness, because she needed it now more than ever. "Was Andi mad?"

Ginny gave Carly a small smile. "A little. But she'll get over it. I think she was more concerned than angry."

Carly nodded. "I shouldn't have gone out alone. I know that now."

Ginny patted her hand. "We all make mistakes."

Carly bit her lip. "I'd like to do something nice for Randy to thank him for watching out for me. I was thinking I could bake something he liked. Do you know what his favorite treat is?"

Ginny grinned. "That's a sweet idea. Actually, there is something he's loved since he was a little boy. Peanut butter chocolate-chip cookies. Let me go get my recipe for you."

Ginny took a recipe card out of a small file box and handed it to Carly. "Would you like me to help you make these?"

Carly shook her head. "No, I want to do it myself. But I'll need to use your ingredients. Do you mind?"

Ginny laughed. "Of course I don't mind. I'll show you where I keep everything."

Ginny showed Carly where everything was and pulled out the cookie sheets for her. Then Ginny went back to work on her jars while Carly began making the cookies.

* * *

Randy arrived at the nursing home later than usual. He'd taken his time driving because even with his sunglasses on, the sunlight bothered his swollen eye. He was happy it hadn't swollen completely shut, otherwise he wouldn't have been able to drive here.

Lunch was already finished and most of the residents were in their rooms or sitting in the community room playing cards or watching television. Randy walked in and quickly signed in, turning his head so the nurse couldn't see his bad eye. The last thing he wanted was to have to explain. She smiled at him, and he headed on to his mother's room.

Halfway down the hall, Renee stepped out of a resident's room and waved at Randy. He stopped, and as soon as he took his hat off, he saw her eyes widen.

"My goodness. What on earth happened to you?" Renee asked.

Randy shrugged. "Just a little disagreement."

Renee studied his eye and the lump on the side of his head. "Have you iced this? It sure looks nasty."

"I iced it last night. It'll be fine."

"Hmmm. I certainly hope the other guy looks worse than you."

Randy laughed. "That's a terrible thing for a nurse to say."

"I'm sure he deserved it," she said, grinning.

"How's my mother today?" Randy asked, wanting to change the subject.

Renee sighed. "She's not in the best of moods. She had a little snit with Mrs. Alden at lunch, and then she began complaining so loudly I had to take her back to her room to finish eating. Maybe you can soften her mood a little with whatever you have in that container."

"Strawberry pie," Randy said. "Let's hope so."

He walked the rest of the way to his mother's room and knocked lightly on the half-open door. "Ma? It's me, Randy." He pushed the door open and walked in. "Ma?" She was sitting at the small table, staring off into space. Her half-eaten lunch was sitting in front of her.

Randy walked over and set the food container and his hat on the counter. "Ma? Hi. It's me, Randy. How are you doing today?"

Evie looked up and stared at Randy, her eyes slowly focusing on him. "Who you say you were?"

Randy put on a smile. "Randy. Your son, Ma." When Evie didn't respond, Randy continued. "I brought you some delicious dessert. Homemade strawberry pie. Would you like a piece now?"

Evie cocked her head. "Looks like you lost a bar fight."

Randy chuckled. "No, I'd say we were even," he said.

"Humph. Just like a man, fighting in a bar," Evie said sourly. "You're just like that no good husband of mine. Bet you were fighting over a girl."

Randy's smile faded. He didn't want his mother getting all worked up. "It was just a little disagreement. Nothing more.

Let's talk about you, Ma. How are you feeling today?"

Evie's face scrunched up. "Why do you keep calling me Ma? I'm not your mother. Who the hell are you, anyway? My poor excuse of a son never comes to visit me. I'd remember if he did. Who are you? Why are you here?" she screeched.

Randy remained calm even though his mother was yelling. "How about a nice slice of pie?" he asked, trying to distract her so she'd calm down. "You love strawberry pie. It's made from fresh garden strawberries."

Evie stood and waved her arms in the air. "Get out! Get out of my room!"

Randy backed away as Renee hurried in. She went immediately to Evie's side. "It's okay, Evie. Everything is fine. This nice young man is visiting you today. He's your son, Randy. He's even brought you a special treat."

"He's not my son!" Evie screamed. "I don't have a son. My Randy doesn't even come visit me. Make him go away!"

Renee looked sympathetically at Randy. "I'm sorry, hon. You should probably leave. It's been a bad day. I'm sure next Sunday will be better."

Randy nodded and picked up his hat. He turned, walked out the door, and hurried down the hallway, all the while hearing his mother screeching loudly.

* * *

Carly drove over to Randy's home with the freshly baked cookies in a container on the seat next to her. It was late afternoon, so she figured Randy would be back from visiting his mother by now. Ginny had told her he visited her every Sunday, which explained why he'd been in such a hurry to take her home that morning. Well, that plus he'd probably wanted to get her out of his sight after last night.

Andi had come back to the ranch house before Carly left, but she'd barely said two words to her. Carly told her she'd be back later and then they could talk. All Andi had done was nod. Carly knew she was angry with her. That was another apology she'd have to make.

She was happy to see Randy's truck in the driveway when she pulled in and parked her car. Sitting there a moment, she studied Randy's mobile home. She didn't have a lot of experience with trailers, but this one didn't look too bad. He'd built a big wooden deck off the front porch and had a nice looking table and chairs and a propane grill sitting on it. There were a few pots of flowers on the deck, and some nice flowering bushes planted around the trailer. Trees grew in a copse over to the right, shading it. It looked like he'd taken time to make the place feel homey.

Picking up the container, Carly walked onto the porch and knocked on the door. Inside, she heard the soft hum of the television, but no one answered. She knocked again.

"Go away."

Carly stood there, unsure of what to do. Was that directed at her, or anyone knocking at the door? Stubbornly, she knocked again. "It's me," she called. There was no answer. She decided she wasn't going to be deterred. "I'm coming in," she said through the door, then slowly turned the handle. It was unlocked. She opened the door and peered in. "Don't shoot me. It's Carly."

Carly walked in. Randy sat slouched on the sofa, a bottle of beer in his hand, staring at the television.

"Don't you ever listen? I said go away."

"I know, but I figured you didn't mean it." Carly closed the door and walked over to the sofa.

"Listen, Carly. It's been a long day. In fact, it's been a long couple of days. I really don't want to talk to anyone, especially you."

Carly sighed. "I guess I can understand that. I came over to apologize again for last night. And I brought you something. Here." She extended the container of cookies to him.

Randy stared suspiciously at the container, then up at her. "What's that?"

"Cookies. Your favorite. Peanut butter chocolate-chip. Here, try one."

Randy accepted the bucket but put it on the sofa beside him. "What did you do? Have Ginny make cookies so you'd feel better?"

Carly frowned and planted her hands on her hips. "No. I made them myself. Just for you. Can't you accept an apology gift, for Pete's sake?"

Randy glanced up at her and rolled his eyes. "Fine. If I eat one of these, will you leave?"

Carly sat down on the sofa beside Randy and curled her legs up under her. "Maybe. Just try one and see." She opened the container and set it in his lap.

Randy picked one up, studied it, and then sniffed it. "Did you poison them?"

"You'll never know if you don't try one," Carly said, grinning.

Randy finally took a bite. Then another.

"Well?"

He shrugged. "They're not so bad." He finished it off in two more bites.

"Not so bad? Hey, they're Ginny's recipe. I think they taste great."

Randy took another and bit into it. "Yeah. They're okay." He glued his eyes to the television again.

"I really am sorry about last night, Randy. Especially your black eye. I hope it heals okay. Do you think you should see a doctor? I'll pay the bill if you do."

Randy shook his head. "It'll be fine. It's not the first black eye I've ever had."

Carly nodded. She turned to see what was on the television. It was in black and white. "What are you watching? It looks like an old movie."

"It's a western."

Carly's eyebrows lifted. "Really? You're watching a John Wayne movie?"

Randy narrowed his eyes at her. "Hey, don't make fun of The Duke."

Carly smiled. "So, is that why you wanted to be a cowboy? Because of John Wayne?"

"Don't all little boys want to be cowboys at one time or another? I just happened to live in cowboy territory, so it was a no-brainer."

Carly laughed softly. "It seems silly to me that you'd watch a movie about cowboys. After all, you are The Duke in real life."

Randy cocked his head and stared at her.

"You ride the range, go on cattle drives, carry a gun for protection, and even get into bar fights to save damsels in distress. You're a real life John Wayne."

Randy snorted. "I wouldn't exactly call you a damsel in distress. More like a spoiled brat who wouldn't listen to good sense."

Carly looked down at her lap. "I already said I was sorry several times. I can't take last night back. I don't know what more to say."

Randy turned and placed his finger under her chin, moving her eyes to look up at his. "I know. And I appreciate the apology. And the cookies."

Carly stared up into Randy's eyes. Even with one swollen, she saw desire growing in them. She reached up and gently brushed away the hair that had fallen into his eyes. She thought he might kiss her, and truth be told, she actually wished he would.

Randy dropped his hand and turned away. Carly sighed.

"Ginny said she was grilling steaks for supper tonight and that you should come over. Maybe you and I could go for a ride afterwards. It's a pretty day out. It should be a nice sunset."

Randy hesitated. "I don't know. It's been a rough day."

"Is your mother okay? Ginny said you go every Sunday to visit her."

"I don't want to talk about her," Randy said sharply.

His tone stung, but Carly nodded her understanding. "That's fine. So, how about supper and a ride?"

"Are you sure you want to go bouncing around on a horse after how sick you felt this morning?"

Carly grinned. "I bounce back pretty quickly from hangovers. Ask Colt. He's seen me have some doozies."

Randy laughed. "I'll bet he has. Sure, I'll come for supper. It sounds good."

"Great." She stood up. "I'll see you at six, then. Okay?"

"Fine."

Carly walked to the door, and turned around. "Thanks for taking care of me, Randy," she said softly. Then she headed out the   door.

Chapter Twelve

Carly pulled Andi aside into the sitting room before supper.

"I know you're angry at me for going out last night after you'd asked me not to. Believe me, I wish I had listened to you. I'm sorry I did it, and that I worried you. I promise I won't do it again."

Andi looked surprised by her apology. "I appreciate that. I realize you're a grown woman and you can make your own decisions, but remember, you were the one who came here asking for help. I'm only looking out for you. Going out to bars and overspending money is what got you into this problem to begin with. Do you really want to repeat that here?"

Carly shook her head. "No, I don't. I'm sorry. I won't do it again. Forgive me?"

Andi smiled and hugged her sister. "Of course I forgive you."

Carly bit her lip. "There's something else I need to tell you."

Andi's smile faded. "Uh, oh. What?"

"Randy got into a fight last night because of me. I don't remember any of it, because I'd had a lot to drink. But he has a black eye and a huge lump on the side of his head."

"Oh, my goodness. That's terrible. Why were they fighting?"

Carly looked down at the floor. "I guess the guy was trying to take me to his home, and Randy wasn't going to let that happen." She looked up at Andi. "He protected me, and I really appreciate what he did. So, could you please tell Luke and Colt not to tease him about his black eye at supper tonight? I don't want to make him any angrier at me than he already is."

Andi sighed. "Well, thank goodness he was there. Do you realize how much danger you could have been in? Did Randy know the guy?"

Carly nodded. "He said he was a local guy. Duane, I think. Honestly, Andi, I don't even remember what happened."

Andi shook her head in disbelief. "I bet it was Duane Utley. He has a bad reputation with women. Geez, Carly, I can't believe you would get so drunk you'd go off with a strange guy. You really owe Randy for this. You know that?"

"I know. It was stupid. I already said I was sorry. I can't undo it, Andi." Tears filled her eyes.

Andi pulled Carly close. "I'm happy you're safe. I'll tell the guys to keep quiet. I know Glen won't say anything. He's too much of a gentleman."

Carly pulled away and wiped her eyes. "Thanks, Andi. Believe me, I'll never do that again."

And Carly meant it. The thought that she could have woken up next to a strange man this morning scared her half to death.

When Randy arrived for supper, he looked around cautiously at everyone, but no one said a word about his black eye. The meal was delicious, and after they were finished eating, Luke and Colt excused themselves to go out and finish up chores. Once they'd left, Carly watched as Beth approached Randy and asked him if his head ached or if he felt dizzy.

Randy shook his head. "No. The headache is gone, and I haven't felt dizzy. I can see fine out of my eye, so I think it's okay."

Beth nodded. "If your headache returns, or you get dizzy, you should go to the hospital and let a doctor have a look, okay?"

Randy smiled. "I will. Thanks, Beth."

Ginny fawned over Randy, bringing him an extra piece of chocolate cake, and winked at him. "I bet the other guy looks worse," she said, chuckling.

Randy laughed but didn't comment.

"I'll go saddle the horses," Randy told Carly.

"If you wait a few minutes, I can help," Carly said.

"You two go riding while the sun's still out," Ginny said. "We can clean up this mess. Glen will help, won't you, dear?"

Glen smiled. "Sure. You two go ahead."

Carly thanked Ginny and walked out to the back porch with Randy. She took her jacket off of its hook and slipped on her riding boots. Then they headed out to the barn.

"Luke and Colt were pretty quiet tonight," Randy said, glancing at Carly. "You must have threatened them so they wouldn't tease me about this black eye."

Carly grinned up at Randy. "Actually, Andi threatened them, not me. But I asked her to. The last thing you needed was for them to give you a hard time."

"Well, it won't stop them tomorrow. But that's okay. I'd give it to them if it was the other way around."

They retrieved and saddled their horses, then headed out. Randy led them to the trail that went down past Luke and Andi's cabin and circled around up to the top of the hill at the center of the property.

"We'll be able to see the sunset before we ride back down to the barn," he told Carly.

They walked the horses most of the way. Carly was happy they were taking it easy. Her stomach was fine, but if the horse trotted, it might get upset quickly. And she was afraid that too much jarring might hurt Randy's eye.

"Did Andi give you an earful about going out last night?"

Randy asked.

"Not really. I apologized to her first, which I think shocked her. I can't blame her for worrying. She's been taking care of me ever since our parents died, and I think she still feels responsible for me, even though I'm older now. It doesn't help that I can be so irresponsible."

"You're lucky to have someone who cares about you so much," Randy said, a faraway look in his eyes. "Not everyone has that."

Carly looked up at him. "You have people who care about you."

Randy turned toward her, a questioning look in his eyes.

"Ginny cares about you, and Luke and Colt do. Andi says nothing but nice things about you and Beth cares. Look at how she asked about your eye tonight. They all care about you."

Randy smiled. "Yeah, I guess I am lucky. Beth is a nice person. And Ginny has always treated me like her own son. Sometimes, I forget how lucky I am."

"I care about you," Carly said softly, averting her eyes.

Randy looked at her curiously. "You do? I thought you hated me."

"I don't hate you," Carly said quickly. "Sure, I think you're a crabby old cowboy sometimes, but when I saw your black eye this morning, all because of my stupidity, I felt so bad. And I was worried. I'm glad nothing worse happened to you."

Randy's face softened. "Well, I'm glad to hear you're on my side. It gets tiring sparring with you all the time."

Carly gave him a wicked grin. "Oh, I didn't say I'm done giving you a hard time. Making you mad is fun."

Randy broke out laughing. "You little devil."

By now they had rounded the trail and were at the top of the hill. They reined in the horses and sat there quietly. The sun was just making its way behind the trees in the distance.

"Can I ask you a question without you getting defensive?" Randy asked.

"Okay."

"Why exactly are you living here? You have a townhouse in Seattle and you had a nice job from what I hear. What happened that made you come here?"

Carly sighed. Did it really matter if Randy knew why she'd come here? After what he'd done for her last night, she figured she should at least be honest with him. "I lost my job in Seattle and got into a little money trouble. I spent too much time partying and too little time planning my life out better. So I came out here to see if Andi would help me. She promised to help if I stopped my reckless behavior and worked to pay off my bills. That's why last night was such a disappointment to her."

"Well, that makes sense now," Randy said quietly.

"So now you know what a loser I am."

"Carly?"

She looked up into his eyes.

"We all make mistakes."

"Yeah, I guess so."

"Look, the sun is going down."

Carly gazed up and watched as the sun slowly fell behind the trees, turning the sky a deep orange. The river below sparkled under the last rays of sunshine. The entire valley was drenched in color for one brief moment before the sky began to darken.

"It's so beautiful," Carly said, smiling up at Randy.

Randy reached over and ran his hand through Carly's hair, pulling her to him. Their lips met. Carly's hand moved up and around the back of his neck and their kiss deepened. Underneath them, the horses stirred nervously, causing their kiss to end too soon.

Randy stared down into Carly's eyes. "I don't know why I

keep wanting to kiss you."

"Maybe because you like it." She grinned and they both laughed.

"We'd better go," Randy said. "Before it gets too dark."

They started walking the horses down the trail. Night sounds drifted around them. Crickets chirped and frogs croaked. A horse whinnied in the distance. A cow bellowed. Yet, all Carly noticed was the pounding of her heart lingering from Randy's kiss.

"Do you want to ride again tomorrow night?" she asked as they rode slowly into the barn.

"Sounds like a plan."

They worked side-by-side unsaddling the horses, brushing them down, and then letting them loose in their separate pastures. Then they stood under the stars, watching the horses walk away in different directions.

"It's sad they have to be separated," Carly said.

Randy grinned at her. "Well, you know how it is. You have to separate the boys from the girls, or there might be trouble."

Carly looked up at Randy's black eye. "Yeah. I suppose there would be."

They walked together to the house.

"It's been an interesting twenty-four hours, wouldn't you say?" Randy asked.

"It sure has." Carly stood there, hoping he'd kiss her again. She really liked it when he kissed her.

Randy bent down and kissed her on the cheek. "Goodnight, Carly."

Carly's eyebrows rose, surprised by the chaste kiss. "Goodnight." She watched as he hopped up into his truck and drove away. With a content sigh, she went inside.

* * *

Monday morning, Randy was busy grabbing and stacking small, square straw bales up in the hayloft. Colt had brought a flatbed truckload of them over from Ray's farm where they'd been cut and baled. Using a conveyor lift, Colt set the bales on the lift and they went up through the open hayloft door where Randy grabbed them with hand hooks and tossed them over on the pile. The straw was used for bedding in the barn stalls for the horses in the winter. The actual hay they fed the cattle and horses all winter was baled in large, round, one-thousand pound bales and set in the fields.

The day was growing warm, and the hayloft was hot and stuffy. Randy had already taken off his shirt and T-shirt, and sweat was running down his back. He stopped a moment and pulled off his work glove, wiping the sweat off his brow. He'd definitely have to go home and shower before supper tonight, or else he'd scare everyone away from the table. Especially Carly.

Randy smiled at the thought of Carly. He was looking forward to seeing her tonight and riding together again. He didn't know how it happened, but in the few weeks she'd lived here, she'd managed to change his feelings for her from indifferent to…what? Desire, certainly. Caring, definitely. Love?

Sheesh. Get ahold of yourself.

"What are you grinning about?" Luke asked, coming up behind Randy.

Randy looked up, startled. He had to get his mind back on work and off Carly. "Nothing. Did you come up here to help or bother me?"

Luke laughed. He went over to where Randy had been tossing the straw bales and began stacking them neatly so they could fit more in the loft.

Randy continued grabbing each bale as it came up and tossing it on the floor. Using hay hooks, Luke lifted and stacked the bales. After about an hour, Colt called up that he had to get another load, then drove off in the truck.

Randy helped Luke stack the rest of the bales and then they both sat on the floor by the door, waiting for a breeze to cool off.

"So, I hear that Duane Utley has a mean looking lump and bruise on the side of his face," Luke said. "I suppose you wouldn't know anything about that, would you?"

Randy glanced at Luke. He'd known it was only a matter of time before he and Colt ribbed him about the fight. "Whatever he got, he deserved. Believe me."

"Oh, I have no doubt he deserved it. He's been a bully his entire life. What surprises me is that you gave it to him."

"Why? You don't think I'm tough enough?" Randy asked.

"Oh, you're tough enough. It's just that you don't usually get into fights. He must have really pissed you off."

Randy shrugged.

"And I'm guessing it had something to do with Carly," Luke said.

"Aren't most fights over a woman?"

Luke grinned. "Now that does surprise me. I thought you and she couldn't stand each other. Has something changed?"

Randy stared at Luke. "You sure are full of questions today."

"Hey, I remember when a friend of mine butted in a few times when Andi first came to the ranch. I'm just watching out for you."

"Looks to me like things worked out pretty well between you and Andi, so my butting in was a good thing," Randy told him.

"No argument there. Don't get mad at me, but I'm not so

sure you and Carly are such a good idea."

Randy frowned. "You think I'm not good enough for Carly?"

Luke shook his head. "No. I'm on your side. It's what Carly could do to you that I'm afraid of."

"You don't have to worry about me. I'm a big boy. I can take care of myself."

Luke chuckled. "Okay." His eyes sparkled with mischief. "Now, tell me. If you marry Carly, and she's already my sister-in-law, then would that make you my brother-in-law? Sounds a bit complicated."

Randy glared at Luke. "I'm not marrying anyone."

Luke laughed. "Right. You get in fights over just any girl."

Randy stood, picked up his T-shirt, and slipped it on. "I'm going to get something to drink before Colt comes back." He headed for the ladder. He heard Luke chuckle softly as he climbed down.

Marriage. Yeah, right. But as he walked toward the house, he smiled when he thought about how nice it had felt kissing Carly.

Chapter Thirteen

The next couple of weeks were the happiest ones Carly had had in a long time. She continued helping Margie increase her sales by making the shop more desirable, and had even talked her into placing some of the older stock on sale for thirty percent off. Recently, a couple of interested buyers had come to look at the shop, but no offers had been made yet.

"It might be easier to sell this business if you liquidate the old stock," Carly had told Margie. "Then there's less inventory for the prospective buyer to worry about."

"I've been thinking of that, too," Margie said. "I had originally thought about having a sale in September, but now I'm not sure if I should wait."

"Now might be a better time to sell off the older stock," Carly suggested. "I'm assuming you won't be as busy in September as you are right now."

"You haven't steered me wrong yet," Margie told her. "Either way, I get to close up this place in the fall. Maybe it would be better to sell out the stock and cut my losses."

Carly spent her time at the shop going through the cost sheets—done all by hand—and re-pricing the older merchandise. Margie put an ad in the local paper, advertising their sale. They had good crowds over the fourth of July holiday week and with the fair coming to town soon, they knew there'd be even more customers stopping in. After the first week, Margie had been pleased by the sales.

"This is better than I'd thought," she'd told Carly. "I'm happy you suggested it."

Carly was pleased she was helping Margie get the most out of her shop before she sold it. Every day, they'd go through and reorganize the shelves to fill in the empty spaces. The store was looking less cramped and was more organized. The local artists were bringing in more of their work, which would help Margie out in the long run. Without having to invest in new merchandise, but still making money off of consignments, she'd earn a bigger profit.

The rest of Carly's time was spent helping Andi with Jessi or helping Ginny in the kitchen. She loved being with her little niece, and often took care of her for an afternoon so Andi could paint. She helped Ginny make her famous strawberry jam and other preserves, too, and decorate jars to sell at the fair in August.

But her favorite time of all was in the evenings when she spent time with Randy. They usually went riding, but sometimes they'd go for a drive and watch the sunset. He took her to a movie one night at the Strand Theater in Superior and he actually sat through a romantic comedy. Carly teased him about it later, but he said he'd enjoyed it.

"It's not John Wayne, but it'll do," he'd said with a grin.

It surprised Carly that he never tried anything other than an occasional kiss. She thought it was sweet. Most men were all over her after only one or two dates, but not Randy. He was being a complete gentleman, something she'd never have accused him of in the past. She was actually enjoying being treated like a lady. Although, she wouldn't have minded a few heated moments with him.

On a hot, muggy Saturday evening in July after Carly had

helped Ginny and Andi clean up after supper, she went in search of Randy to go riding. Because of the heat, she'd worn jean cut-offs and a tank top. She'd slipped on her boots and hat, figuring it would be too hot to ride in jeans tonight.

The sky looked fierce with dark clouds and thunder in the distance when she walked outside. She figured that riding was out of the question for tonight. She poked her head in the barn, hoping Randy had stayed anyway, even if they just sat and talked a while. He was waiting, in his usual jeans and plaid cotton shirt, grinning at her. The bruise around his eye had faded and the red lump was gone. Standing there, he looked absolutely adorable.

"Well, aren't you cute in that little get-up," he said, scanning her with his eyes. "Looks like a thunderstorm is on the way. No riding tonight."

Carly walked over to him. "Aren't you hot in all those clothes? Don't you ever wear shorts?"

Randy stared at her as if she was crazy. "A cowboy in shorts? It may look cute on you, but I'd look like an idiot."

Carly laughed. She drew closer to him and could smell his spicy aftershave. She found it cute that he now showered before supper each night. He never used to. She knew he did it for her benefit, but she didn't dare tease him about it or he'd be ornery and stop. "So, what do you want to do on this stormy night?" she asked, her lips close to his.

Thunder rumbled overhead. Randy looked down at her, his eyes connecting with hers. "I thought we'd go dancing."

Carly pulled back in surprise. "Dancing? Where? I'm not dressed to go out."

"You're dressed just fine," Randy said. He backed away and pointed to the hayloft ladder. "Ladies first."

Carly glanced at the ladder and then gave Randy a curious look. "What are you up to?"

"You'll see."

She laughed and headed up the ladder, very aware of him directly beneath her as they climbed. Once they were both up there, she looked around. The big door was open and there were tiny twinkle lights strung up in the rafters. Randy had moved the bales around so there was an open space near the door. A long chair cushion had been placed over two straw bales and another bale acted as a table with a red cloth over it. On it sat a bottle of wine chilling in a bucket of ice and two glasses.

Carly clapped her hands with glee. "This is so sweet."

"Ah, but you haven't seen the best part yet." He placed his hand on the small of her back and led her to the makeshift table and chairs. Then he turned on a radio that sat over to the side. Country music drifted throughout the hayloft.

"I love it," Carly said. "Even if it is country music."

Randy laughed. "Well, you always say you want to go out dancing and have some fun. No reason why we can't do it right here."

Thunder rumbled again, right over the barn. It was so loud, it shook the barn walls. The sky was darkening fast from storm clouds. In the distance, lightening flashed across the sky. Carly moved closer to Randy.

"We even have our own light show outside," he teased.

They sat down on the cushion and Randy opened the wine and poured it.

"Here's to pretty girls," he said, clinking her glass.

"And romantic cowboys," Carly said, smiling up at him.

As they took their first sip, rain began to pour down. Cool air drifted into the hayloft, refreshing the stuffy air.

Carly sighed. "That feels so good. I hope we don't lose power from the storm, though. It would be dark up here."

"I'm prepared for that, too," Randy said, pointing to a

battery powered lantern.

"Well, aren't you just the perfect little Boy Scout," Carly teased.

Randy chuckled. "Would you like to dance?"

Carly nodded. He took her hand and led her to the small space he'd cleared. He placed one hand on the small of her back and held her other hand, pulling her close. They slowly began swaying to the soft music.

They danced and sipped their wine as the storm rumbled outside. Neither of them noticed it. Randy changed the station to one that played music from the thirties and forties. "There're just too many sad country songs," he said. "I don't want to hear about breakups and heartaches tonight."

Carly agreed. She gazed up into his eyes as she lifted his hat from his head, and took hers off too, setting them down. Then she slipped her arms around his neck and he ran his around her waist. Carly laid her head on his shoulder. "Thank you for this," she said softly. "I haven't been this happy in a long time."

Randy kissed her softly on the cheek. "Me either," he whispered.

"Who would have thought," he said as their bodies moved together to the music, "that you and I would be close like this."

Carly looked up at Randy. "Yeah. We're like oil and water."

"Day and night."

"Cats and dogs." Carly grinned.

"Sweet and sour," Randy said.

"And to think, you never even looked at me twice when I was here before," Carly teased.

"Well, that was before," Randy said, running his hand up her back and into her hair. He loosened the band that held her ponytail and pulled it out. Carly's hair fell loosely down her back.

"What changed?" Carly asked.

"You did," Randy said, twirling a strand of her hair around his finger. "You were always beautiful, no doubt. But now I see there's so much more to you. You aren't putting on a show anymore. You're real. I love the way you help Ginny around here without a fuss. And how sweet you are with little Jessi. And all you've done for Margie's shop. She adores you, you know."

Carly grinned. "Remember, she pays me to do all that."

Randy shook his head. "No. You've done much more for her than just work there. You've changed. You've grown up. I see the real you, and I like what I see."

"Even after I caused you to get a black eye?"

Randy chuckled. "Especially after the black eye. Hey, you baked cookies for me. What more could a man want?"

They stopped dancing but held each other close. Desire filled Randy's eyes. He ran his hand tenderly across her cheek and up through her hair. Slowly, he lowered his head, covering her lips with his.

Carly's spine tingled as Randy claimed her lips. She rose up on tiptoe and pulled him closer. Their tongues met and danced to the music as their kiss grew deeper. Randy's hand slipped down to her waist and found the bare skin between her shorts and tank top. He slowly caressed her skin as his hand slid up her back. Carly's desire grew at the touch of his hand on her skin. She pushed closer against him.

Randy ran kisses down her neck, nipping her at the base of her throat, driving her crazy. He dropped a kiss on her bare shoulder, and then pulled away and gazed longingly into her eyes.

"I want you so badly," he whispered.

Carly took a breath. "It wouldn't take much to get me to say yes right now." She reached up and slipped her hand up the back of his neck, into his hair. Randy sighed.

He pulled away, dropping his hand from her back and reaching for her hand instead. "It's so tempting," he said, his eyes still dark with desire. "But rolling in the hay isn't as romantic as it sounds."

Carly laughed. "Sounds like you've had some experience doing it."

"I never kiss and tell," he said, smiling. The crinkles around his eyes looked sexy as hell to Carly.

"Let's wait until the time is right," he said. He raised her hand to his lips and kissed it.

Carly's heart melted.

Randy grabbed the long cushion off the straw bale and set it on the floor near the big door. He motioned for Carly to lie down beside him, their heads propped on the pillow. He wrapped his arm around her shoulders and she laid her head on his chest.

"Let's enjoy the light show awhile," he said, kissing the top of her head.

Carly couldn't remember when anyone had done anything this romantic for her. She lay beside him, content.

* * *

Sunday afternoon Randy drove to visit his mother with a smile on his face. He couldn't stop thinking about Carly, and last night. It still amazed him how close they'd grown over the past month, but he was happy they had. It had been a long time since a woman made him feel so alive, so filled with the desire to please. He'd actually spent two hours rigging up the lights yesterday in the hayloft so he could surprise her. He couldn't remember the last time he'd done something like that for a woman. And it hadn't been easy keeping it from Colt and Luke. They would have teased him mercilessly if they'd seen him doing it. But it had given him so much joy to see Carly's face light up when she saw the effort he'd put into it.

Joy. That was something he hadn't felt in a long time.

He was glad they hadn't gone too far last night. It would have been too easy to do so. Instead, he'd enjoy romancing her until the time was right. He wanted this to be more than just a roll in the hay. He wanted this relationship to be special.

Special? Romance? She was really getting to him.

Randy smiled at that thought. He didn't care. For the first time in his life, he was thinking of having it all. Love, marriage, family. And much to his surprise, it was Carly who'd brought these feelings to the surface.

Love? Do I really love her?

The thought scared him, but then, taking a big leap in life was always scary. He'd take it slow and figure out what exactly he felt for her.

Randy pulled into the nursing home parking lot, grabbed the container Ginny had given him yesterday, and walked into the building. He was surprised when Renee headed him off before he even reached the check-in desk.

"I need to talk to you for a moment," Renee said, leading him into a small alcove where there was a table and two chairs. She motioned for him to sit.

"Is this about Mom's doctor appointment last week?" Randy asked.

Renee nodded. "You know how she's been losing weight, despite us trying to get her to eat more. And she's been very tired of late. Sometimes, it's impossible to get her out of her chair and down to the dining room for supper."

"What did the doctor find?" Randy asked.

"He said her heartbeat is irregular, but he wants her to have more tests. I took her there personally, because she was being such a pain about going. No one wanted to fight with her.

Anyway, I told the doctor to schedule the appointment for the specialist but that I'd have to talk to you first."

Randy frowned. "Won't her insurance cover it?"

"Well, that's the problem. First, they'll have to approve it, and then it only covers eighty percent. I know you pay for her supplemental insurance, so I wanted to make sure it covers the rest; otherwise, it will come out of your pocket."

Randy sat back in the chair. He already paid the extra money for his mother to be in this facility over what her insurance paid, plus he paid for her supplemental insurance. His money was stretched to the limit. But if his mother needed extra medical attention, he couldn't say no.

"Go ahead with the appointment, and I'll pay whatever isn't covered," he told Renee. "Did the doctor give any hint of what might be wrong?"

"No, but all the symptoms point to her heart weakening. Loss of appetite, shortness of breath, fatigue, even her being ornerier than usual. Her body has gone through a lot over the years between her drinking and then her stroke. She may just be wearing down. But I'm not saying the doctors can't help her. We won't know anything until the specialist in Missoula sees her."

Randy reached over and patted Renee's hand. "Thanks for being honest. And for being so good to my mother. I know how difficult she's been, but you still hang in there. I really appreciate it."

Renee grinned at Randy. "We both know it's her disease that makes her difficult. It's my job to make her life as comfortable as possible. But I'm happy to help her if for no other reason than for you. God knows you need someone on your side."

Randy chuckled. "She wasn't exactly all that easy to get along with when she was well. But she's lucky to have you looking after her."

Renee nodded toward the food container. "Something good in there that will entice your mama to eat?"

"Blueberry pie. Freshly picked berries from Ginny's garden."

"Well, if she won't eat it, I will," Renee teased.

Randy thanked her again and headed down to his mother's room.

Evie was sitting in her usual chair, watching television with the sound down low. She looked so tiny she was practically lost in the chair.

"Ma, it's Randy," he said from the doorway. When she didn't answer, he walked in, took off his hat, and set it and the container on the counter. He drew closer to her. "Hi, Ma. How are you feeling today?"

Evie slowly turned and looked up at Randy. Her eyes showed no emotion. Randy thought she looked even paler than usual.

"Leave me alone," Evie said dully. She turned back to the television program.

Randy sighed but didn't give up. He pulled one of the chairs over next to hers and sat down. "What are you watching?"

Evie didn't respond.

"I brought you some homemade blueberry pie. Thought you might enjoy a piece."

Evie stared at Randy. He could tell she had no idea who he was. "I'm tired. Why don't you people just leave me alone?"

All the joy Randy had felt earlier faded away. As he stared at his mother, memories of his childhood crowded out any happiness. She'd never been a pleasant woman, drunk or sober, and he'd always known he was nothing but a burden to her, especially after his father left. He'd fended for himself his whole life, always giving her part of everything he'd earned even as far back as when he'd swept sidewalks or run errands for townspeople. But no matter how much he'd give her, no matter what he did for her, it had never been enough. She'd called him worthless. *You ain't nothing but a two-bit ranch hand— just like your father.* He'd never been able to earn his mother's approval in the past, and he sure as hell wasn't going to get it now, because she didn't even know who he was.

Randy stood and moved the chair back beside the table. "I hope you feel better soon, Ma," he said gently. He walked back to the counter and picked up his hat. He looked over at his mother, but she didn't turn her head. He placed his hat on his head and walked out the door.

Chapter Fourteen

When Randy didn't show up Sunday afternoon to go riding before supper, Carly drove to his home to check on him. She knew he'd gone to visit his mother, and she was worried he'd had a bad visit and was brooding in front of his television again. Sure enough, when she knocked on the door and let herself in, he was sitting on the sofa with a beer in hand, watching an old movie.

"Bad day?" Carly asked, slipping off her sneakers and walking over to the sofa. She sat down beside Randy and curled her legs up under her.

"It could have been better," Randy said.

"Sorry. I thought you were coming out to the ranch to go riding before supper."

Randy took a swig of his beer. "I really didn't feel like seeing people today."

Carly reached up and placed her hand on his freshly shaved chin, turning his face toward her. "You didn't feel like seeing any people? Not even this person?"

Randy stared into her eyes. He smiled. "Well, I guess one person is okay."

Carly smiled wide and laid her head on his shoulder. Randy circled his arm around her. They sat there for a few minutes, watching John Wayne save the day again.

"We could go for a drive," Carly suggested. "Or to that coffee shop in town for a latte. It's been ages since I've had a latte."

Randy glanced at her. "What do I look like, some sort of city boy or something? I don't drink lattes."

"You would if you tried one. I'll bet you'd even love them," Carly teased.

"I'm fine with sitting right here."

"Do you want to talk about what upset you so much today?"

"Nope."

"I've become a good listener," Carly said.

"I don't want to talk about my mother, okay?"

Carly sighed. "Okay."

Randy sipped his beer.

"Tell me about your childhood," Carly said. "What was little Randy like?"

Randy frowned at her. "That's the last thing I want to talk about. If you want to be chatty, talk about your own childhood."

Carly lifted her head and looked at Randy. "Okay. I grew up in a beautiful home in a nice suburb in Seattle and my parents let me try everything my little heart desired. They owned the gallery and spent lots of money, which we later found out they couldn't afford. Then it all came crashing down when they died in a car accident and Andi had to sell everything to pay off their debts, including the gallery. We had enough to buy the townhouse and Andi put us through college, and that was it. I had a happy childhood until they died, but Andi did her best to take care of me," Carly said. "I guess I got my bad spending habits from them."

Randy turned and ran a finger gently across Carly's cheek, brushing a loose strand of hair behind her ear. "I'm sorry your parents died when you were young. I sometimes forget that I'm not the only one who's had hard times." He kissed the tip of her nose.

"Hey, you're not getting off that easily," Carly said, pulling him closer and kissing him. "Better?"

Randy smiled. "Much better." He stood, pulling her up with him. "Let's go riding," he said.

"Really? Should you be drinking and riding?" she teased.

"I only had one beer. I'll be fine," he said, laughing.

Carly looked around. "Or, we could stay here, you know, away from people." She raised her eyebrows seductively.

"That's why we're going riding. I don't trust myself here. You can't seduce me on a horse."

"Don't challenge me," Carly said. "You'd be surprised where I could seduce you."

Randy pulled Carly to him and kissed her again. "Thanks."

"For what?"

"For barging in and making me feel better. I'm always happier when I'm with you."

"Happy to do it," Carly said. "Come on, cowboy. Let's go riding."

"Anything you say, ma'am."

* * *

Carly was flying high. She hadn't felt this happy in a long, long time. Randy made her feel things that no other man ever had. She couldn't pinpoint exactly what it was. But the fact that she was so happy, and they hadn't even made love yet, told her just how special their growing relationship was.

Is this what it's like to be in love?

Carly wondered if that was the difference. She'd had close relationships with men before, and at times, like with Colt, she'd thought she was falling in love. But then something would happen and she'd pull away fast. The funny thing was, with Randy, she didn't want to run away. In fact, she wanted things to continue and for them to grow even closer.

I don't even care that he lives in a trailer.

Carly had to laugh at that. The old Carly liked men who had money to spend, dressed to the nines, and lived in nice places. That Carly would have turned her nose up at a man living in a trailer home. Not that Randy's wasn't nice, because it was, but the old Carly had been a snob and a selfish brat.

Randy's right. I have changed.

The new Carly didn't miss the old Carly at all. Maybe, that was why she was so happy.

Thursday evening after supper, Carly went into the barn in search of Randy so they could go riding. They had ridden regularly nearly every evening if weather permitted. It was mid-July and most days were hot, so it was nice going riding in the cooler evening air before sunset. Tonight, she was wearing jeans and a T-shirt, despite the heat. She would have preferred wearing shorts, but as the sun dropped in the sky, the bugs came out and feasted on her. She also brought along a light jacket to cover her arms.

At supper, Randy had been staring across the table at her, teasing her with his eyes. She'd tried ignoring him, because she hadn't wanted everyone else's attention at the table too, but it was hard. He was so darned cute. He had showered before supper, and tonight his hair was still damp and curling up at his neck. He smelled delicious and she loved seeing him smile at her with those crinkles framing his sexy eyes.

"You two have something to share with the rest of us?" Luke had asked, making both Carly and Randy look up in surprise.

"Stop teasing, Luke," Andi told him.

"Yeah. Randy might give you a black eye," Colt added, chuckling.

Carly had turned back to her food, her face feeling flushed. Even though she knew it was obvious that something was going on between her and Randy, no one ever spoke about it. She figured they were all so surprised that they still couldn't completely believe it.

Now, as she walked into the barn, she was smiling wide. At the other end, a tall man with broad shoulders had his back to her and she walked up quietly behind him and grabbed him around the waist. "Gotcha!" she yelled.

The man spun around and Carly stepped back, stunned. "Colt? I thought you were Randy."

Colt stared at her a moment, then laughed. "You got me, all right. You scared me half to death."

Carly giggled. "Sorry, Colt. I thought you were Randy. What are you still doing here?"

"I had to put some things away. I'll be going home soon. Are you two going riding again?"

Carly nodded. She climbed up on a railing by a stall and sat. "Yeah. Have you seen Randy? He's usually out here by now."

Colt shook his head. "Nope, but I'm sure he'll be along." He picked up his saddle and blanket that he'd used earlier and carried them into the tack room, then returned. He glanced over at Carly. "You seem to be enjoying your stay here."

Carly gazed at Colt. She hadn't spent much time around him, especially alone, while she'd been here. She'd figured he'd been avoiding her for Beth's sake, although she really didn't believe that Beth had a problem with their past relationship.

"I am enjoying it here," Carly said. "More than I would have ever imagined. I like working with Margie at the shop, and I love being around Andi and Jessi and everyone."

Colt smiled. "That's good. I know Beth has enjoyed riding

with you. What did you think of the house when she took you there?"

Carly couldn't help but smile back at Colt. He was handsome, sweet, and there wasn't a mean bone in his body. She wished she'd treated him better when they were together. He deserved better. But he ended up with Beth, and that was the best thing that could have happened to him.

"I love your house," Carly said. "The loft is wonderful. It has such a beautiful view out the tall windows from up there. You and Beth have done an amazing job with it."

"Thanks."

Carly jumped off the rail and walked closer to Colt. "Can I ask you a question?"

"Sure."

"Someone recently pointed out to me how phony I used to act around men, but he thinks I've changed since coming here. Is that how you felt when we were together? That I was acting like I cared about you, but that it wasn't real?"

Colt lowered his eyes, looking embarrassed. "Well, I don't know, Carly."

Carly walked closer and placed her hand on his arm. "I'm sorry. I didn't mean to embarrass you. I was just curious. I'd hate to think that you didn't know how much I cared for you then. I really did, you know. But I also realize now that I acted like a spoiled brat and that I didn't treat you as well as I should have."

Colt looked up into Carly's eyes. "I knew you cared about me then, Carly. At least, at first you did. As for being phony, well, I did watch you flirt with other men while I was with you in Seattle. It's just your way. You love the attention. It really didn't bother me because you always went home with me."

"You always made excuses for me, Colt. But I don't want people making excuses for me anymore. It's time I take responsibility for my own actions. And I'm sorry that I didn't understand that when we were together."

"Thanks, Carly. You know? You have changed since coming here. You're not out drinking or partying anymore and you just seem content with a simpler life. I guess that's what Randy sees, too, huh?" He winked at her.

Carly smiled. "I guess so. I think everything turned out the way it was supposed to, don't you? You and I would never have made it as a couple. You and Beth are perfect for each other."

"Yeah. I think you're right. You and I wouldn't have lasted. I honestly couldn't think of being with anyone else besides Beth."

Carly reached up and hugged Colt, and he wrapped his arms around her. "You're the sweetest guy I've ever known. I'm so happy for you and Beth. And I'm glad we can still be friends."

"Me too," Colt whispered into her ear.

Carly kissed his cheek before slowly pulling away.

"Well, I'd better head home before Beth starts wondering where I am," Colt said. He waved to Carly and walked out of the barn.

Carly sat on a straw bale, waiting for Randy. It was hot inside the barn, even with the doors on both ends open. She wondered what was taking him so long. She figured she'd wait a few more minutes, and then go looking for him.

* * *

Randy stood at the barn door with his fists clenched. After supper, he'd gone to put away some tools in the shed before coming to meet Carly in the barn. He'd smiled all the way to the barn. He'd been staring at Carly throughout supper, thinking how beautiful she looked even after a day of helping Ginny pick vegetables in the garden and then cooking supper.

He'd been looking forward to riding with her tonight, even though they did it most evenings. He enjoyed hearing about her days at the gift shop, or listening to her describe the latest cute thing Jessi had done. No matter what type of mood he was in at the end of the day, she could always cheer him up. But then, just as he'd walked up to the barn, he'd heard voices and peered inside. There stood Carly, only inches from Colt. He watched as she touched his arm, and the tender way Colt had looked at her. Then she'd hugged Colt and kissed him on the cheek.

She hadn't changed after all. She was still flirting with other men. Still flirting with Colt.

Hot anger spread throughout Randy. He backed away, not wanting to see any more. He turned and strode off to his truck and drove away.

What an idiot I am to have thought she'd be interested in only me. Randy sped his truck down the highway, chastising himself for trusting Carly. He'd known what she was like, but he'd led himself to believe she'd actually changed. He'd thought that she was falling in love with him. *Ridiculous!* Carly loved only one person—herself.

Randy pulled off at the exit for The Depot, parked, and walked inside. It wasn't very busy, but there were a couple of guys playing pool and a few people eating a late supper. He stopped at the bar and ordered a beer, and then headed to his usual spot by the pool tables.

The young waitress came over to say hello. She smiled seductively. "My shift is over. You want some company, cowboy?"

Randy smiled back. "Sure. Sit on down."

Two can play at that game, Carly.

* * *

Carly went to work on Friday morning still wondering what had happened to Randy. Last night, she'd sat for over an hour waiting for him, before finally giving up. When she'd left the barn, she noticed that his truck was gone. She wondered where he'd gone to and why he hadn't told her he was leaving. Then a thought had struck her—maybe something had happened to his mother and he'd had to leave quickly.

Carly had gone inside the house and asked Ginny if she'd heard from Randy. When Ginny had told her no, Carly used the house phone to call Randy's place, but he didn't answer. After several tries, she'd given up and gone up to her room. She'd thought of driving out to his place to check on him, but then made herself stay home. If he'd wanted her to know where he'd gone, he'd have told her.

Now, as she walked into the gift shop and waved hello to Margie, she still wondered about Randy. She'd seen his truck at the ranch before she'd left for work, but he was nowhere to be found. Then, she'd noticed that Black Jack wasn't in the pasture, and figured he was off checking on something in another pasture. But why hadn't he called her? Why had he left her hanging last night?

The morning at the shop was busy with tourists passing through town and some coming in for a weekend at a local dude ranch. When things slowed down later in the afternoon, Carly went on a coffee run and brought back lattes and muffins for both her and Margie.

"Oh, this is a treat," Margie said, sipping her coffee. "I rarely splurge for fancy coffee. This is delicious."

"I used to pick up a latte or cappuccino on my way to work every day in Seattle," Carly said. "That's one thing I really miss. But now that I'm watching my spending, I only do this once in a while."

"Will you be going back to Seattle when summer is over?"

Margie asked.

Carly shrugged. "I don't have a job to go back to, but I do have the townhouse. I suppose I could find a new job."

"A smart girl like you would be snapped up quickly," Margie said. "You have a talent for sales and business. I wish I could talk you into buying my little shop. You'd do quite well here, with all your good ideas."

Carly smiled over her coffee cup as she glanced around the shop. She'd never even considered owning her own business before. It was something that would have been out of reach financially for her in Seattle. Yet, it seemed crazy that she made money for other people and earned only a fraction of what they made off of her. "That's an interesting thought," she told Margie. "But I'd never be able to afford to buy a business. I have enough trouble just keeping my head above water now. But it would be nice to live closer to Andi and watch the baby grow up. I'd miss them if I left."

"And what about a certain cowboy? Wouldn't you miss him, too?"

Carly looked over at Margie in surprise. "How do you know about that?"

Margie grinned. "I've seen how your eyes light up when Randy comes in. And the fact that he goes out of his way to stop in here to see you tells me he's serious about you. How could he not be? Where else would he find such a smart and pretty girl?"

"You're too sweet," Carly said. Her expression grew serious. "You said once that Randy had a difficult childhood. Was it really that bad?"

Margie sighed. "Randy was always a good boy despite his upbringing. His mother grew up here and worked at a local bar from the time she graduated high school. She's only a couple of years younger than I am, so I've known her all my life. I don't think she ever planned on settling down or having a family—she was quite the party girl. She was about thirty when Randy's father came around. He drifted into town and was hired on as a ranch hand for a local dude ranch. It wasn't long before she became pregnant with Randy. That's when I think they got married, probably reluctantly. And boy, those two fought like cats and dogs. But they drank a lot too. Then Randy's dad just up and left and never came back. I think Evie always resented having Randy around. Yet, no matter how badly she treated Randy, he always took care of her. He gave her money even when she was well and could still work. And then after she had a stroke, he made sure she was in the best care facility around here. He's too good to her, if you ask me, after the way she treated him."

Carly frowned. "No wonder he doesn't like to talk about his mother. And he's usually in a bad mood after visiting her on Sundays."

"Well, his mother does have some serious health issues. Her stroke, and all her years of drinking, left her with nerve damage and memory loss. I doubt that she even knows who he is when he visits."

"That's sad," Carly said, her heart aching for Randy. It was as if he'd lost his mother already, even though she was still alive. "That must be really hard to deal with."

"I only know how badly she's doing because I visit an old friend of mine in that same nursing home regularly. Her room is across from Evie's. I hear Evie yelling at the nurses sometimes. It's awful. And even though I've known Evie her entire life, when I say hello to her, she just stares at me with a blank expression." Margie shook her head. "It's very sad."

"You know, it's because of the kindness of the Brennans that Randy was able to do so well," Margie continued. "Jack Brennan treated him like his own son, and Ginny has always been so kind to him. He deserved all the kindness he could get, and he's grown into such a nice man." She smiled at Carly. "He's worth the occasional bad mood. He's a hard worker and a good person."

Carly nodded. Randy had been so kind to her over the past few weeks, despite their rocky beginning. She was sure he had a good reason for not meeting up with her last night. She'd find out why tonight and hopefully they could go riding as they usually did. Carly smiled as she looked forward to seeing him.

Chapter Fifteen

That evening when Carly came home from work, she noticed that Randy's truck wasn't in the driveway. She didn't think too much of it, though. It was close to suppertime, so she figured he was home, showering. She went inside and changed her clothes before helping Ginny and Andi fix the last bit of supper.

When suppertime came and went, and Randy hadn't arrived, Carly didn't know if she should be angry or worried. No one made mention of the empty chair across from her, but she felt their eyes on her throughout the meal. Afterward, as she helped clean up the supper dishes, Ginny placed a calming hand on her arm. "He probably went to The Depot for supper, dear. He used to eat out some Fridays and Saturdays."

Carly nodded. She knew Ginny was just trying to make her feel better, but it didn't. Randy had been eating with the family every night, even on Sunday, since she and he had grown close. He was avoiding her, but she didn't know why.

"Are you okay?" Andi asked later as she got ready to go home with Luke and Jessi. "I can stay awhile and talk if you want me to."

"I'm fine," Carly lied. "You go along home. I'm working tomorrow anyway, so I should get to bed early."

Andi hugged her and they left. No sooner had their truck

disappeared, Carly was out the door. She wasn't going to sit here and wait for answers. She had to go to Randy's place and find out what was wrong.

On the way to Randy's, Carly decided to check The Depot's parking lot for his truck first. Sure enough, it was sitting there. Carly's blood began to boil. *What kind of game is he playing with me?*

She walked into the crowded bar. The band was tuning up their instruments, getting ready for a night of dancing and fun. Carly stood in the entryway, scanning the crowd. From the corner of her eye, she spotted Duane Utley by the bar, staring at her. She ignored him and continued searching until she spotted Randy sitting at a table near the pool tables. Some young little thing with a short skirt and low-cut top was leaning over him. Carly strode across the room and stopped right in front of Randy. The waitress turned and glared at her.

Cripes. She's even younger than I am.

"Will you excuse us a second?" Carly said, looking down at her.

The girl squared her shoulders and tossed back her blond hair before retreating to the bar.

Carly sat down opposite Randy. "I see you've made a new friend."

Randy leveled his gaze on her. "So? What do you care?"

Carly's brow creased. "What do you mean by that?"

Randy took a sip of beer. "Why are you here?"

"You didn't show up to go riding last night. And then you missed supper tonight. I came to find out what was going on."

Randy snorted. "Oh, I was at the barn last night, but I decided three's a crowd."

"What are you talking about?"

"I was there in time to see you hanging all over Colt."

Carly thought back to last night. "All I was doing was talking to him."

"Right, with your hands." Randy shoved his chair back and leaned in close to Carly. "I'd thought you'd changed, but I was so wrong. You're still flirting with anything in pants. Hell, it doesn't even matter to you if he's married."

Anger rose inside of Carly. She couldn't believe he was saying this to her. "We were hugging, you idiot. Friends do that. I'm not after Colt. I wouldn't do anything to jeopardize his marriage. How can you even believe that about me? I thought you knew me better."

"Yeah, well I thought so too. But apparently people don't change. You certainly haven't." He nodded over to the bar. "Hey, your old buddy, Duane, is over there. Maybe you'd like to take a run at him again. I'll bet he's willing."

Carly stared at Randy in disbelief. She stood. "You're right. People don't change. You're still the nasty cowboy I've always thought you were. Go ahead and have your little underage waitress. You're perfect for each other. She's young, and you're an idiot. It's a good match." Carly turned, and with as much dignity as she could muster, she walked across the bar and out the door.

* * *

Randy watched Carly leave as he swallowed the lump in his throat. He knew he should go after her and apologize for what he'd said, but his pride wouldn't let him. After all, he had seen her all over Colt. That much was true. The rest he'd said, however, had just been mean.

The waitress came over to the table as Randy stood.

"Who was that awful bitch?" she asked. Randy sighed. He took out a twenty, dropped it on the table, and walked out of the bar without a word.

Carly's car was already gone. He sat in his truck for a while, wondering what he should do. He'd been stewing for two days about what he'd seen in the barn and that had made him lash out at Carly. He should have let her explain. He should have given her the benefit of the doubt. Instead, he'd let himself run off at the mouth. She was right. He was an idiot.

Yet, that little voice inside his head had told him not to believe her. Heck, he hadn't believed in anyone for a very long time. Why should he start now? His mother had taught him early on that no one could be depended upon. Everyone lied. Everyone took advantage of you. People only looked out for themselves and didn't give a damn about others. But the Brennans had proved her wrong on all counts. They'd never used him, lied to him, or taken advantage of him. His mother had done all those things, but the Brennans never had.

So, why don't I believe Carly?

Randy drove toward the ranch, not sure what he was going to do. As the driveway came into view, he drove on instead of pulling into it. A short distance from there was Colt's driveway. Randy turned into it, still not sure why. He drove up to the house and shut off the lights. He needed to talk to Colt. He would believe Colt.

Colt opened the door just as Randy stepped up on the front porch. "Hey, Randy. This is a surprise. Come on in."

Randy hesitated. He saw Beth inside, sitting on the sofa in front of the television. He'd probably interrupted them watching a movie. He waved at her and she smiled and waved back.

"I just came to ask you a question," Randy said, feeling unsure now. "Can we talk out here a moment?"

"Okay," Colt said, looking confused. He stepped outside and shut the door. "What's on your mind?"

Randy paused, wondering how stupid he would sound to

Colt. He cleared his throat. "Okay. I'll just say it. The other night, I saw you and Carly in the barn. Carly said you were just talking, but I saw her hug you. It looked to me like she was flirting with you. Was she?"

Colt's eyebrows drew together. He crossed his arms. "We were just talking, Randy. Nothing else happened."

"I'm sorry, Colt, but it looked like more than talking to me. She had her hands on you."

"Sheesh, Randy. She only hugged me. You know, like friends do. Do you honestly think I would cheat on Beth? Or hurt you?"

Randy ran his hand across the back of his neck. Now he felt like a full-fledged idiot. "You're right. I'm sorry, Colt. Carly said the exact same thing, and I should have believed her. It's just that with her history of flirting with men, well, I was afraid that's what was happening."

Colt nodded. "I understand. But Carly has changed since she and I were together last summer. She's grown up. She's not the self-centered person she was a year ago. And I know she cares what you think about her. To be honest, Randy, the two of you together is a surprise to all of us, but you both seem so happy. Why do you want to ruin it by not believing her? She didn't do anything wrong."

"You're right. I should have believed her. I'm sorry about bothering you, Colt." Randy turned to leave.

Colt placed his hand on his shoulder. Randy turned. "We're family, Randy. I'm glad you felt comfortable enough to come and ask me instead of just being angry about it. I hope you can make it right with Carly."

"Thanks, Colt." Randy waved and headed to his truck. Tomorrow, he had a lot of apologizing to do.

* * *

Carly lay in bed that night unable to fall asleep. She was angry and frustrated with Randy. When she'd walked out of the bar, she had to force back her tears so she could drive to the ranch. But as soon as she'd entered her bedroom, she'd let them fall. Now, anger had replaced the hurt and she wished she could smack some good sense into him.

The fact that he wouldn't believe her upset her the most. She could almost understand his misinterpreting what he saw in the barn between her and Colt. After all, they'd been lovers once. But he should have known that she wouldn't flirt with Colt. Hadn't she already told him she wasn't out to get Colt back that first night in the loft? Even so, when she'd told him tonight that it was just a friendly hug, he should have believed her. What kind of relationship could they build if he didn't trust her?

Her thoughts turned to what Margie had told her about Randy's childhood and the way his mother had treated him. She could understand how his upbringing could have a lot to do with his trust issues. But she'd never given him any reason not to trust her. If anything, she'd always been brutally honest with him.

And then there was the troubling fact that at the first sign of a problem, Randy had bolted and completely locked her out. If she hadn't confronted him, he probably wouldn't have ever told her what was wrong. She didn't know if she could be with a man who ran away every time there was a problem. She may have broken up with a lot of men in her day, but she'd always done it face-to-face instead of slinking away. Well, in most cases she had.

Carly sighed. Was this karma for all the hearts she'd so casually broken? And wasn't it ironic that it was the crabby cowboy who'd broken hers?

Chapter Sixteen

Carly was exhausted by the time she awoke early Saturday morning. She wished she didn't have to go to work so she could sleep in. But she'd promised Margie she'd be there, so she pushed herself out of bed and went to shower.

When Carly got down to the kitchen, only Ginny and Glen were there, drinking coffee. Everyone else had already eaten breakfast and gone off to do chores. Carly poured a cup of coffee and sat down at the table. There were muffins in a basket, as usual, and Carly ate one spread with Ginny's delicious jam.

The three of them talked about how nice the weather had been lately, what was ripe in the garden, and how busy the gift shop was. Carly watched how Ginny and Glen interacted with each other. The slight touch of a hand, a gentle smile. They teased and joked, and when they looked at each other, their eyes twinkled. They were the perfect couple and seemed so comfortable together; it was as if they'd been together for years. She wondered if they fought, and then dismissed that idea. They would discuss their differences, not argue. That's what mature people did. Like Luke and Andi, and Beth and Colt. She'd never seen either couples argue, either. Maybe that was what it was like when you found the right person. Maybe, that was why she and Randy weren't right for each other.

Oil and water.

* * *

Once at work, Carly was too busy helping customers and straightening merchandise to dwell on Randy. Customers came and went. Carly sold another framed print of Andi's. It was of the sun setting from the view on the top of the hill at the ranch. People loved that print, and the one she'd painted of the valley at the summer pasture, also. Both reflected the beauty of Montana with warm colors and lush scenery. Now that the framed prints were displayed at the front of the store, they sold well.

Later that afternoon when the crowds had thinned out and only a couple of families were milling around the store, the bell over the door rang and Carly glanced up. Randy stood there, a tall coffee cup in his hand and a contrite look on his face. When Carly didn't move, Randy walked over to her.

"I brought you one of those fancy coffees you like so much," Randy said, handing the cup to Carly.

Reluctantly, Carly took it. "Why are you here?"

"Can we talk?"

"I'm busy," Carly said, walking away from him to the counter.

Randy followed. "Just a few minutes, Carly. Please."

Margie walked up to the counter. "Hi, Randy. You go along and take a break, Carly. You deserve one. I'll be fine in here."

Sighing, Carly walked to the front door and stepped outside with Randy right behind her. She went to the other end of the porch and leaned against the support beam. Randy stopped and faced her.

"I came to apologize. I acted like a jerk last night. I was so angry that I didn't want to hear what you had to say. I should have believed you. I'm sorry."

Carly stood there, still holding the coffee. "What made you decide I was telling the truth?"

"I went over to Colt's last night and had a talk with him."

Carly's mouth dropped open. "You went over to Colt's house to ask him if I was lying to you?"

Randy frowned. "Wait. It wasn't like that. I wanted to ask him to make sure."

"To make sure I wasn't lying? So, you wouldn't believe *me* when I told you, but you believed Colt."

"Colt's never lied to me."

Carly looked Randy right in the eye. "And neither have I. Yet, you didn't believe me."

"Carly. I didn't come here to fight with you. I came to apologize. I'm sorry. Can't you accept that?"

Carly shook her head. "No, I can't. First, you run off when you think I've done something you didn't like, and then you don't even believe me when I tell you the truth. How can we have any kind of relationship if you don't trust me? I've never given you any reason not to trust me, Randy. Yet, you don't."

Randy stared into Carly's eyes. "I'll admit I have trouble trusting people. I have my reasons. And you're right. You've never given me a reason not to trust you. But you have to admit, your history with men and relationships aren't exactly sterling. You've played men before. I hated the thought that I was being played."

Carly's face grew hot. "My life before coming here has nothing to do with you and me. Yes, I've had relationships with other men, and yes, I haven't been an angel. Colt and I were lovers. Get over it. We aren't anymore. Does that mean that every time you get mad at me, you're going to throw it all up in my face? What about you? You mean to tell me you've been a perfect angel your whole life? What about that little waitress last night? Did you sleep with her?" Carly shoved the coffee at Randy and spun around to leave.

"Wait a minute, Carly."

Carly turned. "No, there's nothing more to say. If you can't trust me, or respect me, then there's no point in continuing this. I've been played by men, too, you know. And I won't be played again either." She walked down the porch and into the shop.

* * *

Randy left the shop and headed back to the ranch to finish up his chores. As he put tools away in the shed, his thoughts kept replaying his argument with Carly. He knew she was right. He should have believed her and never gone to ask Colt. He hadn't realized how angry it would make her.

"You know nothing about women," he said aloud in the empty shed.

"None of us do. That's why we get in so much trouble," Luke said with a laugh.

Randy spun around and glared at Luke. "What? Are you checking up on me now, too?"

"Oh, settle on down. I was just coming in to get something. It's not my fault you were talking to yourself."

"Well, go get it then," Randy grumbled.

"Trouble in paradise? I left those twinkle lights up in the loft in case you want to romance Carly some more," Luke said with a wink.

Randy threw Luke a nasty look. "You can tear them down. There won't be any more romancing going on around here."

"You two fighting already? Well, it was only a matter of time. You're both pig-headed. One of you was going to piss off the other sooner or later."

"You're really not helping," Randy told him.

Luke slapped him on the back. "Sorry. I was just giving you a hard time. Do you want to complain to someone? I'll listen."

"No. There's nothing to talk about."

Luke shrugged. "Suit yourself." He rummaged through the bins of nails and grabbed a handful, then picked up a hammer. "I found some loose boards on the back side of the barn. Seems like stuff falls apart around here all the time."

"There's still some work to do up in the summer pasture. More fence wire needs replacing in spots. I was thinking I'd head up there Monday and stay the week, if that's okay with you," Randy said.

Luke stared at him a moment. "You're not running away from a little blond woman, are you? A word of advice. Women don't like that. They'd rather talk it out."

"I'm all talked out," Randy said. "You want me to fix those fences, or what?"

"Suit yourself," Luke said. "Need any help up there? I could come up for a couple of days."

Randy shook his head. "No, you stay home. You've got someone to be home with. Besides, you're growing soft."

Luke snorted. "I could take you on any day of the week."

"Right." Randy grinned at him.

"Okay. You go off to the summer pasture. But if Carly asks, I won't take the blame for you going. I don't want that little spitfire mad at me," Luke said.

Randy shook his head. Carly was a spitfire when she wanted to be. Unfortunately, she was no longer his spitfire.

* * *

Carly finished her day at work in a daze after her argument with Randy. As she drove to the ranch, she fought back tears as her anger slowly turned into hurt. What Randy had said about not trusting her because of her past relationships with men had cut her deeply. She was no saint, and she was the first to admit it. But she'd always been honest with Randy. He'd seen the real her. And she'd thought he'd been falling for her because of it. But she'd been wrong.

Carly couldn't stand the thought of sitting across the table from Randy at supper or making small talk. She told Andi and Ginny she didn't feel well and went directly to her room where she stayed all night.

Lying on her bed, she re-examined every relationship she'd ever been in. Despite what people thought, she wasn't a one-night stand type of girl. She'd always been with only one man at a time. The problem was, she'd never wanted to make a lifetime commitment with any of them, and the relationship would eventually end. Last year, Colt had scared her off by proposing marriage. She'd only wanted to have fun then. But now, her feelings about commitment were changing. Seeing how happy Colt and Beth, Luke and Andi, and even Ginny and Glen were had made her more open to finding that one special person to spend her life with. Why on earth she'd starting thinking Randy might be the one, she had no idea. They were so opposite of each other, there was no way they could ever fit together perfectly. But, he'd made her so happy for the past few weeks. At least until everything crumbled.

Maybe it was for the best.

Carly was relieved when Randy didn't join them for supper on Sunday night. But on Monday night, when Andi didn't set a place for him at the table, she wondered why and finally asked.

Andi had looked at her curiously before answering. "He's up at the summer pasture for the week, fixing fences. I'm surprised he didn't tell you."

Carly wasn't surprised at all. He ran away again. That

seemed to be a pattern with him.

The week dragged by for Carly now that she wasn't looking forward to evening rides with Randy. Beth went riding with her on Tuesday afternoon, and although Carly enjoyed her company, it wasn't the same. Carly filled her empty hours watching Jessi for Andi while she painted, and canning with Ginny. And in the evenings when the sun set, she'd go up to the hayloft and sit by the door, staring out at the starlit sky, wondering what Randy was doing, despite herself.

* * *

Randy sat on the front porch of the summer cabin gazing up into the evening sky. Every day he filled his hours working out in the hot sun. He'd strung new barbed wire on what seemed like miles of fencing, he'd replaced some broken boards, and he'd driven around the pasture to check on the cattle. But in the evening, after he'd heated up something from a can to eat and had a beer or two, he'd find himself staring up at the sky, thinking of Carly.

He wondered what she'd been doing all week, and if she missed him. Why would she? He'd given her every reason to hate him and then he'd run off again to hide. He knew it, Luke knew it, heck, he'd bet that Carly knew he'd run away from her.

When did my life become such a mess?

Randy had never had a serious relationship with a woman his entire life. If he wanted an excuse why, all he had to do was look back at his childhood and it was right there. His mother had never been happy and had done nothing but complain about his father even long after his dad had disappeared. Men had come and gone, but none stayed around for long. He hadn't actually seen a healthy relationship until he'd started hanging around the Brennan ranch, but even by the age of eight, he'd already been scarred deeply enough not to believe in love or to trust other people completely. Now, as an adult, he knew it was ridiculous to hold on to those past feelings and use them as an excuse for not getting close to a woman, but it was still hard. Sure, he'd had women in his life and they'd had fun, but nothing serious. Then Carly came along, and after two years of ignoring her, he'd finally fallen under her spell. And for the first time, he'd felt he might actually be able to sustain a serious relationship. Until the past had crept up on him and threw doubt in the middle of his happiness.

Maybe I'm not meant to be happy.

What a sad thought.

Why was he so hung up on Carly's past? She was a grown woman, and beautiful, so of course there had been other men. And then there was her relationship with Colt. He didn't really believe that was the reason he didn't trust her. He'd just used it as a reason. When he'd first met Carly two years ago, he knew she was trouble. She flirted easily and got her way by pouting those pretty lips. She really knew how to play a guy, and Colt had fallen for it hook, line, and sinker. That had turned Randy off so quickly, he'd never given her a second thought. But she was different now. More humble. Less self-centered. Her real beauty had shown through her exterior beauty. And Randy had seen that inner beauty shine through. So, why in the world did he let things get so far off track?

Sitting there on the porch, Randy grew angry with himself. He'd been up here alone long enough. He was tired of eating food out of a can, tired of having too much time to think, and most of all, tired of being alone. It was time to go back home.

Chapter Seventeen

Randy returned to the ranch Saturday afternoon but didn't eat supper with the family until Monday. He'd needed more time to decide what to do about Carly. Unfortunately, Carly had already decided for him. At supper that first night, she'd looked right through him, not even acknowledging his presence. He was disappointed, but he couldn't blame her. For now, he'd let it be. He had other problems to handle, and if that was the way she wanted it, he'd give her some space.

He had gone to see his mother on Sunday, but it had been another frustrating visit. Like Carly, she'd completely ignored him. His mother looked even thinner and paler, if that was possible. When he'd spoken with Renee, she had no new news to tell him. She'd said they were watching her blood pressure and trying to entice her to eat more, but that was about all that could be done until she saw the specialist a week from Friday. Hopefully, the doctor would have news for them then.

Tuesday night, after another meal where Carly had completely ignored him, Randy went out to the barn to put away his saddle and bridle that he had used earlier in the day. As he stepped out of the tack room, he was surprised to see Carly standing in the far door of the barn.

The two stared at each other. Randy was afraid to speak, for fear that Carly would turn on her heel and run. Instead of fleeing, Carly walked farther into the barn.

"I thought you were Colt," she said, stopping several feet away from him. "And no, I wasn't looking for him to jump his bones. Beth asked me to tell him she was leaving for home if I ran into him."

"Colt's in the tool shed," Randy said.

"Thanks." Carly turned to leave.

Randy took a step closer to her. "Carly, wait."

Carly turned and waited for him to speak.

Randy cleared his throat. "Can we talk about what happened? I told you I was sorry I didn't believe you before. I'm not sure what more I can do to convince you."

Carly brushed her hair over her shoulder and looked at him haughtily. "Don't worry about it." She turned and started to walk away.

Randy strode across the distance that separated them and placed a hand on her shoulder, stopping her. Carly stiffened but didn't turn around. "Tell me what I can do to make it up to you," he said, standing close behind her. Her perfume wafted up to him, and reminded him of the night in the loft when he'd held her tight. He loved how she felt in his arms, how warm and soft her body felt against his, and how sweet her lips tasted. He missed spending time with her, riding in the evenings, and talking with her. "Please, Carly. Talk to me."

Carly's shoulders sagged and for an instant, Randy believed she might turn around and give him another chance. But then she stood straighter and said, "There's nothing left to say." She pulled from his touch and walked out of the barn.

Randy watched sadly as Carly ran toward the tool shed. There was nothing more he could do or say. She'd already made up her mind. They were through.

With a heavy heart, Randy returned to his work.

* * *

Carly fled from Randy with tears in her eyes. She ran across the yard to the tool shed, but instead of going inside, she ran behind it and hid in a copse of trees. How could one touch from his hand have so much power over her? She still felt the warmth of it on her shoulder. He'd stood so close, she'd felt his breath, warm on her neck. It had all been too much for her. For a split second, she'd almost given in. But instead, she'd held firm and walked away.

Carly wiped her tears away and sat on the green grass with her back against a tree trunk. She wondered what it was about Randy that made her feel so heartsick about losing him. She'd dated dozens of men and let them go, never once looking back or feeling heartache. Yet, she and Randy had done nothing more than kiss, and she felt she'd lost the love of her life.

The love of her life. How could that be?

Carly thought back to when she'd first met Randy two years before and how he could barely stand to be in the same room as her. When she'd come here this summer, he did everything in his power to make her feel unwelcomed. Then it had all changed. Her life was changing and so was she. She'd stopped acting like a spoiled little city girl and that had altered Randy's opinion of her. Somehow, her opinion of him had shifted as well. He was no longer the crabby cowboy to her. He'd turned into a sweet, caring man who didn't take advantage of her and actually spent time getting to know her. Most men wanted to get her into bed as quickly as possible. Not Randy. He was willing to wait until the moment was right. That was one of the many reasons she'd opened her heart to him. Then he'd lost faith in her over one little misunderstanding and ruined everything.

Carly heard the shed door close and knew that Colt had left.

She decided not to go after him. She figured he'd be heading home soon anyway. She heard one truck, then another, start up and drive off, crunching gravel down the driveway. She was sure Colt and Randy had left for the night.

Wiping away the last of her tears, Carly stood up and walked slowly toward the horse corral. Evening was settling in as the sun made its way behind the hills. Carly stood up on the fence rail and whistled for Abby. To her surprise, Abby came running. Carly ran her hand down the horse's nose and across her smooth neck. "At least you still like me," Carly said softly to Abby.

"I like you, too," a deep voice said behind her. "You're okay, for a sister-in-law."

Carly turned and smiled when she saw Luke standing a few paces behind her. She hopped off the fence and walked over to him. "You aren't supposed to eavesdrop on conversations between a girl and her horse," she said.

Luke chuckled. "Sorry. I was going to head home and noticed the barn door was still open. Are you all done in there for the night?"

Carly's smile faded. "I wasn't in there. Randy was. I think he's already left."

"Yep. His truck is gone. I'll go close things up then." Luke walked over to the barn and went inside, and then he came back out and slid the door into place. He walked back over near Carly. "Have you two made up yet, or am I going to have to butt in?"

Carly looked at him, surprised. "What do you know about it?"

Luke grinned. "Hey, I have eyes. You two were hot and heavy for each other and now you don't even look at him during supper. And even though Randy will kill me for saying this, I know that he was hiding from you when he went up to the summer pasture last week. Is there anything I can do? I'm a good listener."

Carly smiled. "I'm sure you are, but there's nothing to talk about anymore. He doesn't trust me, Luke, plain and simple. So there's no reason to continue. It's never going to work out."

Luke studied Carly a moment before speaking. "You know, Carly, you should never say never. A month ago, I'd have said there was no chance that you and Randy would be a couple. And two years ago, I would have sworn that I'd never fall in love with a city girl again. But, I did, and Andi and I are happier every day. And you and Randy were close. So, don't be so hasty to let it go, okay? Randy's a tough guy, and he rarely shows his feelings, but when I see you two together, I see something in his eyes that I've never seen in him before. Not even when we were ten years old and he had a crush on little Melody Aimes." Luke winked. "He cares about you, Carly. He just sometimes doesn't know how to show it."

"Why Luke, I never knew you were such a romantic," Carly said, watching Luke's face turn red with embarrassment. "No wonder my sister fell for you. And here all along I thought it was just because you were a hunky cowboy."

Luke rolled his eyes. "Well, don't go telling anyone. You'll ruin my reputation as a tough guy."

Carly walked over and hugged Luke tight. "You're secret is safe with me," she whispered.

"Think about what I said, okay?" Luke said after Carly pulled away. "Randy can be a bear to deal with sometimes, but he's a good guy. Maybe you can give him another chance."

Carly sighed and nodded. She waved as Luke stepped up into his truck and drove off toward his and Andi's cabin. She'd like to believe that Randy still cared for her, but she couldn't live her life always defending her every action around other men. If he were jealous of Colt, then he'd be jealous of everyone she ever hugged or smiled at. It would be hard to deal with.

Maybe it was best to let it go.

Carly walked slowly to the ranch house and quietly stepped inside the back porch. She slipped off her boots and was about to walk into the kitchen when she saw Ginny and Glen in there. They were standing close, their arms around each other, gazing into each other's eyes. Carly didn't want to interrupt such an intimate moment, so she stepped back into the shadows.

Ginny and Glen were such an adorable couple. In her fifties, Ginny was still vibrant and pretty, and Glen was sweet and distinguished with his silver hair and bright blue eyes. They'd been dating for almost as long as Andi and Luke had been together, and Carly wouldn't be surprised if they ended up married. She glanced into the kitchen quickly to see if they were gone, and saw them kissing, then Ginny laughed and Carly watched as they walked hand-in-hand into Ginny's bedroom behind the kitchen. Carly smiled. It was heartwarming to know that love didn't have an age limit. She wished love were as kind to her as it had been to everyone else here at the ranch. She tiptoed to the staircase, bent down to pet Bree behind the ears, then headed up to her room.

Chapter Eighteen

Carly went to work on Wednesday but had a hard time concentrating all day. She kept thinking about what Luke had said about giving Randy another chance. She wanted to believe they could get past his being jealous, but she wasn't sure. And then there was the way he ran away every time life became difficult. He'd done it twice in the past month. How could they ever have a relationship if he ran away every time they argued? Randy had admitted to her he had trust issues, but would he be willing to work on them? She wasn't sure if he would, or if she could be with him if he didn't.

She ignored Randy at supper that night again, but it was difficult. He kept staring at her while he ate, and even when she looked away, she felt his eyes on her. Thankfully, he excused himself as soon as supper was over and hadn't even stayed for dessert. Carly let out a relieved sigh when he left. She hoped things would settle down between them eventually so they could at least be friendly, or else suppertime was going to be uncomfortable every night. And it only made it worse everyone was staring at them, as if anticipating something would happen. It was unnerving.

Carly had trouble falling asleep that night so it was late in the morning by the time she came downstairs. The kitchen phone had been ringing several times, and it echoed all the way up to her room. When she entered the kitchen, Andi was feeding Jessi an early lunch and Ginny was cooking. Both women had worried expressions on their faces.

"What's up with all the phone calls this morning?" Carly asked, pouring a cup of coffee.

"I'm sorry, dear. I hope they didn't wake you," Ginny told her. "People have been calling here, looking for Randy. I guess he's not answering his phone."

Carly's heart quickened. "Did something happen to Randy? Isn't he here, working?"

"Oh, no, dear. Randy is fine. But he's not here today. He called me early this morning to say he wouldn't be working the next couple of days. I'm afraid his mother passed away during the night. He's probably off making arrangements."

Shock fell over Carly. She knew Randy had a tenuous relationship with his mother, so she was afraid of how he'd react to her passing. "How was he when you talked to him?" she asked Ginny.

"He was shaken up. He said something about her heart condition and that no one expected this to happen so soon. I know she's been sick a long time, but a death is always a shock no matter what the situation."

Carly thought about how withdrawn and surly he was after he visited his mother on Sundays. If she knew him at all, she had a pretty good idea where he was and why he wasn't answering his phone.

"I'm going over to check on him," she said, setting down her mug.

"Oh, honey. That's such a good idea. He could use someone at a time like this," Ginny said.

Carly saw Andi nod agreement. "Send him our love," Andi said. "If he needs anything, call us, okay?"

Carly nodded and headed upstairs for her purse and car

keys. She slipped on a pair of flats and ran back downstairs. Randy might be a jealous, infuriating grouch, but she couldn't let him be alone at a time like this.

She pulled into his driveway a few minutes later and, sure enough, his truck was parked by his home. She knocked on his door twice, and when he didn't answer, she opened the door and walked right in. As she'd suspected, he was sitting on his sofa with a beer in his hand, staring at the television. He hadn't shaved, his hair was mussed, and his clothes looked rumpled. She figured he must have put on yesterday's clothes after they'd lain on the floor all night.

He looked up when she walked in but didn't say a word. The phone started ringing as she stood in the entryway.

"Are you going to answer that?" Carly asked, walking closer to the sofa.

"Nope."

Carly drew closer and sat down on the sofa beside Randy. "I'm sorry about your mother."

Randy took a long swig of his beer before turning his head to look at her. His eyes looked glazed over, as if he still hadn't accepted what had happened. He nodded at her.

The phone stopped ringing and the room grew quiet. An old movie played on the television set, but the sound was off. Carly watched the movie for a minute, then turned to Randy and said gently, "I don't think John Wayne can help you with this."

Randy gazed at her. "Why are you here?"

Carly sighed. "Because I was afraid you'd be sitting here, hiding out, and drinking beer."

Randy shrugged.

"And because Ginny and Andi are worried about you. You're not answering your phone. People are calling the ranch to find you."

"I don't want to talk to anyone right now."

"Why?"

Randy stare at her with tired eyes. "Because people will want to tell me how sorry they are, and expect some sort of emotion from me. How can I show any emotion if I don't even know how I feel? Right now, I don't feel anything."

Carly's heart swelled. She had no idea what it was like to feel nothing for a family member. She loved her sister, and she'd loved her parents. She cared deeply for the entire Brennan family and would be heartbroken if anything happened to any of them. But from the little she knew about Randy's family, it was understandable that he had trouble dealing with his feelings about his mother's death.

She moved closer to him and reached up, brushing his unruly hair from his eyes. He lifted his hand and took hers, bringing it to the side of his face. He held it there, his eyes closed, as if savoring her touch.

"You don't have to feel anything if you don't want to," Carly whispered. "Forget what other people think, and feel any way you want."

Randy chuckled and opened his eyes. "Hard ass," he said, kissing the inside of her palm lightly and then letting it go.

The phone rang again, but Randy made no move to answer it.

"It could be important," Carly said, standing up.

"Don't answer it."

Carly ignored him and answered the phone. After she spoke with the person on the other end of the line, she hung up and turned to Randy. "That was the funeral home director calling. He'd like for you to come over there and make arrangements."

"I don't want to," Randy said, staring at the television.

Carly walked over, picked up the remote, and hit the power button. "You have to," she said. "I'll go with you and help." She offered him her hand. He took it, and reluctantly stood.

"Do you know how to plan a funeral?" he asked.

"No. But I'm sure the people at the funeral home will help us figure things out."

"Fine."

"You'd better go take a shower and brush your teeth first," Carly told him. "You can't go there smelling like a barn and with beer on your breath."

Randy frowned at her. "You know, you're really bossy."

Carly smiled. "Yeah, I know. Go on and get ready. They're expecting us."

Randy looked like he didn't have any fight left in him. He turned and headed for the bathroom.

They spent the afternoon at the funeral home, making difficult choices. Every time Carly asked Randy for his opinion, he'd answer that he'd be fine with whatever she chose. Carly had no idea how much money Randy wanted to spend, and she didn't want to ask him outright. So she considered prices carefully on the items she chose.

"Where would you like to have the service?" the funeral director asked Randy. "Did your mother belong to a church?"

Randy shook his head. "I don't think an actual service will be necessary. There aren't many people who will come to it."

Carly asked the director to excuse them a moment and she pulled Randy aside. "Are you sure you don't want a service? You could have it in their chapel here."

"My mom wasn't that well-liked in town. The room would be empty," Randy told her.

"Some people will come. Ginny and Glen, Andi, Luke, Colt, and Beth will be there. And I'll bet some of the nurses from the nursing home will attend. What about a graveside service?"

Randy shrugged. "I suppose."

Carly told the director what they'd decided and he said it would be fine. He suggested an officiant to speak at the service and Carly asked if he would set it up. As for a dress for his mother to be buried in, Randy told him to call Renee at the nursing home and she'd send over one of his mother's nice dresses.

After that, they went to the florist and picked out flowers for the casket. Carly hesitated when the clerk pointed out a beautiful spray of flowers that was very expensive.

"Is there a price range you want to stay with?" she quietly asked Randy.

"Buy whatever you think will be nice," he told her. "I'll take care of it."

Carly decided on one that was still lovely but less costly. Since the service was going to be short, she felt that it would be fine.

It was after five o'clock by the time they'd finished making the arrangements. The funeral director said they'd be able to have the funeral on Saturday afternoon, since it was a small affair, so Randy agreed on that day. When they pulled up to his home, Randy looked exhausted. Carly felt drained too. She'd never realized how much went into planning a funeral, and she thought about Andi and how she'd had to plan two funerals when their parents had died. It must have been difficult, especially since she'd had no one to help her.

They still had to write up an obituary for the newspaper, and something that would help the officiant make the service more personal. Carly sighed at the thought of getting Randy to write up something about his mother. He wouldn't even talk about her. How in the world would she get him to write something?

Randy immediately sat down on the sofa and lost himself in a television movie. Carly knew he could care less about the movie; it was just a way for him to escape.

Carly called Ginny to tell her when the funeral was going to be held. Ginny offered to call around and inform people who knew Evie and might wish to attend.

"And I left you something in the refrigerator for supper," Ginny said. "I figured Randy wouldn't want to leave home after all he had to do today."

Carly smiled at Ginny's thoughtfulness. She was so amazing.

Carly also called Margie to tell her she wouldn't be at work for the next couple of days and the time of Evie's funeral.

"Darling, don't you worry a bit about it," Margie told her. "And I'll be there on Saturday for the funeral."

Carly remembered that Margie had said she'd known Evie all her life. "If you know of any nice stories about Evie when she was younger, could you write them down so they can be shared? I think Randy would like to hear those."

"I would love to do that," Margie said. "I do know stories, and there are a few that I'm sure everyone will enjoy hearing."

Carly thanked Margie for helping. When she hung up, she realized how close she'd become to Margie in the short time she'd worked for her. She'd gone from looking down her nose at Margie's shop to actually enjoying working there. She was thankful for having the chance to work with Margie these past few weeks. It had helped to make her a better person.

"I'll bet you're hungry," Carly called out to Randy from the kitchen.

"I'm fine. Besides, there's nothing in the fridge."

Carly opened up the fridge and saw the pan of lasagna Ginny had left there. She'd also left a loaf of French bread, a stick of butter, and a jar of canned string beans.

"Oh yes there is. Ginny brought over a pan of lasagna while we were gone," Carly said.

"Ginny. I should have known she'd do that," Randy said, a small smile appearing on his face. "She knows her lasagna is my favorite."

Carly glanced at Randy and saw him smile. It warmed her

174 | Deanna Lynn Sletten

heart. She thought about Randy as a young boy, spending summer days at the Brennan ranch. How he must have loved all he endless food and treats there, and the love doled out so freely. Ginny knew Randy as well as her own sons. His favorite cookies and his favorite foods. She probably knew his every mood, when to give him advice and when to leave him be. Just like a mother would. Carly thought it was sad that Ginny probably knew Randy better than his own mother ever had.

"I'll put it in the oven," Carly said. She also placed the string beans in a pan with water to heat up on the stove and sliced the French bread and placed it in a basket, lined with paper towels. She placed that on the oven to warm the bread.

"Do you have a pad of paper around her somewhere?" Carly called out.

"In the top drawer by the fridge."

Carly retrieved the paper and a pen, grabbed two beers out of the fridge, and then went into the living room and sat down close to Randy. She handed him one of the beers.

"I thought we could write down a few things for your mom's obituary while the lasagna is cooking," Carly said.

Randy drank his beer but kept silent.

"When was your mom's birthday?"

"Do we have to do this now?"

Carly nodded. "If we finish it now, you won't have to think about it the rest of the night."

"Okay. May 22, 1950."

Carly wrote it down along with her death date.

"What about her parents' names? And did she have any siblings? Are any of them still around here?"

"I didn't know my grandparents. They died when I was very young. Their names were Albert and Bernice Crenshaw. Ma had two older brothers, but they left the area long before I was born. John and Emmett were their names. I have no idea if they're still alive."

"Okay," Carly said. She wrote down their names in case they decided to add them. "Are your grandparents buried in the same cemetery as your mother will be?"

Randy shook his head. "She didn't get along that well with them, so no. From what little I've heard about them, they were mean and nasty people. Her brothers left home as soon as they were old enough and so did my mother. I figured she wouldn't want to be buried near them."

Carly sighed. "Okay. What about your father? Should I mention him?"

"It would be best if you didn't. My mother hated him after he left. I doubt she'd want him mentioned at her funeral."

The oven timer buzzed and Carly went to pull the lasagna out. She stirred and poked the beans with a fork, and they felt ready too. She dug around and found plates and silverware, and set the table. There were no napkins, so she used paper towels.

"Supper's ready. Come and eat," she called to Randy.

He came and sat at the small table in the kitchen. Carly served him a portion of lasagna and green beans and urged him to have some warm bread. She sat with him and picked at her food, and he did also. It had been a very long, heart-wrenching day, and they were both drained.

"Is it okay?" Carly asked.

"Yes, it's fine." Randy looked up at her. "I'm just not hungry. But it was nice of you to cook it up for me."

Carly smiled at him. "I'll put the leftovers in the fridge so you can heat it up another night and enjoy it. Ginny does make delicious lasagna."

Carly began picking up the kitchen. She opened the dishwasher, but there were no dishes in it. "Do you use the dishwasher, or do you hand wash dishes?"

"I rarely cook anything, so I've never used the dishwasher," he said. "I always eat at the ranch or over at The Depot."

"I'll hand wash them, then," she said. After filling the sink with hot water, she found a container to store the lasagna and put it in the refrigerator. Then she slipped the dishes in the sink and began washing them with a new sponge Randy had pulled out from under the sink.

"Let me help," he said, pulling a dishtowel out of one of the kitchen drawers.

"You certainly have a lot of kitchen supplies for someone who never cooks," Carly said. "Dishtowels, storage containers, pots and pans. Where'd they all come from?"

"Ginny, of course. When I bought this place and moved it on the property, she gave me all sorts of things she said I'd need to make my new place a real home. Most of it I've hardly used. But it was nice of her to make sure I had it all, just in case."

"Ginny is pretty special," Carly said as she finished washing the dishes. "She's never judged me no matter what I've done, and she's always welcomed me like family. I wish I could be half the person she is."

Randy stopped wiping the clean dish in his hand and turned to Carly. "You just spent the day helping me plan my mother's funeral. You didn't have to do that, but you did. I'd say you are pretty special."

Carly felt her face heat up in a blush. "I was happy to help," she said quickly.

After finishing the dishes and putting everything away, Carly had no other excuse to stay. "I'd better head back to the ranch so you can get some sleep," she said, walking into the living room to retrieve her purse. "It's been a long day for you."

Randy followed her into the living room, and when she turned around, he was standing right in front of her. "Thank you for helping today," he said. "If you hadn't come here, I'd probably still be on that sofa, drinking beer."

"I'm glad I could help," Carly said softly. He looked so lost and sad, she couldn't help but want to comfort him. She reached up and hugged him. He hugged her back, holding her tight. Carly's heart melted for this tough cowboy who'd had such an unhappy life, yet somehow had turned into a giving, caring man despite it all.

Randy gently kissed her cheek, and pulled away, running his fingers slowly down her arm until they reached her hand. He held it firmly, as if he didn't want to let go. The he gazed into her eyes.

"Stay," he whispered. "Please. I want to hold you close tonight."

Carly saw the pain in his eyes. She understood how it felt to want someone by your side when you were hurting. She nodded.

Hand-in-hand, Randy led Carly to his bedroom. He walked over to the other side of the bed and undressed as Carly slipped out of her jeans before sliding under the covers. She'd left her other clothes on, because she understood that this wasn't about sex, it was about needing the comfort of someone beside you.

Randy shut off the light and crawled under the covers. He reached for Carly, pulling her to him. She curled up with her back against his chest, his arm wrapped around her waist. He kissed her gently on the shoulder, which made her heart melt. Then he lay his head down, and right before he fell to sleep, Carly heard him sigh.

Chapter Nineteen

Randy awoke the next morning, savoring the warmth of the soft body beside him. He smiled. He'd been so exhausted the night before that he'd thought he'd dreamt Carly had stayed. But it hadn't been a dream. She was here, lying beside him, sleeping.

He raised up on his elbow ever so gently so as not to wake her, and gazed down at her sleeping form. Carly was lying on her side, facing him, her long hair spread out behind her and her face serene and lovely. His heart filled with a warmth he'd never felt before for any other woman. Carly had come to him on a day when he'd needed someone the most. She'd helped him with a difficult task, and even stayed to comfort him when he'd asked. How could he have accused her of not being honest with him? There was so much more to her than he'd ever given her credit for.

"What are you staring at, cowboy?" Carly asked, looking up at him.

Randy smiled. "I've never woken up with a princess lying beside me before. I'm savoring the moment."

"Are you teasing me?"

"No. Not at all. You are a fairytale princess to this cowboy." He lowered his head and gently kissed her lips. "Unfortunately, I can't keep you here forever," he whispered.

Carly traced her fingertips along the back of his neck, causing delightful chills to dance down his spine. "Well, maybe if you ask really nice," she said, grinning.

He kissed her again but forced himself to pull away after a time. "We should get up. Reality will come crashing in pretty soon."

Carly sighed. "Yeah. And Andi's probably wondering where I am about now. I should get back to the ranch."

Randy lay back in bed. "I'd rather hide out all day. I don't want to go anywhere or talk to anyone."

Carly leaned over him, her eyes twinkling. "Not even me?"

He reached up and slid his hand through her silky hair. "You I would make an exception for."

Carly's eyes lit up. "Why don't we take the horses out and ride as far back onto the ranch property as we can go for the day? I'll pack a lunch and we can stay away from people. How about it?"

Randy didn't have to think twice about it—he loved that idea. "Let's do it. But we should finish writing up the obituary first."

Carly sobered. "I have everything I need. I'll write it up at the ranch and drop it off at the paper, if you'd like me to. I also asked Margie to think of some nice stories about your mom as a young girl. Margie knew her pretty well when they were growing up."

Randy stared at Carly in awe. "I'd have never thought of asking Margie. That was a good idea. Thank you. I couldn't have done this without you, Carly."

Carly smiled. "It's no problem. I'll go do what I have to, and you get ready and meet me at the ranch, okay?"

They planned to meet around noon at the barn and Carly quickly slipped on her jeans and, after one more kiss good-bye, headed out.

* * *

There was a bustle of activity in the ranch house kitchen when Carly entered. Ginny and Andi were in the middle of boiling strawberries to can, and little Jessi was nestled in her baby swing, rocking back and forth. Bree sat on the floor near Jessi, dutifully guarding her as she swung. Andi turned as she continued stirring the gooey mixture at the stove.

"Hey, you made it home," she said, smiling. "How's Randy?"

It took Carly a moment to digest her question. She'd thought Andi would be upset with her for not calling, but she supposed that Andi had guessed she'd be with Randy. "He's doing fine. I think it's still a bit of a shock for him. We made all the arrangements. I still have to write up the obituary for the newspaper and something for the officiant to say at the service. After that, we're going riding. He really doesn't want to talk to anyone today."

"Riding is a wonderful idea. I know Randy likes his privacy," Ginny said. She stood at the counter, preparing the empty jars. "I'll make a lunch for you to take along."

Carly smiled. "Thanks, Ginny. That would be wonderful."

"Oh, and you can send the obituary directly to the newspaper office through their website. That will save you some time," Ginny told her.

Carly thanked Ginny for telling her that. It would make things easier for her. She doubted that the obituary would get in the paper for Saturday, but at least it might be in Sunday's paper.

Carly quickly showered and dressed in jeans and a T-shirt. She pulled her hair up into a ponytail and dabbed on a little makeup. Then she sat down on the bed and started up her laptop to type the obituary and send it in.

By the time Carly came downstairs again, the women had already filled the jars and were now cleaning the pans, getting ready to make more preserves.

"I packed your lunch," Ginny said. "It's on the table in an insulated bag. It should slide into a saddlebag easily."

Carly went over to her little niece and ticked her belly, then kissed her lightly on the cheek. Jessi waved her arms in the air with delight and smiled. Then Carly hugged Ginny. "Thanks so much for everything," she told her. "And for the lasagna last night too. Randy is so lucky to have you in his life."

"We all are," Andi said from the sink as she washed fresh raspberries from the garden.

"Yes, we all are," Carly agreed.

Ginny blushed. "Stop it, girls. You're embarrassing me."

Carly giggled and headed out to the back porch. She looked out the window and saw Randy's truck. Quickly, she slipped on her boots and grabbed a light jacket from one of the many hooks. Picking up the lunch from the table, she said good-bye to Ginny and Andi and hurried out the door.

Randy had already saddled the horses by the time Carly walked into the barn.

"I thought you said I had to saddle my own horse from now on," she teased him.

Randy glanced up and smiled. He looked refreshed after his shower, and when she drew near, she smelled the light, spicy scent of his aftershave. That was quickly becoming her favorite scent.

"We can make an exception for today," he told her with a twinkle in his eyes.

Carly handed him the lunch bag and he slid it into one of the saddlebags. Then he left for a moment and came back with an old wool blanket that he kept in his truck.

"Can't have a picnic without a picnic blanket," he told her. He slipped it into the other bag.

They rode off up the trail in the center of the property with Randy leading the way. The day was sunny and warm, and Carly was happy to be outside on this beautiful day.

They rode side-by-side once they made it to the top of the hill. Pine trees grew in groves on the edges of the trail, as did red cedar, birch, and maple trees. Carly loved the aroma of the trees and inhaled deeply, smelling a mixture of pine and cedar.

"I love how rich the scent of the pines are up here," she told Randy.

"You should come up here after a rain," Randy said. "The cedar and pine scents are thick in the air."

They rode a long time, both of them enjoying the peacefulness of the forest. A bald eagle soared high above them and landed in a treetop. Smaller birds flew by and squirrels scurried about. They didn't talk as the rode. They were both content to enjoy the beauty around them.

After about an hour of riding, Randy led them to a small stream that ran along the edge of the trail and was lined with trees.

"Here's the perfect place to stop," he told her. "We can rest the horses and they can get a drink of water."

Carly looked around her at the crystal-clear stream, the trees, and the green grass that grew at the water's edge. "It's lovely," she said, beaming at Randy. "It's like a fairytale land."

Randy slipped off his horse and walked over to help Carly down. He reached up and placed his hands around her waist as she slid out of the saddle. They stood there a moment with his hands holding her and his eyes sparkling. "Then you belong here, princess."

"I used to hate it when you called me that," she said, gazing up into his eyes. "But now I kind of like it."

Randy chuckled. He pulled the saddlebags off Black Jack and set them under a tree by the river. "I'll go water the horses."

"I'll set up the lunch," Carly said.

She found a nice spot under a willow tree right by the stream. It was cooler up here in the higher elevation, so she slipped on her jacket and then spread out the blanket on the grass. She pulled the food from the bag and laid it out. Ginny had packed roast beef sandwiches, cut-up strawberries, peanut butter cookies, and four bottles of water. After skipping breakfast and riding for the past hour, Carly was famished and the lunch looked delicious.

"You'd better hurry over here or I may eat everything myself," she called to Randy.

He tied the horses to trees and strode over. Sitting down on the blanket beside her, he took off his hat and brushed his hair from his eyes. "It looks delicious. I'm starved."

They sat under the tree eating their lunch as the horses grazed and the stream rippled over stones in the water. Sunlight filtered through the tree branches and felt nice on Carly's back.

"The stream is so lovely," Carly said after a time. "Is it larger in the spring?"

Randy nodded. "Yep. It's practically a river after the snow melts on the mountain and it all comes rushing down. When we bring the cattle up here in the spring, the cattle drink from it as well as a watering hole off there in the distance." He pointed to a large, open pasture opposite them. "We're always hopeful for rain before a fall cattle drive; otherwise, we may not have enough water as we move the cattle along."

"Are we near the summer cabin?" Carly asked, wishing she could see it.

"No. We'd still have to ride another couple of hours to get there."

"Oh," Carly said, disappointed.

"We can visit it another time, though," Randy told her. "It's quicker if we drive in the truck, and easier too. That way we can get back home before dark."

"What if I want to stay up there? It sounds cozy and cute from what I've heard Andi and Beth say."

"I'm not sure you'd like it much," Randy said. "There's a generator for power, but no indoor plumbing, so you'd have to use the outhouse. You don't seem like the type of girl who'd enjoy that."

Carly shuddered. "An outhouse? Maybe you're right. We could just visit for a day sometime."

Randy laughed.

Carly cocked her head and looked at Randy. "I know you don't like talking about your childhood, or your mother, but if you want to talk, I'd be happy to listen."

Randy glanced up at the blue sky where puffy clouds slowly sailed by, then looked at Carly. "I don't like to think about that time of my life. I mean, it wasn't great, but it could have been worse. And I was lucky enough to have met the Brennans. They made up for whatever bad stuff happened."

Carly's brow creased. "From what I've heard, you were so good to your mother. You made sure she was in a nice nursing home and you visited her every week. How were you able to be so nice to her after having such a terrible childhood?"

Randy sighed. "It's hard to blame her for being a bad parent when she didn't know any better. From what I could gather, her parents had been even worse. My mother never laid a hand on me, but she had a tongue that could hurt severely. I always knew that I was in her way and that she really hadn't wanted me. She said that all the time. And as I grew older, she said I reminded her too much of my father and that made her dislike me even more—especially since I was a ranch hand, just like he'd been."

"That's terrible," Carly said, aghast.

Randy shrugged. "I spent my whole life trying to make it up to her for being stuck with me, but I never could. I guess that was one reason why I continued to help her, even when she grew meaner and more bitter. When the alcohol-related dementia began, and then the stoke hit her, I couldn't blame her for her anger. She barely knew her name anymore, let alone mine. I felt it was only right that I help her."

Carly placed her hand on his arm and looked up into his eyes. "You were a good son, even if she didn't appreciate you. I hope you know that."

Randy gave her a half-smile. "I learned to be that way because of the Brennans. They treated me like part of their family from the start. Without them, I could have grown up bitter and angry. So I figured if I could make my mom's life a little nicer, even if she didn't realize it or appreciate it, at least I'd feel better about it than if I had ignored her in her later years."

Carly gazed at Randy in awe. She didn't know if she could have been so giving to someone who'd treated her so bad. He was a much better person than she'd ever given him credit for, and her feelings for him deepened.

After they finished eating and putting away the food, Randy sat with his back against the tree trunk and his legs stretched out in front of him. "This is a great spot for a nap," he said, yawning.

Carly came and curled up beside him. "I'm glad we did this," she said softly. "It's so nice and peaceful here. And we get to spend time together, alone."

Randy wrapped his arm around her and Carly dropped her head on his shoulder. "Does this mean you forgive me for not believing you?" he asked.

Carly glanced up at him. He'd shaved today and the smooth skin on his face made him look years younger. He looked adorable, staring down at her with those amazing amber-brown eyes. "Yes. Promise me you'll believe me from now on, though, okay?"

"I promise," he whispered.

They lay against the tree a long time and Carly fell asleep curled up next to Randy for a while. She awoke suddenly and looked around, dazed, before she realized where she was. She heard Randy laugh.

"I fell asleep, too," he said. "I must have been more tired than I'd thought."

They both stood up and stretched. Randy wrapped his arms around Carly and pulled her close. "I don't know what I would have done without you these past two days," he said, gazing down into her eyes. "Thank you for being here for me."

Carly reached up and wrapped her arms around his neck. "I wouldn't want to be anywhere else," she said.

Randy dropped his head and kissed her lightly on the lips. Carly sighed. It felt so good to be in his arms again.

The late afternoon sun was heading west so they knew that it was time to go home. They packed up the horses and headed out, but they rode slowly. Carly could tell that Randy wasn't looking forward to going home, or spending tomorrow at the cemetery. It was going to be a rough day. But she'd be there to help   him   get   through   it.

Chapter Twenty

Randy stood quietly at his mother's graveside while the officiant spoke. He talked about life and death, read a passage from the Bible as well as the obituary that Carly had written, and then said a prayer. The polished wood casket gleamed in the sun and the flowers that lay upon it were beautiful. Randy reached for Carly's hand and held it tight. He couldn't have put together such a nice funeral for his mother without her help, and he appreciated her being here beside him now.

Randy was surprised at how many people had actually come to the service. The entire Brennan clan and Glen were there, as Randy had expected, but there were also several townspeople and a few people who had worked with Evie years before. Renee, and two other nurses from the home had come, as had neighbors of the Brennans who Randy had known for years. Margie had come as well, and when the officiant asked if anyone would like to speak, she stepped forward. Margie told everyone she'd known Evie since she was very young, and said she'd been a cute little girl and had been homecoming queen in high school her senior year. She told a story of how Evie had found a baby bunny on Easter morning when she was only seven years old, and that she'd been convinced it was the real Easter Bunny. Everyone laughed, and it made Randy smile. He hadn't known these things about his mother, and it shed light on the person she'd once been. He was grateful to Margie for sharing them.

After the service, Randy walked around the circle of people and thanked each one for coming. Ginny invited everyone out to the ranch for a late lunch, since no reception had been planned. This surprised Randy. He hadn't expected anyone to come to the funeral, let alone to a reception. Most of the attendees said they'd be there and soon everyone was in their cars and trucks, heading back to the Brennan ranch.

"Did you know Ginny was having a luncheon?" Randy asked Carly, who had ridden along with him.

"You know Ginny. She took it upon herself to do it. Andi, Beth, and I helped her prepare the food last night. She wanted to do something to help."

Randy had stood dry-eyed at his mother's funeral, unable to feel any emotion for the woman who'd given birth to him, but at the thought of Ginny wanting to make this day easier for him after all she'd done for him his entire life, his eyes filled with tears. He quickly pulled the truck to the side of the road and parked, swiping at his eyes.

"Are you okay?" Carly asked, scooting closer to Randy.

Randy had only cried once in his adult life. It was the day Jack Brennan had died and he'd felt as if he'd lost a father. He dropped his head in his hands, embarrassed at his tears. "Sorry. Men don't cry. But the thought that Ginny would go to all this trouble for me…well…it just hit me."

Carly wrapped her arms around him. "Real men do cry. You have nothing to be sorry about."

They sat there a few minutes, holding each other tight. Randy took a deep breath and wiped his eyes one last time, and then he drove the rest of the way to the ranch.

Almost everyone who'd been at the service was at the ranch house by the time Randy and Carly pulled up. Ginny and Glen had set out a couple of extra tables in the sitting room and the food sat buffet-style on the kitchen table. There were sandwiches, large bowls of cut-up fruit, a vegetable tray with dip, and cake and cookies. Everyone walked around, eating and visiting with each other, and once again offering their condolences to Randy.

Randy found a quiet spot to stand in the corner of the kitchen and watched as everyone in their Sunday best milled around. He watched Carly talking to Ray's wife, and then helping refill the sandwich tray. She blended in and moved around so confidently, as if she'd been here her entire life. And she looked beautiful. She'd worn a somber, short-sleeved, black dress that grazed the top of her knees. Her hair was pulled up into a twist, and her makeup was very natural. He loved the wild-looking Carly with plunging necklines and tight jeans, but this more subdued Carly was even more beautiful than he could have ever imagined. She was forever surprising him.

"What are you staring at?" Carly said, coming up to him and grinning.

"You. Just you," he replied. He bent down and placed a kiss on her cheek. "Thank you."

"For what?"

"For everything. For just being you."

Carly reached up and gently caressed the side of his face. Then she turned and left to help Andi and Beth put out more food.

* * *

Carly's heart swelled with affection for Randy throughout the day. At the graveside, he'd been so strong, standing there quietly throughout the service. When he'd reached for her hand, her heart had melted and she was happy to be there to support him. He'd looked so handsome in his dark suit, and she'd thought that even his mother would have been proud of him today. And when tears had filled his eyes on the ride back to the ranch, Carly had fought to hold back her own. She knew how proud he was, and that he saw tears as a sign of weakness, but she thought differently. It proved he had a kind heart, even if he tried to hide it behind his tough cowboy persona. He may not have been able to feel emotion for his mother's death, but he'd finally let out what pent-up emotion he did feel, and she knew he'd feel better for it.

The guests soon left, and Carly watched as Randy said good-bye to them all. She was happy that so many people had attended the service. She could tell it meant a lot to Randy. He was well-liked in the area and today his friends had been there for him.

Carly helped the other women put away the leftover food while Glen and Colt picked up the extra tables. Luke had changed into work clothes and gone out to do evening chores. After the work was finished, Carly watched as Randy hugged Ginny and thanked her for putting on the reception.

"It's the least I could do," Ginny said sweetly. She hugged Randy a second time. "You're family. That's what family does."

Carly fought to hold back tears. She'd always cherished the warmth of the Brennan family, but today had just proven to her again what wonderful people they were. She thought about her own parents, and how much she missed them, but how having Ginny in her life, as well as Luke, Colt, Beth, and Randy, had made her life even fuller. For years, it had only been her and Andi, but now, they had an entire family to rally behind them, no matter what happened. It warmed her heart just thinking about it.

Carly walked with Randy outside to his truck. The sun was beginning to make its way behind the hills in the distance. It had been a long, emotional day and Carly was suddenly very tired. When they reached the truck, she instinctively reached out and wrapped her arms around Randy. He held her close.

"I missed waking up next to you this morning," he said.

"Me too," Carly whispered.

They stood there a few minutes, just holding each other as twilight settled over the ranch.

"Do you want to spend tomorrow together?" Carly asked.

"That would be nice. First, though, I have to pick up my mother's things at the nursing home. I told Renee to give away her clothes, but there are a few personal items and a couple of pieces of furniture that I need to get. Colt said he'd ride along and help me move the heavy items."

Carly nodded. "Well, you know where to find me." She gave him a small smile.

Randy hugged her once more, and then kissed her softly on the lips before getting into his truck and driving away.

* * *

That next few days, Carly and Randy spent all of their free time together. They went on rides after supper or spent time after dark in the hayloft, staring up at the stars and listening to music. Each evening as Randy prepared to leave for the night, it became increasingly difficult for them to say good-bye. Carly had never denied herself a physical relationship before, but with Randy, it was different. She wanted him to make the first move. It was refreshing to be with someone who wanted the moment to be right when they were both finally ready to be together.

It was early August and Ginny and Andi were working hard to prepare for the fair held at the Missoula Fairgrounds. Ginny was finishing canning the last of her preserves to sell and Andi was helping her, as well as sorting and pricing the prints of her paintings. Andi shared the booth with Ginny and her friends and sold her prints there. Carly helped both of them as much as she could when she wasn't working at the gift shop or spending time with Randy. Margie and she had marked down even more of the shop's stock, and sales were thriving. Carly was seriously considering buying the gift shop and staying in Montana. She wanted to be closer to Andi, Luke, and Jessi, as well as the entire Brennan clan. And she also wanted to be near Randy. She'd never felt as close to a man as she felt toward Randy, and she thought that if she stayed, they might have a chance at building a relationship. But there was a big problem that kept her from acting on her desire to buy the shop—her finances were a mess. She still had a huge amount of debt to pay off. She hadn't yet figured out how she could afford to buy Margie's gift shop.

She said as much to Andi one afternoon as the two women sorted prints of various sizes into boxes for next week's fair while Jessi napped. Andi looked up at her in surprise.

"You mean you're really considering staying here?" Andi asked.

"I'm thinking about it. But I'm not sure how I'd earn a living so I can pay off my debt."

Andi looked thoughtful a moment. "Let's go look at where you are with your bills," she suggested. They went into the dining room where Andi's laptop sat and she brought up the Excel sheet that tracked Carly's debt and payments. It didn't look hopeful. Even though the majority of Carly's checks went toward her debt, and Andi and Luke had paid for the electricity and gas to be turned back on at the townhouse, she still owed a lot of money.

Carly sighed. "It's hopeless."

Andi looked at her sister curiously. "Does Randy have

anything to do with you wanting to stay?"

"Yes," Carly said honestly.

"Are you two that serious?"

Carly hesitated. In her mind, they were, but she couldn't speak for Randy. "We haven't discussed it, but I think if I stayed, he and I would have a good chance of being together."

"Are you sure about that? Or is this like your other relationships, like the one you had with Colt?"

Carly bit her lip. Only Andi could say these things to her without her feeling defensive. She knew that no matter what, Andi always had her best interests at heart. But sometimes it was hard to admit that she was so flighty with relationships. "I'm sure. Randy is different. He doesn't fawn all over me or treat me like a glass doll. Our relationship is based on mutual respect, and that's a first for me. I cared about Colt, but I was too busy playing the diva to take our relationship seriously. I feel different with Randy."

A smile spread across Andi's face. "You mean my little sister has finally grown up?"

Carly grinned. "I hope so. I was such a flake—with men and with money. I hope I don't act that way ever again."

Andi laughed, and so did Carly.

"Well, let's take a good hard look at these finances again and consider your options. If you're completely serious, maybe we can make this work."

Carly's eyes lit up. "Really? How?"

"Well, we do have the townhouse paid off. If you don't go back, we could sell it and split the profits. And what about all those designer clothes, shoes, and handbags you own back in Seattle? You could sell those. It would be a start."

Carly's heart beat faster. Maybe her dream was possible after all. If she could start fresh with her finances, she might just be able to buy the shop and stay. Then a terrifying thought occurred to her. Would Randy want her to stay?

"What if everything doesn't work out?" she asked Andi, her excitement waning.

"We'll work the numbers to see if it does. There's no harm in trying. At least it will give you an idea if you can afford to stay."

Carly nodded. Andi had thought she was afraid of the numbers, not of the fact that Randy might not want her to stay. But she could still be here with her family. She had no idea where she'd end up this fall, but at least she could weigh her options and, hopefully, Randy would be one of them.

Chapter Twenty-One

Randy was planning a surprise for Carly and he felt as excited as a schoolboy as he tried to keep it to himself. The past week had been busy and they'd hardly been able to spend time together. She'd not only worked her three days at the gift shop, but she'd also helped Ginny and Andi at the fair booth on her days off. He'd gone there one afternoon to wander the fairgrounds and take her to lunch, and as he waited for her, he'd watched her work. She was a natural born salesperson. He watched proudly as she talked people into buying much more than they had intended and they left happier than when they'd entered the booth. Andi's prints were selling well, and he'd heard Andi say more than once that it was because of Carly's help. The two other women who shared the booth with Ginny, Mary and Sharon, were also pleased with Carly's salesmanship. Their sales were high, and they were happy there'd be very little to pack up when the fair ended on Sunday.

Saturday morning Randy caught up with Carly beside her car before she left for work at the gift shop. He and Colt had spent all morning training two young horses that their neighbor, Ray, was paying them to break. He was hot, dusty, and smelled like horse sweat, but he wanted to ask Carly a question before she left.

As he strode up toward her car, she smiled at him. "Hey,

cowboy. Why are you so dirty? Were you working for a change?" she teased.

Randy grinned. "Watch it, or I'll give you a big sweaty hug and ruin your nice clothes."

Carly laughed. She looked pretty in her skirt, heels, and blouse. Her hair was wavy down her back and she'd clipped the top part back, off of her face. The hairstyle accentuated her lovely cheekbones and big, blue eyes.

"I wanted to ask you something," Randy said, being careful not to rub up against her even though he wanted nothing more than to pull her into his arms and kiss her. "How would you like to go out to supper tonight, and maybe even dancing?"

Carly's eyes lit up with delight. "Dancing? Really? I'd love to. Where would we go? To The Depot?"

Randy pushed his hat back on his head and gazed down at her. "Actually, there's a little place this side of Missoula on the river that I thought you might like. They have delicious food and a band in the lounge on weekends. You can get all dressed up and we can act like grown-ups for a change instead of the cowboy and the princess."

Carly beamed up at him. "I'd love to. It sounds wonderful." She stepped even closer to him and placed her hand on his bare forearm. "So, is this an official date?"

The touch of her hand made Randy's heart skip a beat. He wondered how such a simple gesture from her could do that. "Yep. I guess it is."

"Well, it's about time, cowboy," she said, then winked at him mischievously. "What time should I be ready?"

"I'll pick you up around six and make the reservation for seven. Sound good?"

Carly stood carefully on tip-toe and placed a soft kiss on his lips. "I can't wait," she whispered. Then she slid into her car and drove off.

"Neither can I," Randy said aloud with a smile.

* * *

Carly was excited all day about her date with Randy. She knew it was silly, feeling so elated, since she'd spent so much time with him, and had even once spent the night chastely in his arms. But this was different. This was a real romantic night out together.

After work, she hurried home and showered. She left her hair down, because she knew how much Randy loved her long hair, and applied a sensible amount of make-up. She didn't want to overdo it, but she wanted to look pretty for him. After that, she searched through the clothes in her closet for the perfect dress. Her eyes settled on a sleeveless, scooped-necked, white dress that fell high above her knees. She pulled the dress out and studied it. The last time she'd worn this was on her twenty-fifth birthday in Seattle when she'd gone out to celebrate with Colt and her friends. She'd drunk way too much that night and had paid for it the next day. She loved this dress though, and wanted to wear it for Randy. It had been a long time since she'd dressed up to go out, and she wanted everything to be perfect.

Carly slipped on the dress, then chose a pair of shiny blue high-heeled pumps to wear with it that were comfortable enough to dance in. She finished the outfit with a simple white-gold necklace that held a small sapphire stone and had once belonged to her mother, along with matching earrings. A few minutes before six, she grabbed a light sweater from her closet and ran downstairs to wait for Randy.

The kitchen was quiet since the women were still at the fairgrounds. Carly was surprised to see Luke sitting at the table, feeding Jessi.

"I see you have baby duty tonight," Carly teased, walking toward the table.

Luke glanced up and whistled softly. "Well, don't you look pretty tonight?"

Carly smiled. She adored Luke. He was a good man and made her sister so happy. "Thanks." She moved closer to the table.

"Careful," Luke warned. "We've started Jessi on mashed peas and she spits them out sometimes. I don't want you to get your pretty dress dirty."

Carly laughed. "Little princesses don't spit out their food," she said, looking at Jessi lovingly.

"This little princess does," Luke said, grinning. "So, do you have a big date tonight?"

Carly nodded. "Randy is taking me to dinner and dancing at a place near Missoula."

"That's nice," Luke said. He spooned more peas into Jessi's mouth. She made a sour face and then sprayed them all over Luke.

Carly laughed. She grabbed a rag out of the pantry and handed it to Luke. "She really doesn't like those, does she?"

Luke shook his head. "I think we'll go back to cereal." After wiping his face, he looked up at Carly. "I'm glad you and Randy are together. Randy has never been this serious about any other woman. I've never seen him as happy as he's been over the past few weeks."

Carly stared at Luke, surprised. Luke minded his own business and hardly talked about personal matters. Knowing how close Luke and Randy were—practically like brothers—it warmed Carly's heart that he condoned their relationship. "Thanks, Luke. That means a lot to me."

"Be good to him, okay?" Luke said softly. "He's had a hard life, and you're the first person in a long time that has made him smile." Then his eyes sparkled with mischief. "Otherwise, he'll be crabbier than usual to be around."

Carly bent down and dropped a kiss on Luke's cheek. "I will. I promise."

The crunch of gravel in the driveway announced a truck pulling up to the house. She glanced out the window and saw it was Randy.

"I'll see you later," she said to Luke as she hurried to the door. Then she stopped and turned, catching Luke's eye. "You're a good friend to Randy, Luke. And a good daddy to Jessi, too. I'm so happy that we're family."

Luke smiled at her, and then she waved and stepped outside.

Randy was just getting out of his truck when Carly walked toward him. His eyes beamed with delight. "You look beautiful," he told her, reaching out and pulling her into his arms. He kissed her lightly on the lips before saying, "You should have waited for me to come inside. I was going to escort you out just like a real date should."

Carly laughed. "I saved you from getting the third degree from Luke. He may have wanted to practice on you since he'll have a teenage girl in a few years."

"Lord have mercy on whoever tries to date Jessi," Randy said, chuckling.

Carly took Randy's arm as he accompanied her to the other side of the truck and opened the door for her. He was wearing a nice pair of jeans and his dress cowboy boots along with a black button-down shirt and a dark gray suit jacket. He'd forgone wearing a cowboy hat, his hair was trimmed nicely, and he had shaved as well. Carly smelled his spicy aftershave as he helped her up into the truck. She turned to him, eye level with him where she sat.

"You clean up pretty good yourself, cowboy," she told him.

Randy smiled and his warm brown eyes twinkled.

They drove off down the highway with country music playing softly on the radio. To her surprise, Carly suddenly began feeling nervous; as if this was the first time she'd ever been alone with Randy. It was silly, she knew, but she wasn't used to playing dress up around him or seeing him look so refined. She'd grown comfortable with him wearing jeans and T-shirts and her wearing cut-offs and tanks. The old Carly had lived for putting on airs and dressing up to entice men and make other women jealous. But she no longer felt the need to hide behind designer clothing and heavy make-up to impress. Randy had proven already that he appreciated her for who she was, not who she pretended to be. Instead of tonight feeling special, she suddenly felt as if she were a different person, a person she was no longer impressed with.

"Something wrong?" Randy asked as if sensing her sudden discomfort.

Carly took a breath as she glanced over at Randy. "It feels funny to dress up and go out. I've become used to us riding horses or sitting in the hayloft, gazing at the stars. I feel kind of like the old, fake me right now."

Randy reached across the seat and took Carly's hand. "You're beautiful both ways. I like seeing you dress up like this, but I adore the jeans and T-shirt Carly too. Just relax and be yourself. We're going to have a great time. I promise."

And Randy was right. They arrived at the restaurant, which was situated beside the Clark Fork River and secluded in a grove of pine trees. Their table was next to a window that allowed for the beautiful outdoor view, and it was lovely and romantic. They both ate the specialty—steak, of course—and Carly drank Chardonnay while Randy drank his usual beer. The intimate atmosphere encouraged them to open up and share stories about their lives, all the while holding hands across the table.

After they shared a decadent piece of cheesecake topped with strawberries, Randy led Carly to the lounge where a band was set up on a platform stage and played a mixture of old pop songs and country. They found a small table off to the side with a candle burning in the center to offset the darkened room. Randy ordered more drinks when the waitress came to the table.

"Better be careful, cowboy," Carly teased. "You know what happens if I drink too much."

Randy chuckled. "Don't worry. I'll cut you off if you get tipsy. No black eyes tonight."

After their drinks arrived, Randy took Carly's hand and led her out to the dance floor. The band was playing a slow song, so Randy pulled Carly close to him and they began to move their bodies to the rhythm of the soft tune.

"Do you still feel strange about tonight?" he asked.

"No. This is nice. Being here with you feels just as comfortable as when we're on the ranch together."

"I'm glad. I wanted you to have a nice night out for a change. A girl needs more than a dusty trail ride every now and then," Randy said, dropping a light kiss on her neck.

Carly sighed and laid her head on his shoulder. She felt so comfortable with Randy. So close to him. Before she came to the ranch, she'd done nothing but go out and dance the night away, often dancing with a new man every night. But here, with Randy, it didn't matter to her if they went out for a fine dinner and dancing or if they ate a picnic lunch on a horseback ride. She just enjoyed being with him. Only him. And for her, that was saying a lot.

I'm actually falling in love with him.

Carly pulled back and looked up into Randy's amber-brown eyes. They were warm and inviting as they gazed back at her. Yes, she was falling in love with him. The thought amazed her, yet warmed her heart all at once.

The music kicked up a notch and Randy led her across the floor in a lively two-step, and then pulled her back into his arms when it slowed down again. By the time they sat down, they were both laughing and out of breath from flying across the floor several times in between holding each other close.

The waitress came by again, but Randy shook his head. "No more for me. I'm driving. Do you want another, Carly?"

Carly said no. She didn't want to ruin this night by drinking too much. She wanted to remember every minute of it.

They danced one last time to a slow song, their bodies touching as they swayed to the music. After that, they walked leisurely out to the parking lot, holding hands.

Carly gazed up at the night sky when they stopped at the truck. "Look at the stars," she said. "The sky is so clear, and they're so bright."

Randy wrapped his arm around her waist and glanced up. "It is a beautiful sky," he said. He turned and looked at her. "But you're much more beautiful to look at." He slowly dropped his head and kissed her softly on the lips. Carly reached up and wrapped her arms around his neck, pulling him closer as their kiss grew more passionate. When they finally parted, Randy said in barely a whisper. "I don't want tonight to end."

"Me either," Carly said, touching her lips to his once more.

Reluctantly, they moved apart, stepped up into the truck, and Randy drove them toward home. Carly slid across the seat and sat beside him, laying her head on his shoulder as he draped his arm around her.

As they drew closer to the ranch, Randy turned and stared into Carly's eyes. "Will you stay with me tonight?" he asked.

Carly gazed up at him. She felt so safe with him, so comfortable in his arms. She knew him better than any man she'd ever been with before, and she cared deeply for him.

"Yes," she told him. She wanted nothing more than to spend the night in his arms.

After a time, they pulled up to Randy's house and stepped out of the truck. Randy came to Carly and wrapped his arm around her as they walked the short distance to the door. They went inside and walked through the dark house to the bedroom. Randy turned on a small lamp beside the bed before returning to Carly.

He gently caressed her bare arms and gazed into her, his eyes dark with desire. He bent down and kissed her softly, then slowly ran kisses down her neck until he found the sweet spot at the base of her throat, making her gasp with delight.

Carly slipped her hands under Randy's jacket and it slid down his arms and onto the floor. Then, ever so slowly, she began to unbutton his shirt, all the while gazing into his eyes. When his shirt hit the floor, she ran her hands over the white T-shirt he wore, across the taut muscles underneath. She felt his muscles flex as he took a breath, and it made her smile. Then she stepped back and turned, lifting her hair up and pulling it to the side to expose the zipper on her dress.

Randy didn't need words to understand her meaning. He stepped up close behind her and slowly unzipped her dress all the way down her back. He dropped a kiss on her neck as he slid his hands inside her dress and around her waist. Carly drew in a breath, delighted at the feel of his hands on her bare skin.

Carly turned and slipped the straps of her dress over her shoulders, allowing it to fall to the floor. She wore only a satiny bra and panties underneath.

Randy's breath quickened. "You're so beautiful," he said huskily. Reaching out, he pulled her to him, gliding his hands slowly down her long back to where her body rounded seductively.

Her desire growing, Carly tugged on Randy's T-shirt and lifted it up, wanting to feel him underneath her fingertips. Randy obliged by pulling his shirt off and they embraced, their skin melding together.

Randy could no longer control his desire. He lifted Carly in his arms and gently laid her on the bed. She slipped off her shoes and they fell to the floor while he quickly discarded his boots and jeans. Lying down beside her, Carly saw him fully for the first time. She marveled at his long, muscular legs, taut stomach, and broad shoulders. She ran her hands over his chest and down to his waist, wanting to touch every inch of him.

But Randy had other plans. He pulled her to him, his own hands exploring her thoroughly. He slipped off her bra and caressed her breasts, seeming to enjoy her gasps of pleasure. When he pulled first one nipple, and then the other into his mouth, sucking and teasing each one with his tongue, Carly's back arched as she moaned with delight. They kissed and caressed until neither could hold out any longer, and when they finally came together, Carly cried out in sweet release.

Chapter Twenty-Two

Randy lay on his side beside Carly, his hand gently caressing the silky skin on her back. She was on her stomach, her head lying on her crossed arms, her sapphire-blue eyes gazing up at him. He was completely in awe of her beauty, but more than that, he was amazed that such a woman would be lying in his bed, still warm from his touch.

"You're more beautiful than I could have ever imagined," he said, leaning over to kiss her lips softly. "How is it I'm so lucky to have you here with me?"

Carly smiled up at him. "You're not so bad yourself," she said, reaching out one arm to trail her fingers along his firm chest. "I think I have to start calling you my hot cowboy."

"Don't you dare," he warned, his eyes glinting mischievously. He tickled her, making her jump and he laughed as he pulled her to him, savoring the feel of her body pressed against his.

Carly stroked the back of his neck, causing chills to tingle down his spine. She pulled him to her, kissing him deeply until he felt his desire rising once more.

"How did I resist you these past two years?" Randy asked, winding his hands through her silky hair and kissing her lightly on the temple.

"How could I have thought you were an old, crabby

cowboy?" she asked, laughing softly. Her gaze followed the length of his body. "You're definitely not old. Maybe crabby sometimes, but sweet too. Like now." She traced her tongue along his lips, and then covered his mouth with hers. "Yes, definitely sweet."

Randy laughed, pulling her on top of him. He loved the shape of her body and couldn't take his eyes off of her. But what he felt was more than lust. He felt a warmth deep down inside for her. His feelings for her were stronger than he had ever had for any other woman in his life. He wanted to not only hold her close and make love to her, but also to protect her and care for her.

I love her.

Randy swallowed hard at the thought of loving her. Yes, he loved her.

He reached up and slowly caressed the curve of her waist down to her rounded hips. Rising up, he kissed her between her full breasts. He felt he could spend the rest of his life lying beside her.

This time they made love slowly and sweetly, savoring every touch, every caress, their lips and hands exploring every inch of the other's body. When their bodies finally came together, they held each other tightly, and fell asleep in each other's arms, neither one wanting to let go.

* * *

All day on Monday, Randy couldn't keep his mind off of Carly. He and Luke had driven the truck up to the summer pasture and were searching the herd to select heifers and cows for breeding. They tagged the ones they selected and the following week they would come back here on horseback. With Colt's help, they would move the selected cattle to a separate pasture where they'd release the bull for breeding.

As they worked, Randy's mind wandered back to spending the past weekend with Carly. He'd delighted in waking up with her lying beside him Sunday morning. He loved the feel of her in his arms, her body soft and warm. They'd gone riding that afternoon and spent the day under the tree by the stream, making love on the blanket with the sounds of birds chirping and the stream splashing over rocks nearby. His heart had filled with love for her each and every time he' touched her, as it did now just thinking about her. This morning, he'd awoken alone, and he'd missed her terribly. She'd slept at the ranch house because she had to go to work this morning, but he hoped she would come and stay with him tonight. Just having her with him made his life feel complete.

Complete. He'd never felt that way with anyone before.

Even though they'd made love, he hadn't told her he loved her and he wondered why he'd held back. Throughout yesterday, the words had sat on his tongue, but he hadn't been able to release them. He loved her. He knew for sure he did. But something deep inside him had caused him to hold the words inside. Was he incapable of expressing his feelings for her? For anyone? He scowled. He hoped it wasn't true. He wanted Carly to know that their relationship was not one born out of just passion—it was based on love too.

"What the heck is going on with you?" Luke said, waving his hand in front of Randy's eyes to get his attention. "First you're smiling like an idiot and then you're scowling. If you don't start paying attention to what we're doing, you'll be stomped into the ground by these cattle."

Randy glowered at Luke but set his mind to his work. He'd have plenty of time to spend with Carly over the next few weeks and to tell her how he felt for her. Right now, he had work to do.

* * *

Carly floated around the gift shop as if she had wings. Her smile was wide and her eyes were bright. She'd brought in coffee and muffins for her and Margie that morning and she'd worked her charms so easily on customers that she was selling more than usual for a Monday.

"You sure are on fire today," Margie commented after Carly had sold yet another one of Andi's prints. "You must have had a wonderful weekend."

Carly beamed at Margie. "I had a fantastic weekend. And I hope it continues that way," she said.

Carly's thoughts kept wandering back to the weekend and the feel of Randy's warm, strong body beside hers. Her heart danced with delight at the memory of his lips on hers, his hands caressing her bare skin, and the joy of their lovemaking. She was no innocent, that was true, but she had never felt about anyone else the way she felt about Randy. Not even with Colt, she had to admit to herself. She'd cared deeply for Colt, but she'd never been truly in love with him. But with Randy, it was different. She could easily be persuaded to spend the rest of her life with him.

The rest of her life. That thought no longer scared her—it thrilled her.

As Carly moved about the shop, she thought about her life and where she was headed. Seattle no longer held any interest for her. Her life and family was here, in Montana. She thought more about moving here, buying the gift shop, and settling down. Could she do that? Could she actually change her party girl ways so completely and become a quiet country girl?

She wondered what Randy was doing at this exact moment, and if he was thinking about her like she was of him. Although no declarations of love had passed between them, Randy's actions had told her everything she'd needed to know. She didn't need to hear the words—she knew how he felt from the sparkle in his eyes and the tenderness of his touch. She hoped he felt the same from her.

We have plenty of time. I'll tell him how I feel very soon.

Carly spent the rest of her day trying to concentrate on work, but it wasn't easy. She couldn't wait to spend another night in Randy's arms.

* * *

That night during supper it was all Randy could do not to reach across the table and pull Carly to him. Every time Randy looked up, he saw Carly smiling seductively at him and he couldn't wait for the meal to end so they could be alone.

"How was work for you today?" Luke asked Carly from across the table. Randy frowned at him. What was he up to?

Carly looked up in surprise. "It was fine, why?" she asked.

Luke's eyes twinkled. "Well, your boyfriend here couldn't keep his mind on what he was doing all day, so I wondered if you were the same way."

Carly's mouth dropped open, and Randy glared at Luke while Colt chuckled at the other end of the table.

"Now Luke, you stop teasing Randy," Ginny said. "I remember it wasn't that long ago when you couldn't concentrate on anything around here except a pretty redhead." She winked at Andi.

Luke's blue eyes softened. "I still can't," he said, gazing at Andi. "And now I have two lovely redheads to distract me."

Everyone at the table laughed and finished eating.

"Speaking of distractions," Andi said, turning to Ginny. "Where is that handsome man of yours?"

Ginny's expression grew serious. "He'll be along later," she said. "In fact, there's something I need to discuss with the entire family tonight after supper."

All eyes turned on Ginny. Family meetings were rare, and from the confused looks they all shot each other, each of them was wondering what she had to say.

When everyone was finished, Andi, Beth, and Carly started to clear the table. They hadn't quite finished when Ginny asked them to sit down. "I can see you are all curious about what I want to talk about, so let's all sit down," she said.

When Carly came near Randy, he pushed back his chair and rose. "I'll leave you all to your family discussion," he said.

"No, Randy. Please sit down. This has as much to do with you as the rest of the family. You too, Carly. You're both a part of this family."

Randy and Carly glanced at each other a moment before she went around to the other side of the table and sat down. Randy had no idea what was going on and why he was included.

"What's up, Ma?" Luke asked once everyone was settled. All eyes rested on the matriarch of the family.

Ginny took a breath and folded her hands in front of her. A small smile appeared on her lips. "Glen has asked me to marry him, and I've accepted."

Luke and Colt's mouths dropped open, but the women all smiled wide.

"Oh, Ginny. I'm so happy for you," Andi said, standing to hug her. Carly and Beth also congratulated her warmly, but the men sat silent.

Andi turned to Luke. "Aren't you going to congratulate your mom?"

Luke looked across the table at Colt. They both the same shocked expression on their faces. Randy knew exactly what the brothers were thinking, because he was thinking the same thing. He was happy that Ginny had found happiness again, but he was also remembering Jack, who had been like a father to him. The thought of Ginny with anyone else but Jack was difficult for him, and he knew Luke and Colt were wrestling with it too.

Ginny looked tenderly at her sons. "I knew this might be difficult for you, so that is why Glen decided to let me tell you without his being here. He wanted you to feel comfortable enough to say what was on your mind without the fear of insulting him. So, boys, if you have something to say, say it now."

Luke looked at his mother and took a deep breath. "I am happy for you. Glen is a wonderful man, and I know he'll make you happy. It's just going to take me a while to get used to."

Colt nodded his agreement.

"I understand," Ginny said. "Glen and I didn't make this decision lightly. I know it changes things around here, but I'm ready to make a change. A lot of things have changed around here the past couple of years, and I'm happy about that. You boys now have families of your own and it's finally time for me to begin to step aside and let the next generation of Brennans take over."

Everyone around the table sat silent as they digested what she'd said.

Luke's brow creased. "What do you mean by you stepping aside?"

"Oh, don't worry. I'm not leaving entirely," Ginny said with a laugh. "But now is a good time to make some changes. Glen wants us to go to his San Diego house at least a few weeks every winter, and to tell the truth, I'm looking forward to it. But if I leave for part of the year, then we need to make a new plan. I won't always be here to cook the meals and do the books for the ranch. So, you all will have to decide how you'll want to handle that. Luke and Colt, you have your own households now. You may just want to eat at your own homes. If not, maybe Andi and Beth will want to be in charge of the meal preparation around here while I'm gone."

Beth's eyes lit up. "I love cooking. And baking, too. I wouldn't mind being in charge of that. I only work three days a week at the hospital, so it wouldn't be too hard for me to make breakfast and supper."

"And I can help," Andi said. "I can make lunch while Beth's at work. To tell the truth, I'd hate for the family meals to go by the wayside. I like eating with everyone."

Everyone at the table nodded that they'd like to continue family meals, too.

Ginny smiled. "I'm happy you want to continue doing that. It's a nice tradition to keep. I will also have to teach someone here to take care of the books for the ranch. Luke already knows how but doesn't always have the time to mess with bookwork."

"If it's okay with everyone, I'd be happy to do it," Andi offered.

Ginny looked around the table. Everyone seemed fine with Andi doing the books in her absence. "That would be wonderful," Ginny said, reaching across Jessi's high chair to pat Andi's arm. "Now, with all that settled, we still need to talk about the ranch's finances."

Randy cleared his throat and pushed back his chair to rise. "I'm happy for you, Mrs. B. Glen is a good man. I'll take my leave now that you've told us the good news."

Ginny pointed for him to sit back down. "This concerns you as well, Randy. Please stay."

Randy reluctantly sat back down. He felt uncomfortable being here at a family meeting. Even though he thought of the Brennans as his family, he was still only a paid ranch hand. He had no business listening to a discussion about the ranch's finances. He shifted in his seat and sent a glance Carly's way. She shrugged, and then reached across the table for his hand, apparently sensing his uneasiness.

"With Glen and me marrying, I'm sure you're all worried about the future of the ranch, but you needn't be. He and I have already agreed to keep our money separate so what belongs to me now will stay in the family and be passed down to future Brennans. Glen has plenty of his own money and he has no need for ours."

Luke cleared his throat. "I'm sure we can trust him."

"I'm sure we can too, but I want to assure you all that the Brennan ranch will always be here for future generations," Ginny said. Then she looked across the table at Randy. "Before Jack became sick and passed away, he and I discussed the future and how the ranch's profits would be divided up when we finally retired. Unfortunately, he didn't live to see this day, but he was certain about a few things he wanted done and now I want to honor his requests."

The silence around the table was deafening as everyone sat, listening to Ginny.

"Jack had always meant for Luke, Colt, and him to split the profits in thirds when you boys grew up and started seriously working the ranch. And that's exactly what we've done. But it was also always his intention to give ten percent of our third of the profits to Randy when we retired. So, starting now, Randy will receive ten percent of my yearly profits from the ranch in addition to his yearly wage."

Randy blinked. Had he heard right? When every eye turned to stare at him, he realized he had. Swallowing hard, he looked directly at Ginny. "I appreciate that, Mrs. B, but I can't take your money. It doesn't belong to me."

"It does now," Ginny said. "Jack wanted it this way and I want to honor his wishes. He always thought of you as a son and he wanted to give you a little something extra. It won't be a fortune, that's for certain, but hopefully it will help make your life a little better." Ginny smiled at him. "So, I'm setting it up so that as long as you are working on this ranch, you will receive ten percent of my one-third until the day you retire."

Randy sat there, stunned. His heart swelled with love for Ginny, the only true mother figure he'd ever had. The fact that Jack and Ginny had long ago planned to include him in the ranch's profits was overwhelming. He fought the tears that threatened to fill his eyes. Carly squeezed his hand, and he found strength in her touch.

"Thank you, Mrs. B. I don't know what to say," Randy told her, shock clearly written on his face.

"You're welcome," Ginny said, smiling across the table at him.

When Randy dared to look around the table, he saw his two closest friends, Luke and Colt, smiling back at him.

"I think it's a wonderful idea, and long overdue," Luke said as Colt nodded agreement. "You work just as hard, if not harder at times, as we do on this ranch. You deserve to be rewarded for it."

"So everything is settled," Ginny said, standing up from the table.

"Not everything," Andi said, grinning. "What about the wedding?"

Ginny laughed and it was then they heard the back door open and Glen peered into the kitchen. "Is it safe to come in, or should I run?"

Everyone laughed and soon there were congratulations all around. Colt found a bottle of champagne left over from his and Beth's wedding and he popped it open and poured glasses for everyone.

"To the future Mr. and Mrs. Glen Parker," everyone

toasted.

"And to all the future Brennans," Ginny said, raising her glass. "May the family continue on for years to come."

"Here, here!" everyone cheered.

Randy sipped his champagne and slipped his arm around Carly's waist. "For years to come," he whispered to her, and they smiled at each other and clinked glasses.

Chapter Twenty-Three

That night, Carly lay in Randy's arms, sated from their lovemaking. It had been an interesting evening all around. After Ginny's surprising announcements, about the marriage and Randy receiving a share of the ranch's profits, she and Randy had walked outside in a daze. They didn't go riding as they'd planned, but instead walked a short distance up the trail and then sat in the grass on the hill and gazed out over the Brennan Ranch.

"Amazing, isn't it?" Carly had asked. "Now you're even more a part of this ranch than you were before."

Randy had nodded, seemingly unable to express how he felt.

"I wish I had known Jack," Carly had said softly. "He must have been a great man. Look at how well Luke and Colt turned out, and all he did for you. Ginny too. They're amazing people."

"Jack was a good man," Randy had said. "He worked hard, but he was kind and always treated people fairly." He'd glanced over at Carly with a grin. "And he would have liked Andi, Beth, and you. He would have appreciated what a little spitfire you can be sometimes."

Carly had laughed at him then, and she smiled now as she lay in Randy's arms.

"What are you grinning about?" Randy asked. "Did I do

something funny?"

Carly shook her head. She reached up and brushed the hair out of his eyes, marveling again at their deep amber color. She thought about his toast to her tonight. *For years to come.* Had he meant it? Did he hope they'd be together, forever?

Carly sighed and Randy rose up on one elbow, looking down at her. "Hey? What's wrong?"

"I was thinking about the toast tonight. What you said. *For years to come.* What did you mean by it?"

Randy's fingers slowly traced the side of Carly's face, along her jawline, and down her neck. "I could easily imagine spending every night with you, for years and years," he said softly.

Carly's heart melted. "I can too," she said.

Randy bent down and kissed her lips tenderly. Carly sighed again. She loved the feel of his hard body against hers, his gentle, yet strong touch, and the way he made her feel so safe and cared for. Could this last forever? She wasn't sure. But for now, she'd take whatever he offered and hope that one day, his offer would be forever.

* * *

That next two weeks went by in a frenzy as Carly and the other women helped Ginny plan a very quick wedding. She and Glen wanted a small wedding on the ranch with only a handful of friends and family in attendance. They decided on the first Saturday in September for the ceremony, which gave them only three weeks to get everything done.

"I feel like we're planning a shotgun wedding," Ginny teased.

Andi had raised her eyebrows at her. "Is there something you need to tell us?"

Ginny laughed. "At my age, definitely not! No surprise babies for me."

Andi designed and ordered the invitations while Beth helped Ginny write up the guest list. They all helped Ginny pick out flowers and Andi talked Ginny into ordering a small cake. "What's a wedding without cake?" she'd asked.

The second week of planning, all the women, little Jessi included, went into Missoula to shop for the perfect dress for Ginny's special day. After trying on dozens of dresses, Ginny settled on a simple, pinky-peach, satin, knee-length dress with a fitted bodice, cap sleeves, and a flowing skirt. The color complimented her skin, making it glow. She also bought creamy colored low-heeled shoes to wear with it. It was the perfect dress for an outdoor wedding in late summer. The other women also bought new dresses to wear, and even Jessi got a new, frilly dress for the occasion.

Luckily, Luke, Colt, and Randy were gone for three days that week up at the summer pasture, corralling the heifers and cows that had been tagged for breeding and checking on the rest of the stock. Glen was around in the evenings to see Ginny, but other than that, he was more than happy to leave the wedding planning up to them. That left the women free to work without interruption on the wedding when they weren't off working at their jobs.

Carly missed Randy while he was gone to the summer pasture and couldn't wait for him to return. But the wedding preparations and the gift shop kept her busy. She and Margie had marked the majority of the merchandise down to fifty percent and the stock was selling fast. That was good for Margie, who was getting excited about leaving for the winter months, but Carly was beginning to worry. What would she do once Margie closed the shop for good? Where would she work? She hadn't yet decided if it was feasible for her to try a business on her own, and there weren't that many places to work close to the ranch.

Carly pondered her problems as she lay awake in her bed at night while Randy was gone. She knew starting a business was risky, and even with the money from her half of the townhouse, if they sold it, she'd need a bank loan to cover expenses. Plus, she still had a mountain of debt to pay off. A big chunk of the townhouse money would have to go toward the debt. If she didn't make a profit from the business during the first few years, she'd have no money to live on.

Finding a job locally that paid enough money for her to pay down her debt wasn't an option either. She could probably find something in Missoula, but that would mean a long commute each day and with gas prices so high, it just wouldn't make sense. Her only other option was going back to Seattle and finding a job. The townhouse was paid for and the bills wouldn't be too bad if she was careful this time. But she didn't like that option either. It would mean leaving Randy behind.

Carly discussed her options with Andi, but even she didn't know what to tell her.

"This is going to be a tough decision," Andi said. "Maybe you should discuss it with Randy."

Carly was surprised that Andi suggested she talk to Randy and said as much to her. Andi had just smiled and said, "I see how you two are together. I wouldn't doubt that if he had his choice, you'd stay here. Maybe forever."

Deep down inside Carly wished that were true, but she wasn't going to saddle Randy with her debts. Even though she'd been careless with her finances the past couple of years, she had always paid her own way and she didn't expect Randy or anyone else to take on her problems. But the thought of leaving the ranch broke her heart. She had only a few weeks to come up with a solution, and it weighed heavily on her.

The men came home Thursday evening and Randy hugged Carly tight despite his being dirty from riding and working the herd. Carly had run down to the barn when she'd seen them ride up and greeted them, and she didn't care one bit that Randy covered her in trail dust when he pulled her to him.

"I'm taking you out dancing tomorrow night," Randy told her. "I have to make up for all the time you haven't been in my arms."

Carly laughed and sat on a stall rail inside the barn, watching as the men unsaddled their horses and brushed them down. Colt and Luke finished quickly, eager to get home to their wives, leaving her and Randy alone. Randy led Black Jack out into the pasture, came back inside, and grabbed Carly, lifting her and twirling her around.

"Miss me?" he asked.

"More than anything," she said.

"Come to my place tonight," he said. "I can't stand the thought of spending another night without you beside me."

Carly nodded. "Let me pack up a few things for work tomorrow. I'll shower at your place in the morning."

Randy waggled his eyebrows. "I'll shower with you."

Carly put her hand on his chest and pushed him back. "You're showering tonight, or else you're sleeping alone."

Randy laughed heartily. "Then I'm going home right now and I'll beat you to bed."

They made love that night so passionately that Carly's eyes filled with tears at the intense emotions she felt for him.

"What's wrong?" Randy asked, concern filling his voice. "Please don't cry."

Randy's deep concern only intensified Carly's emotions and the tears ran down her face. "I'm sorry," she said. "I've never felt this way about anyone else in my life."

"That's a good thing, isn't it?" Randy said softly, gently

brushing away the tears on her cheeks.

Carly nodded. "I'm just so afraid of losing you."

Randy frowned. "Why would you think that? I'm not going anywhere."

"I know," Carly whispered. "It's silly. Just hold me, please. I missed being held by you."

Randy reached for her and pulled her close in his arms. Carly nestled her head on his chest and curled her body around his. "I'll be with you as long as you'll have me," Randy whispered to her. He kissed the top of her head.

Carly hoped that would be for a very long time.

* * *

True to his word, Randy took Carly out dancing at The Depot Friday night and Colt and Beth even came along for a little while. They took turns dancing around the floor to the live music, and even though Colt was an excellent dancer, Carly enjoyed herself more when she was in Randy's arms. After years of not feeling an emotional attachment to any one man, the intensity of her feelings for Randy scared Carly. She'd never thought of herself as the kind of woman who'd feel lost without a man beside her, but she was becoming that way. Her days were complete only when she saw him, and missing even one night in his bed was almost heart wrenching for her. If this was love, it was both beautiful and agonizing, she decided. Either that or she was going crazy.

Yep. This was love!

They spent the weekend together, riding the hills, picnicking by their stream, and making love every night. On Sunday, as they relaxed lazily by the stream after having another one of Ginny's wonderful picnic lunches, Randy asked, "Can I ask you a serious question?"

Carly's head had been on his chest as they lay under the tree, but she lifted it and looked into his eyes. "Sure."

"When we were fighting about my not trusting you, something you said has stuck with me all this time. You said you've been played before by men. Do you mind if I ask what you meant?"

Carly sighed and sat up. "I said that because I was angry, but it's not a story I like thinking about. In fact, I've never told anyone, not even Andi. It's too embarrassing."

Randy sat up and reached for her hand. "You don't have to tell me if you don't want to."

Carly looked up into the blue sky, as if searching for answers. Finally, she said, "I should tell you. If we're going to have a serious relationship, this is something that you should know. I just hope it doesn't lower your opinion of me." She took a breath. "Last year, after I broke up with Colt, I started seeing another man. He was the whole package, or at least I thought he was. He'd actually tracked me down after I met him at the gallery, and I had thought that was so romantic. We dated a few weeks. He took me out to all the best restaurants and we went to dance clubs every weekend. He seemed to have an endless supply of money, and he had a beautiful apartment in the city and a really good job. I thought I'd won the lottery with him."

She stopped a moment, sadness creasing her face.

"What happened?" Randy asked.

"I didn't hear from him for over a week, and that was unusual. So that weekend, I dressed up in my sexiest dress and went to his apartment to surprise him. But I was the one who was surprised."

Randy frowned. "He was seeing another woman."

Carly slowly shook her head. "No. I found out that day that I was the other woman. His wife answered the door with their baby daughter in her arms. I panicked and lied, saying I worked with him. She told me she lived in the suburbs all week and had decided to come into town shopping for the weekend. I left as fast as I could."

"Oh, Carly, that's awful. How could he do that to you, and to his wife?"

Carly dropped her head. "I felt so terrible. I had no idea he was married. I may be a lot of things, but I'd never purposely date a married man or break up a marriage. He used me. I promised myself that I'd never let another man use me that way again."

Randy raised his hand and gently lifted her face so their eyes met. "And then I blamed you for flirting with Colt. I'm so sorry, Carly. No wonder you were so mad at me."

"Promise me you'll always be honest with me," Carly said. "Even if you think I don't want to hear it. I would never lie to you, and I hope you won't to me."

Randy pulled her to him and they lay down on the blanket by the tree. "I promise I'll never play you, Carly. I want us to have an honest relationship, too." He kissed her on the top of the head, and Carly sighed.

* * *

Carly was half-way through her workday on Monday when her cell phone rang. It startled her at first, before she realized what was making the chiming noise and she pulled it out of her pocket. She rarely ever received calls on her cell phone anymore, since there was no reception at the ranch. Only Andi occasionally called her to ask her to pick up a carton of milk or some such thing. But when she looked at her phone, it wasn't Andi. It was a call from Bayside Gallery in Seattle where she used to work.

Carly answered the phone tentatively. The owner, Mr. Barnett, was on the other end of the line. As he spoke, Carly's expression grew more serious. By the time she said good-bye, she was even more confused about what her future held.

When Carly arrived back at the ranch after work, Andi was in the kitchen alone, sitting at the table addressing wedding invitations. Carly smelled a chicken cooking in the oven, and saw a pan on the stove, but Ginny and Jessi were nowhere around.

"Where is everyone?" Carly asked, sitting down across from Andi.

"Ginny's folding laundry in her room and Jessi is taking a late nap in the office," Andi said. "I'll have to wake her up soon, or she won't sleep well tonight." Andi looked up at Carly and set down her pen. "You look awfully serious. Is something wrong?"

"I had a call today from Mr. Barnett at the gallery," Carly said.

Andi's eyebrows rose. "What did he want?"

"He asked if I'd be interested in coming back to work at the gallery. He apologized for being so hasty about letting me go, and said he'd give me the manager's position back along with a nice raise."

"Wow, that's incredible," Andi said. "What did you tell him?"

"I didn't know what to tell him," Carly said. She rose and started pacing around the room. "I don't even know if I want to go back to the gallery, or Seattle. I told him I'd have to think about it."

"Come sit down and let's discuss this calmly," Andi said, waving Carly back to the table.

Carly sat down again, but she still felt agitated. "I don't know what to do, Andi. I'd like to stay here, but after next month, I won't have a job. How will I pay off my bills? There really isn't anyplace around here where I could earn as much as I would at the gallery."

Andi patted her arm. "I know, hon. If you went back to the gallery, you'd be able to pay off your debt quicker. You wouldn't have any rent, only the bills to keep the townhouse running. Paying off your debt would be a big burden off your shoulders, and then you could decide what you wanted to do."

Carly nodded agreement. "I'd never earn the kind of money here that I could earn there. And it would be nice to get rid of those bills."

"That really is the best solution to your problem," Andi said.

"I know it is." Carly looked sadly at Andi. "But what about Randy? What will happen to us if I leave?" A tear ran slowly down her cheek. "What if I lose him?" she said in barely a whisper.

Andi stood and pulled her sister into a hug. "I'm sorry, Carly. This is going to be a difficult decision. You need to talk to Randy about it—and soon."

Carly pulled back and wiped the tears away. "I will. I'll talk to him tonight." She gazed around the room. "I don't want to leave here, Andi. I love being here with all of you. And if I leave, I'll miss out on Jessi growing up. She'll forget who I am."

Andi sighed. "I'd miss you if you left, too. But you have to do what's right for you. When do you have to give Mr. Barnett your answer?"

"He said to let him know as soon as possible. He'd like me to come back by the middle of September."

Andi placed her hand gently on Carly's arm. "Talk to Randy. You two will figure something out."

Carly nodded and walked up the stairs to her room to change before supper. If she hadn't put herself into such a terrible financial mess, her answer would have been easy—a flat out no. But she didn't have the luxury of throwing away a good job. She hoped talking to Randy would make things clearer.

Chapter Twenty-Four

Randy quietly closed the back door to the ranch house and strode off quickly to his truck. He hopped in and drove away, not allowing himself to think about what he'd overheard until he was parked in front of his own house.

Carly was thinking of leaving.

He hadn't meant to eavesdrop on her and Andi's conversation. He'd walked into the mudroom with the intention of saying hello to her before he headed home to shower. The two women had been so intent on their conversation, neither of them had heard him come in. And when he'd heard what they were talking about, he'd hesitated to tell them he was there.

"I'd never earn the kind of money here that I could earn there." Carly had said. He knew it was true. He also knew she had a lot of debt that she needed to pay off. If she stayed here, it would take her a long time to pay it down. Even so, it had been hard for him to hear her talk about leaving. When he'd heard Andi say that her returning to the gallery was the best solution for her, and Carly agreeing, Randy couldn't stand to listen any longer. He'd left quietly.

I'm going to lose her.

Randy's heart felt heavy.

He walked inside, undressed, and stepped into the warm

shower. His thoughts turned to how happy they'd been together these past few weeks. Their time together had been too short. He wanted more—needed more—time. But how could he ask her to stay when she could do so much better with her life if she went back to Seattle? After all, he had nothing to offer her. He was just a ranch hand and he'd never be anything else.

That dreaded thought nagged at him. How could he have ever thought a woman like Carly, so beautiful, intelligent, and motivated, would ever even consider staying in this insignificant place and leading a small life? She would just wither away, angry and bitter, because of everything she had given up to be with him. He could never love her enough or give her enough to make up for her losing a promising life just to be with him. He wasn't worth it. Echoes of his mother's words reverberated in his ears. *You ain't nothing but a two-bit ranch hand—just like your father.* He knew that was true, yet he'd hoped for so much more. He'd hoped for Carly. Now, he had to face reality—*he* wasn't enough to keep her here.

No longer hungry despite his long day of working, he dressed and grabbed a beer out of the fridge. He couldn't bear to look at her across the table tonight, knowing he was soon going to lose her. So he stayed home, hiding out, unable to face Carly.

A little while later, there was a knock on his door and Carly walked in, looking concerned. She had a covered plate in her hand. Randy glanced up, keeping his expression unreadable.

"You missed supper tonight," Carly said, coming closer. "What happened? Everyone was wondering where you were."

Randy took a sip of his beer and said casually, "I wasn't very hungry and I was too tired to come back to the ranch tonight."

Carly studied him a moment. "Ginny sent a plate of food along. Do you want me to heat it up?"

"Nah, don't bother. Just put it in the fridge."

Carly went into the kitchen and set the plate in the refrigerator, glancing at the empty beer bottles on the counter. She walked back over to the sofa, sat down close to Randy, and asked, "What's going on? You never miss supper on a week night."

"Nothing's going on. I told you, I wasn't hungry." He sat there, staring at the silent television, not even aware of what was on the screen.

Carly sighed. She reached up and touched Randy's face, making him turn to look her in the eye. "There's something we need to talk about."

Randy already knew what she wanted to discuss, and he wasn't looking forward to hearing what she was going to say. He knew that no matter what was said, he had to let her go. Holding her here would be selfish and senseless. Eventually, she'd resent him for making her stay, and leave anyway. Carly would never want to be a ranch hand's wife. She had too much going for her to settle for someone like him. But looking into her eyes was breaking his resolve. He quickly glanced away.

"Okay. Talk," he said.

Carly curled her legs under her and turned to look straight at him. "The owner of the gallery in Seattle called me today. He asked me to come back to work as the manager again, and even offered me a big raise. He apologized for letting me go. I need to make some hard decisions. *We* need to make some decisions."

Randy kept his eyes on the television screen. "Sounds like a great opportunity for you. What's there to decide?"

Carly grabbed the remote from the sofa and turned off the television. "Randy. Look at me! This is important. This involves the both of us."

Randy stood and walked across the room. He turned to face

Carly. "No, Carly. This is your decision. I live *here*. I'll always live here and work here. Nothing is going to change for me. It's you who has to decide what you want to do. And it sounds to me like going back to Seattle is the best choice for you. You'll make enough money to get out of debt and you'll be back with your friends in the town you love. What's the downside to that?"

Carly stood and stared at Randy. "The downside is we won't be together. I don't want to leave, Randy. But pretty soon my job at the gift shop will be over, and I don't know if I'll be able to find another job around here. Especially one that pays as much as the gallery does. I need your help making this decision. I don't know what to do."

The desperate look on Carly's face tore at Randy's heart. He wanted to pull her to him and beg her to stay, but he couldn't do that. He held onto his resolve. "Listen, Carly. You and I both know that going back there is the best decision for you. There's nothing here for you as good as what you can have there. You have a future in Seattle, a good one. Why would you throw that away to stay here?"

Carly's eyes filled with tears. "Because you're here."

Randy swallowed the lump that had formed in his throat. "We've had some good times together, but now it's time to face facts. I promised you yesterday that I would be honest with you, so, that's just what I'm going to do. We both know that you'd leave eventually. You don't belong here. Would you really be happy living in a trailer with me here in the middle of nowhere? Of course not. So, let's be satisfied with the fun times we've shared and move on."

Carly stood there, stunned. Tears rolled down her cheeks. "You don't mean that. What about *for years to come*? You said you'd be with me for as long as I'd have you. Was that all a lie? Didn't you mean any of it?"

Randy didn't know how much more of this he could take before he caved. He was doing this for her. He knew he had to be strong. But his heart broke with every word he said to her. "I meant every word, but the reality is that you and I are two different types of people. We'd never be able to make each other happy. I'm not like Luke or Colt. I'm not the kind of guy to settle down with one woman for the rest of my life. Go back to Seattle. Your life will be so much richer and fuller without me holding you down."

Carly stared at him. "Why are you pushing me away? Even if I do go back, you and I can still be together. It's not that far away. We can visit each other. There's no reason why we can't work this out."

"It would never work, Carly. You know that as well as I do. Let's just be mature about this and let it go."

Carly blinked back tears. Randy stood there, stiff and unyielding. He watched as Carly spun on her heel and ran out the door. He continued standing there as he listened to her car start and drive away. Only when he knew for sure she was gone did he fall onto the sofa and drop his face into his hands.

* * *

Tears spilled from Carly's eyes as she drove down the highway, away from Randy's place. She swiped them away several times, but more just took their place. When she finally made it back to the ranch, she couldn't bear to go inside and face anyone. She ran inside the barn and climbed up the ladder to the hayloft. It was hot and stuffy up there, so she used all her strength to push the door aside a little to let in fresh air. Then she sat down on the floor and cried.

Why was Randy pushing her away? It made no sense. He'd acted so cold, as if telling her to go had meant nothing to him.

After all they'd been through together, and the wonderful times they'd shared these past few weeks, how could he let her go?

Carly thought about what he'd said. *I'm not the kind of guy to settle down with one person for the rest of my life.* She didn't believe that about him. He was kind and caring and had so much love to share. She'd felt that love. It was she who had never thought she'd be the kind of woman to settle down with one man for the rest of her life. But with Randy, she could picture the two of them together, laughing, fighting, and making up. *For years to come.*

Maybe he'd thought she could never commit to one guy. She had a bad track record with men, that was true. But she'd changed. Randy had changed her by showing her what a spoiled brat she was and making her take responsibility for herself and her actions. Hadn't he seen how much she'd changed?

We both know that you'd leave eventually. Those words had jarred her the most. What made him think she'd leave? Did he still believe she was that shallow? Was she? Or was he so afraid of commitment that he didn't even want to try?

Evening settled over the ranch and the air drifting through the barn door cooled. Carly found the blanket Randy had kept up here for the nights they laid on the floor and looked up at the stars. She wrapped it around her and sat against a straw bale, staring up into the starry sky.

Maybe Randy was right. Maybe it wouldn't have worked out between them. Or maybe he was running away—again. She loved him. She truly did. But she couldn't make him love her back. She couldn't make him want her as much as she wanted him.

Carly sat up there a long time, thinking about what to do. She really had no choice. He didn't want her to stay, and he didn't want them to continue their relationship. She'd go back to Seattle, work, and take care of her obligations. In truth, she had no other choice, but it broke her heart to think about leaving.

* * *

Randy had made up his mind, and nothing, or no one, was going to change it. Carly needed to go home to Seattle, and he wasn't going to do anything to get in her way.

He did his best to avoid her the next day, but he had no excuse to miss supper every night until she left. Ginny and Glen's wedding wasn't until Saturday, and Carly would definitely stay until then. After that, he wasn't sure how much longer she'd stick around. So, when suppertime rolled around, he went inside, sat, and ate as fast as he could without looking up. Just as he had before, when he hadn't wanted anything to do with her. Except now, it was harder—much harder—to ignore her.

The week dragged by, but Carly didn't even try to talk to him. He figured she must have realized that he was right. Her leaving was the best thing for her. But it still didn't make him feel any better knowing he was right. His heart lurched every time he saw her, which was often.

Plans for the wedding were underway and everyone was recruited into helping with the outdoor decorations and setting up tables for the guests. Ginny and Glen had decided to have the ceremony outside under a big oak tree that had been standing on the ranch for over one hundred years. A tent was set up in the yard for the reception, in case of rain, with tables and chairs for the supper and a dance afterward. The men did the grunt work and then Beth, Andi, and Carly decorated to make everything perfect for Ginny's special day. Tables and chairs were covered in cream-colored cloths and wide, wine-colored ribbons were tied around each chair. Twinkle lights trimmed the tent and were also strung in a crisscross pattern inside it. When Randy strung the lights, he couldn't help but think of the night he'd surprised Carly with lights in the loft two months before. He wished they could go back to that night, when they were both happy. Maybe things would have worked out differently. Unfortunately, they couldn't go back.

It was difficult not to pass by Carly throughout the day, and several times, Randy accidently caught her eye, and then looked away quickly. But she never said a word to him. He wasn't sure if that made it better, or worse.

The day of the wedding dawned sunny and clear, and as everyone bustled about, they marveled at the beautiful day they'd been graced with. The flowers arrived as well as the cake, which they kept in the kitchen until after the supper. The ceremony was planned for five o'clock with the supper to follow. By four-thirty that afternoon, everyone was dressed and ready. Colt and Luke greeted the few guests who'd been invited as well as the minister. The meal was being catered, so all the women could enjoy the evening as well. The two-piece band that had played at Andi and Luke's wedding was there to play the march down the aisle and also for the dance after supper. It was an exciting time and everyone was in good spirits.

At exactly five o'clock, everyone was in place and Luke and Colt walked their mother down the aisle to Glen. Andi was Ginny's matron-of-honor and Glen had asked a long-time friend of his to come from Seattle and be his best man. They all stood there, under the giant oak tree, as the minister read the wedding vows. A gentle breeze rustled the leaves while puffy, white clouds drifted above them in the deep blue sky. Ginny looked lovely in her peach dress as did Glen in his brown suit. It was the perfect setting for two people who had found love the second time around.

Carly stood with the other guests holding Jessi in her arms. Randy was across from her and stole a glance at her. She looked beautiful in a satin, burgundy dress that fit her curves at the waist before flaring out into a full skirt that stopped right above her knees. Her hair was pulled up into a twist, showing off her lovely face. The color of the dress complimented the light tan on her skin, and to Randy, she looked like she glowed. It looked so natural for her to be standing there, holding Jessi, that he thought for a moment what a wonderful mother she would be. Then she glanced up, catching him staring at her. The look that crossed her face was both sweet and sad as she gazed at him. Reluctantly, he turned away, just as the minister announced that Ginny and Glen were now husband and wife.

* * *

Carly looked over at Randy as he stood across the lawn from her and was surprised to see him watching her. He looked so handsome in his dark, navy suit. She knew it was the same one he'd worn to Andi's wedding and his mother's funeral, but it didn't matter—he looked handsome just the same. His hair was freshly cut and he'd shaved. Her heart skipped a beat at how much she loved him, yet sadness fell over her at the thought that he would never be hers.

Randy turned away and her heart fell. She looked over at Ginny and Glen just as they kissed for the first time as husband and wife. Carly smiled. Ginny was such sweet soul and she deserved to be happy. She hoped that one day she'd be as happy as Ginny was with Glen. And as happy as Andi and Luke, and Colt and Beth were. She'd thought she'd found that kind of happiness with Randy, but she'd been wrong.

Carly sighed as she turned and carried Jessi over to the tent where she set her in her high chair. People milled around, and

Andi found her and took over watching Jessi. When Ginny and Glen came near, Carly hugged them each in turn and congratulated them.

"I'm so happy for you both," she said, smiling at them.

Ginny grasped her hand and smiled wide. "You're next, dear. We want to see you happy, too."

Carly's smile faded. "Maybe someday."

Ginny pulled her into a hug and whispered into her ear. "Just give him a little time, dear. It'll be worth it in the end."

Carly stepped back and looked at Ginny, clearly surprised. Ginny winked, and then more people came up and took the couple's attention away.

Carly wondered how Ginny knew about her and Randy's situation. She swore that the woman had special powers. Carly had not told anyone that he'd told her to leave, not even her sister. And with all the commotion over the wedding, it had been easy to hide their broken relationship from everyone. She'd planned on telling Andi tomorrow that she'd be leaving the following week, and also telling Margie on Monday. The shop was quieting down, so she knew Margie wouldn't need her help anymore. Besides, Margie would be closing up the shop by the end of September and leaving too.

Supper was being served so Carly sat down at a table with Luke, Andi, Jessi, Colt, and Beth. Luckily, Randy had chosen to sit at another table. The caterers had done a nice job and the food was delicious. The centerpieces on the tables, made up in fall colors, were lovely, and the cake, when it was served a while later, was delicious. Everything, from the weather to the cake had turned out perfect for Ginny's day, and it made Carly happy for her.

After supper, a few of the tables were cleared away and a wooden dance floor was placed in front of the two-piece band. The music began, and Ginny and Glen danced the first dance.

Everyone clapped and cheered at the newlyweds. After that, Ginny took turns dancing with each of her sons, as well as Randy, and Glen danced with Andi, Beth, and then Carly. Other couples came onto the dance floor and soon it was full as people slow-danced or two-stepped alternately as the music changed. As the song Glen and Carly were dancing to stopped and a slow song began, Glen expertly handed Carly over to Randy, who'd been standing nearby.

"Now here's a fellow your own age you can dance with," Glen teased, and then walked away toward his bride.

Before she knew what was happening, Randy took her into his arms and they began dancing slowly around the floor. Carly could have walked away, but she didn't want to make a scene— it was best if she just finished the dance with Randy.

Carly tried to look everywhere but at Randy. She watched Andi and Luke dancing, holding each other close, and Beth and Colt were cuddling on the floor as well. Other couples around her looked happy as they slowly danced around them. Randy's hand felt warm in hers, and his other hand on the small of her back made her spine tingle. She wanted nothing more than to place her head on his shoulder as he pulled her close. But she didn't dare. She stood stiffly, moving to the music, barely touching him.

Finally, as the song ended, she glanced up at him and saw he was gazing down at her. Their eyes met and held, but no words were said. What she saw in those eyes made her heart break. A sadness, deep and powerful, reflected in his eyes. But before she could say a word, Randy pulled away, turned, and walked away through the crowd.

It was really over.

Chapter Twenty-Five

On Sunday, Carly and Andi began the task of cleaning up the remnants of the night before. They had refused to let Ginny help in any way, and had told her to pack for her honeymoon instead. Glen was taking her on an Alaskan Cruise, something she'd always wanted to do. They were leaving for Vancouver, BC, Canada on Tuesday where they were boarding the ship, so Ginny had plenty to do to prepare.

As they folded tablecloths and chair covers, Andi spoke up. "I noticed Randy left early last night. Is everything okay with him?"

Carly closed her eyes and took a breath. She had watched him leave right after their dance. It had broken her heart to watch him walk away into the night. The fact that he couldn't stand to be around her, even for a short time at Ginny's reception, made her feel even worse.

"Carly?" Andi asked, looking at her strangely. "What's wrong?"

Carly opened her eyes and looked directly at her sister. "I'm leaving on Wednesday to go back to Seattle and work for the gallery again."

"What does Randy think about that?"

Carly sighed. "He thinks it's a wonderful idea."

Andi stared at her sister. "So, does that mean you two are going to have a long-distance relationship for a while?"

Carly shook her head. "No. He doesn't want me, Andi. He said as much."

Andi's mouth dropped open. "I can't believe that."

"It's true. He said he isn't the type of guy to be with only one woman and it would never work out between us. He told me that I'd end up leaving him eventually." Tears filled Carly's eyes. "It doesn't matter what I say to him. He's made up his mind that we're through, and he's sticking to it."

"Oh, Carly. I'm so sorry." Andi pulled her into a hug. "I had really thought you two would stay together. I had no idea he felt that way."

Carly stepped away. "That makes two of us." She wiped her tears and picked up another tablecloth to fold. "I guess I'm not the type of woman that men want to commit to. At least, not him."

"That's not true, Carly. One day you will find the right man to spend your life with. It will happen."

Carly shrugged. "I guess. Until then, it's back to Seattle." She turned to Andi. "Please don't say anything to Luke about this. I know Luke. He'll go right to Randy and knock him over the head. It's best if nothing is said."

Andi nodded. "Okay. But maybe that's what Randy needs. After all, it was Randy who told Luke that if he wanted me to stay, he should tell me. And that turned out fine."

Carly smiled at her sister. Yes, it had turned out very well. "I know, but this is different. Luke loves you, but Randy apparently doesn't love me like that. Please don't say anything."

"I won't," Andi promised.

Carly wiped away the last of her tears and went back to work cleaning things up. It was going to be hard to leave the ranch and everyone she loved here, but it was for the best.

* * *

Monday morning, Carly broke the news to Margie that she was leaving.

"Oh, darling, I'm going to miss you so much. But you're right; I'll be closing up the shop at the end of this month and heading out to see my daughter for the winter. I'm going to put the building up for sale too. Hopefully, someone will be crazy enough to buy it."

Carly glanced around the shop, regretting having to leave. It was hard to believe that only three months ago, she'd resented having to work in a place that she'd felt was below her standards. It hadn't taken long before Margie found a way into her heart and so had the little shop. That she'd been able to help Margie turn it around and make a bigger profit than usual, made Carly proud.

"It's a shame you can't buy this shop and keep it going as an art gallery for the local artists," Margie said. "It will sure be missed by the artists and the tourists alike. But I can't blame you. You have a good job waiting for you back in Seattle."

Before Carly left the shop that afternoon, she gave Margie a hug and thanked her for everything she'd done for her. "I'm going to miss you, Margie."

Margie told her to call on her whenever she was back visiting. "I'll be spending my summers at my home here, and you're always welcome to stop by."

As Carly walked out the front door and listened to the bell tinkle for the last time, she felt as if another piece of her heart was breaking away.

* * *

Early Monday morning, Randy packed up his truck with supplies and drove up to the summer pasture. He'd told Luke he was going to check on the cattle and make one last fence check before winter. Luke had stared at him strangely but hadn't said a word. Luke knew as well as he did that the fences were fine and the cattle were too, but Randy didn't care. He had to get away from the ranch for a few days, and the summer pasture was his only escape.

As he drove up to the cabin, his thoughts turned to Saturday night and his dance with Carly. She'd looked so beautiful that when Glen had brought her to him, he'd been unable to resist holding her in his arms one last time. He loved the way she felt up against him, how her body swayed perfectly with his, and the sweet smell of her lavender-scented perfume. He could have caved at that very moment and begged her to stay, but he'd stayed strong. Yet, as the last note of the song played, she'd looked up at him with such soulful eyes, he'd felt his heart break. That was why he'd had to get as far away from her as possible. He'd ended up in his truck, driving home, where he'd drowned his sorrow in beer for the rest of the night.

He was running away—he knew it. But this time it was for someone else's own good. Carly's life would be so much better without him in it. He knew that for certain. He only wished he could make himself believe it.

* * *

Carly rose early Wednesday morning and had breakfast with the Brennan clan one last time before preparing to leave. Ginny and Glen had said their good-byes to her on Tuesday before they'd left for the airport for their honeymoon. Now, she hugged Beth, Colt, Luke, Andi, and Jessi good-bye before packing up her car with Luke's help.

"It's too bad Randy's not here to say good-bye," Luke said, loading up her last bag in the back of her car. "He headed up to the summer pasture yesterday."

That didn't surprise Carly. He had run away again.

"Tell him I said good-bye, will you, Luke?"

Luke nodded. "I'll do that."

With one more round of hugs, including a hug for Bree, Carly walked over and opened her car door. She stood there a moment, taking in one last look of the ranch, already feeling the sorrow of missing it. She gazed up at the trail that led to the summer pasture, then with a sigh, slipped into her car, and drove away.

Chapter Twenty-Six

The cold November wind cut through Randy as he and Luke stood in a wide-open, snow-covered field repairing a strip of fence. Earlier in the day, a neighbor had called to say that he'd seen some of the Brennan cattle wandering along the highway. Colt, Luke, Randy, and Glen had spent the afternoon rounding up the missing cattle. Now, the other two men were out checking to make sure there were no more strays while Randy and Luke fixed the fence the cattle had knocked down for their escape.

"Damn stupid cattle," Randy said through gritted teeth. He stood in knee-high snow, his hands and face frozen from the icy wind. Winter had come early and the snow had fallen relentlessly over the past two weeks. It didn't matter how many layers he wore—he still froze.

"Well, nobody ever said cattle were smart now, did they?" Luke teased.

Randy glared at him. How he could keep his sense of humor after a day like today was a mystery to him.

It was almost suppertime by the time they'd nailed the last board up and strung the last bit of barbed wire. Randy sighed with relief when they jumped into the warm truck. He dropped his wet gloves down on the floor by the heater to dry them and rubbed the cold from his hands.

"Tell me again why we live in this godforsaken place?" he asked Luke.

Luke laughed as he maneuvered his truck along the freshly plowed road toward the ranch house. "Because it's so beautiful."

Randy grunted. "Yeah, in the summer. But it's winter more than half the year."

Luke glanced over at him. "You know, you've been ornerier than usual the last couple of months. Want to talk about it?"

Randy ignored Luke and stared out the window at the white-covered terrain. The last thing he wanted to do was talk.

At supper, the conversation centered around the early winter, the cattle running off, and Glen and Ginny's escape to San Diego in January after the holidays. Randy still felt the chill of the day in his bones. It felt like he'd never warm up. And as he looked around the table, the icy chill of reality only made him feel worse. Everyone here had someone to go home with tonight and keep them warm. Everyone but him.

He glanced across the table at the empty seat that only two months before Carly had sat in. He missed her beautiful smile, her stubborn personality, and the way she felt when she pressed up against him. He missed how she made him laugh, and warmed his heart. Most of all, he missed kissing her. He forced himself to look back down at his plate so he wouldn't feel so alone at his end of the table without Carly.

Later, Randy went to the barn to check on the horses in their stalls before he left for home. He gave each horse a bucket of grain and then ran his hand up Black Jack's warm nose. He hadn't had a chance to ride Black Jack much since the cattle drive in October and also when they'd moved the cattle for transport to auction. Fall had passed quickly and winter had hit overnight, with cold temperatures and piles of snow. Yet even though he had plenty to keep him busy, he thought of

Carly almost every hour of every day. He'd gone back to his old routine of watching an old movie before going to bed on weeknights and going to The Depot every Friday and Saturday night for a burger and a few games of pool, but it was just a way to pass the time. The cute little waitress still flirted with him, and so did a few of the women who frequented the bar, but he ignored them all. If he couldn't have the woman he wanted, he didn't want anyone at all.

"Hey there," Luke said, coming up behind him. "Are you out here brooding some more?"

Randy turned around and stared at Luke. He was his best friend and he respected the hell out of him, but he sure could be annoying when he wanted to. "Why are you still here? You should be at home by the fire with your beautiful wife and daughter."

Luke cocked his head and looked at him thoughtfully. "I'll be heading there soon. Just wanted to check on you and make sure you were okay."

"Well, I'm just fine," Randy said, turning back to his horse.

"Are you?"

Randy turned his head and looked at Luke. "What do you want, Luke? If you have something to say, just say it."

Luke pushed his hat back on his head and stared straight at Randy. "Okay, I will. You know I don't butt into your business often. But I have to say, you're a complete idiot."

Randy's brow creased. "What?"

"You heard me. You're an idiot. You had the chance of a lifetime to be happy and you threw it away for whatever stubborn reason. Ever since, you've been glowering at everyone, complaining about everything, and acting the crankiest I've ever seen you be."

Randy stubbornly set his jaw and headed toward the door. "I'm not listening to any more of this."

"You can run away from me, but you can't run away from the truth."

Randy spun on his heel and strode right up to Luke, his eyes flashing. "What does that mean?"

Luke crossed his arms and stood his ground. "Go ahead. Run away. Just like you did two months ago to the summer pasture so you wouldn't have to watch Carly leave. But it really hasn't helped, has it? You can't run away from the fact that you still care about her."

"You don't know a thing about what went on between Carly and me," Randy said. "Mind your own business."

"You're right. I don't know much about the two of you. But I can tell you something I do know. When you and Carly were together this summer, you were the happiest I've ever seen you. And now you're the worst version of yourself. It doesn't take a rocket scientist to put two and two together."

Randy sighed and his shoulders sagged. "Just let it go, Luke, okay? Carly is where she belongs and so am I. It would never have worked out between us."

Luke frowned. "What do you mean by that?"

"Carly's a city girl. She deserves a life with a nice home and nice things. I can't give her that. I'm just a ranch hand, and that's all I'll ever be."

"That's ridiculous. I'm just a ranch hand, and it doesn't bother Andi."

"That's because you own this ranch. So does Colt. You have more to offer than I do."

Luke snorted. "Okay, so I'm a glorified ranch hand who not only does the same type of work you do, but I get to worry about expenses and making enough of a profit to keep the ranch running another year. You and I do the same thing, Randy. Heck, sometimes you work even harder than I do. But at the end of the day, we both go home smelling of the same dirt, sweat, and manure. So, why in the world would your being a ranch hand have anything to do with Carly loving you?"

"You just don't understand, Luke," Randy said sadly.

Luke walked over and put his hand on Randy's shoulder. "You're wrong there. I understand better than anyone does. A couple of years ago a pretty city girl was stranded on this ranch, and I wouldn't believe that I was good enough for her. Then my best friend came to me and said that if anyone was ever worth begging for, it was she. I took his advice, and look how well it all turned out."

Randy dropped his head. "That was different. Andi is different. I knew she loved you."

"And I know Carly loves you," Luke said softly.

Randy looked up at him, surprised.

"You know, I was the last person to ever believe that you and Carly would get together. But then I saw how much she changed over the summer, and how devoted she was to you and the look in your eyes every time you two were together. You love her, you idiot. And she loves you. And all I can say is if you don't get in your truck and go find her and beg her to spend the rest of her life with you, then you are the biggest idiot I've ever known." Luke patted his shoulder and grinned, then turned and left the barn.

Randy stood there in shock for a few minutes before getting into his truck and driving home. He didn't know if he should be angry with Luke, or if he should take his advice to heart. He showered and went to bed, too tired from his long day and the emotional toll of Luke's words to stay awake another minute. But sleep eluded him. He tossed and turned, Luke's words replaying in his mind.

Luke was right—he was an idiot. He'd let the only woman he'd ever loved go without asking her what she wanted. His whole life he'd been told he wasn't good enough by his mother, and he'd believed it. But Carly had showed him differently. She'd helped him when he'd needed someone the most, and loved him in spite of the many times he'd pushed her away.

It was high time he changed.

With renewed energy, Randy hopped out of bed and dressed. He put a change of clothes and a few personal items in a duffle bag, grabbed his coat and hat, and headed out to his truck.

* * *

Carly stood at the counter in the gallery going over sales figures with the owner, Mr. Barnett. She was dressed impeccably, as usual, in a silk, sapphire-blue blouse, black skirt, and black heels with her hair falling down her back. It was ten in the morning and the gallery was quiet. Everly, who'd been relieved that Carly had returned as manager because she'd hated the responsibility of being in charge, was near the back of the shop dusting glass display cases.

Carly gazed out the window that faced the street. The day was cold and cloudy with a light drizzle falling. She sighed. It was just another dreary day in downtown Seattle.

Since coming back two months ago, Carly had made many changes in her life. Before she'd gone to the ranch last summer, she'd spent almost every night out eating and drinking with friends and dancing and partying on the weekends. She'd flirted recklessly with men, shopped without worrying about how much she spent, and never gave a thought as to where her life was headed. That had all changed. Now, she rarely went out after work, opting to eat at home. She'd realized that she'd learned how to cook quite well from helping Ginny and Andi in the kitchen, so most nights she'd make dinner and sit on the sofa, watching an old movie on television.

No longer caring about the excesses in her life, Carly had gone through her closet of designer clothes, shoes, and purses and taken more than half of them to an upscale consignment shop downtown. Already, she had earned a small fortune from selling several items and she'd put all the money against her debt. Her income from the gallery was quite good too, and she was able to place large chunks of it each pay period toward what she owed. It felt good to finally be in control of her life, at least financially.

The electronic bell over the door rang as a young couple entered the gallery. The sound always reminded Carly of the bell on Margie's gift shop door. She often wondered how Margie was doing and if she was enjoying her time with her daughter in California. She felt heartsick with memories from her time in Montana, and how much she missed everyone at the ranch—especially how desperately she missed a certain cowboy.

Despite her best efforts to forget him, she still thought of Randy every day. She often replayed their last conversation in her mind, still unable to believe that after all they'd been through together, the good and the bad, he'd been so willing to let her go. Sometimes, when she'd talk to Andi on the phone, she'd ask about Randy, but it seemed there wasn't much to tell. He was working on the ranch as usual—nothing had changed. It broke Carly's heart to think that their time together could be wiped away so easily. For her, it hadn't been easy to let go of him at all.

The couple showed interest in a painting on the back wall, so Carly walked over and began talking to them quietly. The bell on the door chimed again, but Carly ignored it. She was sure Everly or Mr. Barnett would help whoever had come in.

After a moment, Everly came up to her and caught her attention. Carly noticed she had an odd look on her face.

"Carly? I think there's someone here to see you."

Carly glanced toward the door, and let out a small gasp. A tall man stood there wearing a sheepskin jacket, jeans, and a cowboy hat. "Randy?" she said in barely a whisper.

She quickly excused herself from the couple and let Everly take over. Walking slowly across the gallery, her eyes caught his, holding his gaze until she stood right next to him. "Randy. What are you doing here?"

Randy took off his hat and pushed his hair back. "We need to talk."

Carly stood there, stunned at seeing him. She glanced around and saw Everly and the young couple staring at them. Mr. Barnett was also watching them curiously from behind the counter. She moved a bit to try and block their view. "You came all this way to talk?"

Randy fixed his eyes only on her. "I came to apologize to you for being an idiot. I should have never let you go. I thought I was doing the right thing, but I was wrong. I'm miserable without you. You're the only woman I've ever truly loved, and instead of begging you to stay, I pushed you away. I'm so sorry, Carly."

Carly couldn't believe what she was hearing. She had wished that one day she would hear those words from Randy, but she hadn't truly believed she ever would. "Oh, Randy," she said as tears filled her eyes.

"Luke told me I was an idiot if I didn't come here and beg you to take me back. And he was right. So here I am. I've never believed I deserved anything good from life, so if any came my way, I ran from it. But for the first time in my life, I'm running toward something instead of away from it. I'm running toward you, Carly. I love you." Randy took her hand in his and slowly dropped to one knee. Behind them, Everly and the young couple gasped, but Randy ignored them and continued, his eyes only on Carly. "Marry me, Carly. I promise I'll love you forever. For years to come."

Carly's other hand drew up to her mouth as her tears slid down her cheeks. "Is this real? Do you really want to marry me?"

Randy stood again and gently wiped away the tears from her cheeks. "Yes, it's real. I love you, Carly. Marry me?"

Carly smiled. "Yes. A thousand times yes."

Randy pulled her to him, and they kissed as Everly and the couple clapped excitedly.

Randy chuckled at their applause, but Carly's expression grew serious. "Are you sure, Randy? It won't always be easy. We're both so stubborn. We're complete opposites, like oil and water."

Randy grinned. "Day and night."

"Cats and dogs," Carly said, a small smile appearing on her face. "Think of the fights we'll have."

Randy dropped his head and whispered in her ear, "Yeah, but think of how much fun we'll have making up."

Carly laughed then and they kissed again.

Randy glanced around. "Can you leave?"

Carly grinned. "Only if you carry me out of here in a way that would make John Wayne proud."

Randy's eyes lit up. He set his hat on Carly's head and in one quick swoop, lifted her up into his arms. From across the room, Everly whooped and clapped with glee.

Carly waved at her friend, and then turned toward her boss. "Sorry, Mr. Barnett, but I have to quit. I'm going home to Montana."

Randy pushed the door open and carried Carly outside. The rain had stopped and the sun was streaming through the clouds. He set her down beside his truck and pulled her into his arms.

"I love you, Carly," he said, staring down into her eyes.

"I love you, too, Randy," Carly told him, smiling. And after one more kiss, they climbed up into the truck and drove off.

Epilogue

Six Months Later

On a beautiful sunny day in May, Randy and Carly stood before the minister up in the hayloft in front of the large, open door and promised to love each other forever as their family and friends watched from below. For anyone else, it would seem like a strange place to get married, but for Carly and Randy, it was fitting. It was the place where their love story had begun, and Carly wanted to continue their good luck by starting their married life there also.

Luke stood proudly beside Randy as his best man while Andi stood beside Carly. Neither Luke nor Andi could have ever predicted nearly three years ago when Andi had first knocked on Luke's cabin door that they would all, one day, become a family. And no one was happier at the outcome as they were.

Ginny watched the two exchange vows with a smile on her face and holding the tiny hand of seventeen-month-old Jessi standing beside her. Glen stood beside her with his arm around her. They had spent three months this past winter at his San Diego home, and upon returning to Montana, he'd moved into the ranch house with Ginny. She loved the ranch and would never have been happy living anywhere else, so he'd put his riverfront home up for sale and they planned on making the ranch house their summer home.

Colt and Beth stood near Ginny and Glen, both smiling up at their happy friends. They were expecting a baby in October and everyone was very excited for them. The Brennan family was growing and soon another generation of Brennans would continue the family legacy and run the ranch. And today, as family and friends shared in their wedding day, Randy felt closer to the Brennan family, his family, than he had ever felt before.

Other guests were there as well, celebrating Carly and Randy's special day. Their neighbors, Ray and Amy, Mary and Sharon and their husbands, Margie, and Randy's friend, Jeremy. Carly's Seattle friends Adam, Chelle and Quinn, and Everly had come, and Mr. Barnett had sent a lovely gift along with Everly for the couple. Even Bree, freshly washed and brushed, wearing a ribbon around her neck, was standing at attention with the other guests.

Last November, it took the couple only a week to pack the items Carly wanted to keep from the townhouse into a rented trailer and drive back to Montana. Carly knew her life was no longer in Seattle; she wanted to be with the man she loved and with her family. The townhouse was put on the market and sold quickly, and the two sisters split the profits from the sale. Carly had paid off her debts and had enough left over to set up a deal with Margie to rent-to-buy the gift shop building so she could open her own business. All winter Carly had worked diligently updating the inside of the store and setting up contracts with artists around Western Montana to sell their artwork in her new shop. Starting June first, the doors to Mountain Gallery & Gifts would be open.

Margie had offered her services to work at the shop part-time for free during the summer, and Carly couldn't have appreciated her more. Carly's dream of opening her own gallery was coming true, and she was so happy to have Margie be a part of it.

The couple decided to forego a honeymoon and instead use their money to begin building a house where Randy's trailer now sat. Since Randy's money was no longer being spent on his mother's nursing home care, and he was earning more from the profits of the ranch, he could finally use it toward building a home. It was Randy's wedding gift to Carly, and she loved the hacienda style home he'd asked Luke to draw up for them. Their lives were changing and growing, and becoming fuller and richer with every day.

Randy gazed down in awe at his lovely bride. He was finally getting his happily ever after, something he'd never dared dream would happen. To think that he, the little boy who had swept sidewalks for money and who'd became just a ranch hand would have a home of his own and a wife to cherish and love. It was more than he'd ever thought possible.

"You may now kiss the bride," the minister said as the ceremony came to a close.

Randy looked down into Carly's eyes and saw her love reflected in them. As their lips met, he smiled, happy that he would spend the rest of his life kissing Carly.

###

About the Author

Deanna Lynn Sletten grew up on the sunny coast of southern California before moving to northern Minnesota as a teenager. That's a story all its own. Her interest in writing novels was sparked in a college English class, and she has been writing in some form or another ever since. In 2011, Deanna discovered the world of self-publishing and published three novels she'd written over the years. After that, she was hooked.

Deanna's women's fiction novels, *Widow, Virgin, Whore* and *Maggie's Turn* have both made the top 100 bestselling book lists on both Amazon and Barnes & Noble in 2014. Her romance novels *Memories* and *Sara's Promise* both won semifinalist in The Kindle Book Review's Best Indie Books of 2012 and 2013 respectively. *Sara's Promise* was also a finalist in the 2013 National Indie Excellence Book Awards.

Deanna enjoys writing heartwarming women's fiction and romance novels with unforgettable characters. She has also written one middle-grade novel that takes you on the adventure of a lifetime. She believes in fate, destiny, love at first sight, soul mates, second chances, magic, and happily ever after, and these are all reflected in her novels.

Deanna is married and has two grown children. When not writing, she enjoys walking the wooded trails around her home with her beautiful Australian Shepherd or relaxing in the boat on the lake in the summer.

Deanna loves hearing from her readers. Connect with her at:

Blog: www.deannalynnsletten.com
Website: www.deannalsletten.com
Twitter: @DeannaLSletten
Facebook: http://www.facebook.com/DeannaLynnSletten
Goodreads: http://www.goodreads.com/dsletten

If you enjoyed **Kissing Carly,** you might also enjoy these
novels by Deanna Lynn Sletten

Kiss a Cowboy (Kiss a Cowboy Series, Book One)
(Romance)

A Kiss for Colt (Kiss a Cowboy Series, Book Two)
(Romance)

Destination Wedding
(Romance)

Memories
(Romance)

Sara's Promise
(Romance)

Maggie's Turn
(Women's Fiction)

Summer of the Loon
(Women's Fiction)

Widow, Virgin Whore ~ A Novel
(Women's Fiction/Family Drama)

Made in the USA
Monee, IL
22 June 2021

72038365R00146